ALLIANCE

ALFRED J. HUNT

Copyright © 2020 by Alfred J Hunt

Library of Congress Registration Number: TXu002187845

First paperback edition November 2020

Book cover by Jordan Jackson

Editor: Anna

ISBN: 978-0-578-78666-7

alhunt63070@yahoo.com

CONTENTS

Dedicated to God

1

DAY 1 | ASSAULT

_1_

The winds of relief blow strong across the barren land, but there is no time for relaxation, comfort, or enjoyment. My legs have gone numb from pain and exhaustion. Each step feels as if there are weights chained to my ankles; tugging and pulling in resistance, rebelling against my conscious effort to move on. My heart is beating like a tribal drum, rapid and fierce as each reverberation flows throughout my veins. Beads of sweat pour down my face and into my eyes, burning like a fire. The sun dances majestically on my saturated body as if it is a river on a hot summer day. Ah, yes. A river, that would be nice. Ice cold, refreshing water engulfing my body . . .

NO! Focus; there is no time for that.

But I can't go on. What started as a sprint is now a walk that may only look like a jog by appearance.

I can't stop. They may be tracking me. If I stop, it may mean not only my life, but the lives of everyone I hold dear and love, and even those I don't. Who knows where they will stop? The world? The screams are still vibrantly ringing in my ears. The sight of blood still *tints my vision. It was pure horror. They never stood a chance. The king must know!*

To run nonstop starting at the southern edge of the Forest of Mezpha, to the Valley of Kurdish, to the Castle Dorian is an impossible feat.

Yet here I am, The Great Herms.

Or so I am called.

Ever since I learned how to walk, no one has been faster than me. I've won every competition I've entered. Some have even rumored that I have wings on my feet. Though this is not true, there have been times where I was sure I was no longer running on solid ground, but rather gliding on air. These are the moments I've worked for, that I live for. I love running. It's just me and the circuit. If I do not finish it is because I could not muster the strength to complete the course. I could not dig deep enough to find the endurance, the confidence, or the will to finish. In essence, I would have to give up on myself, and I am too determined to ever give up on myself. This is why I have always been and always will be the best. If I am not eating or sleeping, I am running. Constantly redefining what I thought were my limits; pushing myself past hunger, pain, and exhaustion.

But this is unlike anything I've ever experienced. Hunger has a death grip on my stomach. Pain is ripping through my sides. Air itself has betrayed me, piercing my lungs with each breath. Each gasp for air seems barely sufficient until the next.

If I just hang on though, any moment, the tops of the castle towers will burst up out of the plains with triumph and glory.

Still, each step feels like my last. From where comes the strength to continue? I do not know. Exhaustion has taken its toll on my body, vomit covers my mouth like wax, and now spots are appearing before my eyes, hiding low in the grass like a crouching lion, then slowly rising up to prey on its victim.

I've heard it said, "Mind over matter". This has proven true in times past, but I wonder how long one can "will" themselves forward until a bodily shutdown occurs? If it can, when does the body overrule the mind? When does the saying, "Body over mind" prove true? After all, we are only humans, and as humans, we are bound by unbreakable limits.

A little further, another step . . .

But with each step comes fret, despair, and hopelessness. Every step forward may as well be ten steps backwards.

If spots had not overtaken my vision, I might be able to see the castle in the distance. Focus Herm, focus! For to rest may mean death.

But to continue may mean death as well.

Either way, death is patiently waiting to give me a warm greeting.

Why should I prolong the inevitable?

<u>2</u>

Commotion quickly arose from the table where the five kings of the land of Sahleam were convening for the annual Gathering of the Lords. It is called "Gathering of the Lords" for this is how the kings addressed one another. Seeing the uselessness of the rising turmoil, Lord Titus slightly raised his left hand and boldly, yet gently, asserted, "Gentlemen, gentlemen, please. Before we instate any mobilization of arms, let us first review our sources to ensure that the collaboration of data aligns in a retaliatory manner."

Insulted by Lord Titus' request, Lord Ekron quickly and calmly proclaimed in a bold, burly voice, "What are you implying, Lord Titus?"

"Nothing of cruel intent," Lord Titus quickly replied. He knew that Lord Ekron was noble and true. And that, like many other characteristics of dwarves, their honesty is brutal. Lord Titus did not doubt the truthfulness of Lord Ekron's report, but rather was concerned of its implication.

"All I am saying is that, thus far, we have only heard of your accounts. I think it behooves us to reinforce the reports, considering the manner of action which would need to be taken."

Lord Ekron may have been short in stature, but his heart, bravery, and temper were bigger than any giant or mountain. "And these are not good enough?" he asserted firmly.

"No, no, they certainly are," quickly replied Lord Titus. "But is it not true that the dominating number of accounts were reported by those who have grown in popularity for crying 'wolf'?"

"First, my word," calmly claimed Lord Ekron, as he was now obviously trying to hold back his temper. "And now, my intelligence . . ." Quickly failing in his attempt, Lord Ekron slammed his hands on the round marble table, shaking its contents as his voice and temper rose along with his posture.

Seeing the uselessness of trying to talk to someone who was not only convinced of a matter, but whose anger was also blinding them of reasonable comprehension, Lord Titus tried to balance the situation with soothing logic. "Surely you have taken this into consideration. All I am asking is to first hear any other accounts by the present lords before taking affirmative action."

After a moment of silence, a small, hesitant meekly voice spoke. "Actually, my lords," stammered a soft voice, "there has been a mysterious disappearance of gatherers a couple of weeks past. We have sent out search parties, but to no avail. If what Lord Ekron is saying is true, then a plausible conclusion could be formulated out of the known facts."

Although Lord Augusta did not dare say what that conclusion was, everyone gathered around the table knew his insinuation. Silence held their voices ransom as the lords carefully and delicately mulled over the truthfulness of the matter.

A sighting and a disappearance in such a short time can only mean an infiltration of the Southern Territory, thought Lord Titus. *It has happened in times past, where one of the creatures would lose their way and invade our land. We have developed tactics to handle such matters. If Lord Ekron and Lord Augusta are correct, then it would mean multiple beasts have infiltrated at the same time and are progressively and collectively moving north. I wonder if the sighting and*

disappearance are related to the matter that was brought to my atten-
tion late last night.

Before Lord Titus could finish his thought, the sconces and wall décor began to shake as someone pounded their way down the hall, screaming a muffled tune at the top of their lungs.

3

"I . . . SPEAK . . . LORD TITUS!" Herms screamed breathlessly as he paraded down the corridor. "DISPATCH . . . AMBUSH . . .MAS-SACRE . . ." he managed to get out while gasping for air.

"Easy, Herms," the guard replied. Holding up both hands, he indicated for Herms to stop and collect himself. But when he saw the door after first entering the hallway, Hermes sprinted for the finish line as he had done in races before. This time, though, it seemed that there was more energy in his reserves than anticipated. Before he knew it, Herms was just yards away from the guards and the door. Trying to stop proved futile as he braced himself for a collision, hoping that the guards would absorb most of the impact.

Herms was not a man of great size or stature. Being a runner kept him nimble, quick, and very slender; although he could eat an absorbent amount of food. Yes, Herms was not one to shy away from a meal, nor to stop before challenging the expansion limits of his stomach. And yet, as a result of his running, he could not gain a pound of weight even if he wanted to.

He was clean-shaven, with short dark hair and green eyes. Herms was always light-hearted and optimistic in nature. Although he was very confident in his running, he was not braggadocious, unsportsman-like, or confrontational. Herms was a loyal friend; a friend that you could always count on, the kind of friend that you, if you were lucky, could only find once in your lifetime.

Stepping to the side, the guards caught Herms easily enough. "Easy, Herms, easy. Catch your breath," Brutus implored him as they got him to stand with his arms above his head. Normally, Brutus and Antheis would immediately detain and silence such an outbreak, but Herms had been a good friend and trusted counselor of King Titus since Brutus and Antheis had enlisted into the national army.

As Herms stood there, his arms shook as he fought to hold them above his head, desperately trying to catch his breath. His legs felt like they were trying to run away from him in order to finish the race, even though Herms knew that they remained beneath him, barely able to hold his posture.

Between the amount of sweat that covered Herms' body, the smell of death and decay that roared in and out of his mouth, and his state of utter exhaustion, Brutus and Antheis easily deduced that something of great importance had happened. Antheis ran off to a nearby room where refreshments were being kept for the Gathering of the Lords, which was taking place just beyond the doors, in order to fetch Herms some water. While Antheis darted down the hall, Brutus continued to encourage Herms to calm down and catch his breath. This did little good, as Brutus saw Herms' arms starting to shake violently. Knowing the importance of keeping your arms above your head when you were out of breath, Brutus decided to fight through the nauseating smell that protruded from Herms' mouth and pores. He couldn't have stepped in to assist Herms at a better time, as at the very moment Brutus grabbed Herms' arms, his legs also started shaking in exasperation from supporting his own weight.

It seemed as if his legs finally had caught up to him. Only now, Herms wished that he would have continued running, or that at least his legs would have continued. The moment that his legs had stabilized themselves, they started to give way at the very notion of trying to hold up his frame. It was not pain that caused Herms' legs to fail him, just utter exhaustion. For Herms knew that nothing he felt today could compare to what he would feel tomorrow, or the next day, or the day after that.

Seeing Herms' legs start to shake, Brutus immediately pressed his body against Herms, grasping more firmly around his elbows and lifting his arms up, elevating Herms slightly to rest his body on his own.

Herms did not notice the pain from such a forceful grip, nor the manhandling of his body. What Herms did notice was how unusually comfortable Brutus' body was. It was like lying on a bed made out of the softest goose feathers and most delicate fabric. He hardly took notice that he was vertical at the moment. The only thoughts that invaded Herms' mind were rest and sleep.

Brutus noticed Herms' trance-like state and continued to whisper words of encouragement into his ear. Knowing that time was running short, Brutus arched his back, bearing more of Herms' weight, and grasped both his wrists with one of his massive hands so that the other would be free to gently slap Herms in order to keep him awake, and, more likely, alive.

4

"Come on, Herms, stay awake. Finish the race. You're almost there. The finish line lies just ahead," Brutus said into Herms' ear as he slapped his face. Although Brutus was built like a bear, trying to hold another grown man's body weight with just one hand would prove difficult for anyone. Thus, every several seconds, Brutus needed to switch which hand was holding up Herms. Even though he was not doing this for a long time, Brutus was starting to feel the effects of the strenuous workout.

"Finish the race, finish the race," Herms heard as he was fading in and out of reality. "You are almost there. The finish line lies just ahead."

The finish line, Herms thought. *The race, the race is not over. I have yet to finish, and the finish line is oh-so-close. To finish the race means to relay the message. Only then will I be finished. Only then will my race be complete. And there has yet to be a race that the "Great Herms" has not finished, nor will there be.* Feeling a couple more slaps, Herms opened his eyes. He was determined to finish the race, even if it meant death from exhaustion. For his death in a successful delivery of the accounts may mean life for the kingdom, and it is better that one man shall die so that an entire kingdom may live.

Yet even in his newfound determination, there was not more Herms could do than to be vertically prostrated on Brutus' body. To be conscience meant to be alive, and to be alive meant the ability to finish the race.

Herms mustered up some strength in order to tell Brutus that he must speak to King Titus, but when he went to speak, all that could come out were pants and puffs of air, for his mouth and throat were completely dry and covered with a waxy film that the vomit had left behind. Putting his head down, he began to think of another means to tell Brutus of his need to speak to King Titus. It was then that he heard faint footsteps. Looking up, he saw Antheis walking briskly and purposefully toward him with three pitchers of water in each hand. Brutus must have taken notice to this as well, for he now took Herms off of his own body and leaned him against the corridor wall, still holding his arms up as he gently and firmly directed Antheis to hurry, because there was not much time left.

5

Oh, the feeling of the cold pitcher pressed against his lips and the sudden rush of cool, refreshing, sweet water entering his mouth. This only lasted a second before the vomit that coated his mouth and throat loosened; the smell, the texture, the taste, all vibrantly coming alive again.

Herms almost choked on the water before he spit it out, spraying it all over the corridor. Brutus and Antheis were taken back by Herms' reaction to the much-awaited salvation, but did not force their thoughts on the matter. They knew that Herms was an accomplished runner and had faced similar (or at least they thought) brinks of exhaustion before. They gave Herms water when he asked for it by opening his mouth, and took it away at the close. Herms would only take half mouthfuls at a time. He needed to get the taste of vomit out of his mouth if he wanted to enjoy the finest water in all the land. It seemed a pity that he was wasting so much of it. In the end, though, it was worth it if he got to finish this race. Swishing the water around, gargling, and then spitting seemed to be his method for an entire pitcher. Then, when the second pitcher came to his lips, he decided to drink.

Oh, what joys, oh what sweet refreshment, oh what pure ecstasy ran through his entire body as that first sip of water ran down his throat and through his veins! *Ah yes, I will make it,* thought Herms. He motioned for a second sip; again, pure ecstasy. Herms had enjoyed many joys and pleasures in his short life up until this point, but all of them seemed like torture compared to what he was experiencing right now. A third sip, the same experience. Only now, Herms felt some of his strength coming back to him. Out of pure excitement and enjoyment of knowing that he would finish the race, Herms freed his hands from Brutus' hold, grabbed the pitcher, and began to chug. Sensations of cold water running through his veins overtook him with each gulp, only briefly stopping to gasp for air. The water splashed against his face like waves against the beach, running down his face, neck, and body like a mighty river trying to sort its way from the peak to the bay. This sweet, refreshing water was revitalizing, reviving, rejuvenating. Herms felt young . . . alive . . . dizzy . . . nauseated.

The last thing Herms remembered was feeling light-headed and seeing spots dance their way down from the ceiling, before he regurgitated most of the water that had brought comfort to his soul and then passed out.

<u>6</u>

Muffled tones and beating drums were all Herms could hear as he slowly came to consciousness. When he tried to open his eyes, he found himself in another battle, this time with himself. His eyes were caked shut with dried mucus that had sealed them like a wax signet.

After a second, he mustered what felt like was all of his strength to open his eyes.

At first, he thought he was in a dream, or still dreaming. Then confusion quickly sprang upon him. Not realizing where he was, he gazed at the white and black infused marble wall. Elaborate sconces dimly lit the room, as a magnificent painting of a herd of horses running with grace and freedom brought a smile to his face. Satisfied with the painting and the lift it brought to his spirit, Herms turned away from the wall to see the rest of the room, and hopefully another painting. To the opposite side of the wall was a window, not much more than an arms' length away, in which he became fixated. The sill itself was skillfully done, with swirling tribal patterns that overlaid and intertwined with each other in a brilliant fashion. Whoever made this was obviously a master craftsman, for the intricate design of the work, and the patience and vision required could have been done by none other. His admiration was quickly followed by a curiously attractive stained-glass window: a green snake on a wooden pole posted on a hilltop with people cascading from it, down the hill and off into the distance. Although the image itself did not make sense to Herms, the purple and blue sky looked to rumble with thunder as the sun passed through it, while the snake's red eyes flashed in approval of the withered and downtrodden men before him and its green scales shimmered with satisfaction. While staring at the configuration, Herms heard a whisper in his mind, *Finissssh the race,* it said. *The finissssss line issss upon you. Don't give up now.*

Race? Herms thought for a second, removing his eyes from the glass portrait as he gave thought. *What race? Was I in a race? And if I have been in a race, why haven't I finished?*

Finissssss the race, the whisper said again. *The finissssh line issss upon you.*

This time, Herms took notice to the unmistakable hiss that was in the voice. After brief contemplation, he looked back at the snake on the pole, believing that the voice was not in his head, but also not believing that the voice was coming from the portrait. Much to his displeasure,

Herms' fear became a reality when he saw a ripple run through the snake's body.

Finisssssh the race, the voice repeated, louder this time.

This time there was no denying it; the snake, or serpent, had said it. *The image is alive,* thought Herms. In that moment, a feeling of dread came over Herms, for although he was a fierce athlete, he was not one for confrontation of any kind off of the track field. It was like they were two different people; Herms, the confident and fearless athlete who never backed down from a challenge, and Herms, the non-confrontational citizen. For that moment he believed what he had seen and heard. But then, to save himself from this increasingly unpleasant situation, Herms tried to use reason and knowledge to outwit reality. Removing his eyes from the figure, he nervously laughed to himself, brushing it off as a silly thought. *Non-living things don't just come alive.*

But at that moment, movement from the window caught his attention. This time Herms knew that he had, in fact, seen a ripple go through the snake's body as it began flicking its tongue and slowly pulling its head away from its confinement.

The voice returned again. *Finisssssh the racccce,* it said in a slithery tone.

Race? What race? Herms thought in a scared confusion.

As Herms' heart started to pound and his breathing became more rapid, an extraordinary thing happened: the snake lifted its head off of the glass, turned, and looked right into his eyes. Gripped with fear, all Herms could do was watch as the snake flicked its tongue, its upper body waving as if in a current.

Finissssh the race, it repeated in a harsh tone.

Sensibility, reason, and knowledge had lost the battle to reality, as there was no doubt that the stained-glass snake was encouraging him to "finish the race".

The only problem was that Herms could not remember any race that he had not completed. Mesmerized by those ruby-red eyes, Herms could not pull away as they glowed like embers, searing his brain. As if those beady red eyes were projecting an event into his mind, Herms started recalling an occasion that seemed like a distant memory. As he watched this imagery, he was sucked into his past; a morning jog, a beautiful day, a cool breeze. Yes, Herms remembered this. What happened next, though, came as a shocking surprise; a platoon, a dragon, an ambush. Herms recalled hearing the screams, seeing a cloud of fire, feeling hopelessness. Then he remembered. He remembered the horrors, the death, the invasion. Chills crept up and down his spine. He had seen enough. He could no longer bear to watch this morning's massacre. But before he could look away, he saw something that he had seemingly forgotten.

He was standing in the forest, looking out into the valley, and watching the platoon as they prepared themselves to resolve the situation. Then he saw a large dragon crouching low near the edge of the forest. Its large, scaly body blended in perfectly with the greens and browns of the forest. Its large claws dug into the earth, apparently waiting to pounce. It reminded Herms of runners in the starting block, anxiously anticipating the sound of the whistle. As he looked upon the creature, realizing the implications of this discovery, the dragon must have heard him adjusting himself for a better look. He thought he was very careful and quiet, but the dragon still noticed; this must be due to its excellent hearing. When he made eye contact with the creature, a peculiar thing happened. Herms felt a connection, a surge of emotion: confusion, anger, and despair ran through his body. As Herms looked on, he did not see a foul, vicious monster. He saw something a bit more. Then, fire ran through his bones. Blinding, piercing pain consumed his body. Still looking into the beast's eyes, Herms heard a familiar voice echo in his head: *run*. At that moment, the dragon blinked, looked straight ahead, and took off.

Herms' eyes began to refocus. His peripheral vision told him that he was back in the chambers, but in front of him were those dark red amber eyes. The scales of the snake had thickened, its jaw had become robust, and two horns sat on top of its head while a fan of smaller horns protruded from behind its jaw, and rows of sharp jagged teeth filled its mouth. Fear overtook Herms as he realized that this was the dragon that he had encountered earlier. His throat became too dry to scream, his body scared stiff. Beads of sweat crowned his forehead as the dragon began to open its mouth.

"Finish," Herms began to hear as he saw a small flame develop within the dragon's fully extended mouth. "*THE* . . ." the voice continued, having lost its hiss and now sounding deep and angry. The flame grew as the smell of fire and brimstone filled his nostrils. "*RACE!*" it finally exclaimed, as the dragon launched a massive fireball into Herms' face.

Herms, not being a warrior, reacted instinctively the only way that he knew how: by clinching his eyes and gritting his teeth.

7

Silence weighed heavy on the room. Thoughts of concern, implication, and retaliation filled the minds of Lords Augusta, Ekron, and Titus as they sat by a glorious fire, mulling over the events that had just come to pass. Fresh tea, biscuits, cheese, and spreads sat barely touched at a nearby table. Instead, Lord Ekron calmly puffed away on his favorite meerschaum pipe. With a long black "s" stem, the bowl sat comfortably at chest level. A stout, prideful lion stood tall on one side, looking over its kingdom, while a stoic eagle that perched on the other side gazed along the way. With one arm crossing his body and the other hand grazing the bowl of the pipe, Lord Ekron's meditations were obvious. He sank low into thought in the high back chair, his tough skin creasing his brow as his eyes gleamed with contemplation, considering all the events that had transpired and trying to piece them together.

Lord Augusta sat just off to the side of the fire, where the poker and shovel would be. Being a Faun, there was no need for him to be in the direct heat of the blaze. His goat-like legs and rather hairy upper body were more than enough to keep him comfortable most days. But he did not walk around uncovered, for that would be improper. No, fauns wore a garment girded around their waste to cover their lower torso, and some type of loose top that they could slide on over their heads. Now, as king, Augusta had leather garments with tribal designs impressed upon them. His belt was studded with an ivory minotaur horn, a great minotaur warrior who was conquered in battle. Lord Augusta also had a minotaur hide that he would wear as his official cape, a constant reminder of the enemy they had to overthrow in order to establish themselves. He had small horns that were almost hidden within his brown, bushy hair. For how hairy fauns naturally were, Lord Augusta kept his face clean, except for a patch of hair that hung from his chin. Leaning forward with his elbows on his knees, and hands folded in front of his mouth, he watched the fire perform its hypnotic dance and play its rhythmic crackle while concern for the land and his people filled his heart.

Lord Titus sat adjacent to Lord Ekron in front of the fire. Out of all the lords, Lord Titus had the most ordinary look about him. He was not very distinctive in appearance, for he looked like a regular man with a regular build who stood at a regular height. His thick, black, medium-length hair and a full, nicely trimmed goatee would help him go unnoticed at the market if he wanted to. In fact, many people probably have encountered his acquaintance and thought him to be nothing more than the baker or the tailor. Lord Titus' differentiation did not come from his appearance or his demeanor, but from his wisdom and his heart. He always listened patiently to people, giving them his full attention. No one had ever come before Lord Titus and felt as though he was higher or better than themselves. He always considered all of his options before giving his advice, weighing each thought with scrutiny, and making sure that it was the best possible option.

Rather than drinking the cup of hot tea that was in his hands, Lord Titus seemed content to stare blankly into the mixture while the pleasing herbal aroma rose within the steam, filling his nostrils with sweet delight.

Finally, looking over to Lord Ekron, Lord Titus said the only appropriate words for the given moment: "I apologize for not taking immediate action upon your word."

Lord Ekron's eyes went from the fire to Lord Titus. "Apology accepted," he replied without taking his mouth from his pipe. After another long puff and exhale, Lord Ekron continued, "Although I do not think that any course of action would have changed the current situation."

This was most definitely true. Although the Lords had yet to discover the purpose for Herms' unusually peculiar actions, they undoubtedly believed that it was related to the news which Lord Ekron brought forth at the gathering of the Lords: that dragons are in the land. This occurrence was not unusual in itself, though. Ever since the Separation of Exaltation, a stray dragon had been known to cross the Addalayin Depths from time to time. At first, this was a great terror, as dragons were maliciously violent creatures with huge appetites. They would come and create havoc by flying over houses, destroying farms, and even snatching a herd driver or two. Land would be destroyed, yearlong crops were ruined with no return, and herds were at the mercy of their appetite. After they had their fill, they would simply fly away, leaving a wake of devastation and destruction. After the first encounter, the Lords gathered to devise a way to prevent such an atrocity from happening again. It was not until a couple of encounters later, though, that a potion was brewed that penetrated and shut down the dragon's seemly impenetrable defenses. Since then, the Lords had met on an annual basis to discuss any issues that affect the entire land of Sahleam.

This same gathering was in session when a persevering commotion had disrupted them. While Lords Titus, Ekron, and Augusta waited for Herms to wake, Lord Cephas of the Sheppen and Lord Benaniah of the Nimrods had volunteered their services to go to the place mentioned by Lords Ekron and Augusta for further investigation.

Although Lord Ekron had a stern look on his face, Lord Titus could not help but notice how his diamond and ruby-studded beard looked like a beautifully calm and starry night. Do not be fooled, though: The jewelry and braids within his hair and beard were not a sign of sensitivity or weakness, but just the opposite, of power and wealth. Dwarves were miners and extraordinary craftsman by trade. That is why the King Dwarf had diamonds and rubies studded throughout his beard—to show the Dwarfs' wealth and power. It is also why the King Dwarf had three braids within his hair and beard (two on the sides and one in the middle); to show their love for art and craftsmanship. It is said that any respectable Dwarf would have several mines that were jewel-infested and lined with beautiful carvings and sculptures.

It was at this point that the Lords were disrupted by a loud grunt, and simultaneously, Herms bolted upright within his bed, shielding his face with his arms.

<u>8</u>

Galloping hooves filled the air as Lords Cephas and Benaniah journeyed toward the southern regions of the land. Typically, when dragons entered Sahleam, the Dwarfs were the first to sight them, since the Mountains of Endor which they inhabited ended just shy of the southern tip. Being well-armed, trained, and accustomed to this type of situation, the matter was normally dealt with in brevity. But somehow they had evaded Lord Ekron's men, managing to make it as far north as the Plains Elah, which were part of Lord Augusta's kingdom.

Fauns were gentle creatures that tried to avoid confrontation, but don't let their petite statue, stubby horns, or goat legs mislead you. They may have tried to avoid confrontation, but their militias were well-armed and trained to defend their land when called upon. The fact was, the Dwarfs had mastered the use of the carnivorous diffusion (an herbal mixture that penetrates the dragon's skin and disables their use of fire after entering the blood stream), thus making any dragon intrusion oblivious to the Fauns' way of life. Besides the first ever intrusion, in which many fauns fell victim, there hadn't been a need for the Fauns to defend themselves against such an enemy. The Plains of Elah were in the middle of Sahleam, which all of the other kingdoms surrounded. If an attack occurred, whoever the foe may be, they would need to get past the Dwarfs, the Sheppen, the Nimrods, or the Humans before being able to lay foot on Faun soil. This is why it was very suspicious that the dragons had eluded the Dwarfs and traveled further north to the Plains of Elah, and why it was imperative for Lords Cephas and

Benaniah to discover the meaning behind these accounts before there was another massacre in Sahleam.

9

There was not much talk between Lords Cephas and Benaniah, although one might not have been able to hear the other over the sound of pounding hooves. Lord Cephas was not one of many words, always listening patiently and given to much contemplation before articulating his thoughts. Sheppen were naturally taller than most, and Lord Cephas was among the tallest of his kind. His long legs and arms did not seem to be supported by much muscle, but contrary to his appearance, Lord Cephas was very strong, as were most Sheppen. Although Sheppen could grow hair on their head, Lord Cephas was bald with the exception of the horseshoe-type pattern that remained on the lower portion of his head. Most of these features would typically go unnoticed, for Sheppen were garbed with a loose-fitting shepherd's cloak. As the lords rode, Lord Cephas' mind was tangled with thoughts about the currents events and their implications.

Lord Benaniah, on the other hand, was a great hunter and tracker, as most Nimrods were. Their puffy cheeks, thin lips, and flat nose gave the Nimrods' faces a circular shape. Their legs were similar to that of a horse's hind legs, thick and strong, great for running and lunging upon their prey. Combined with their keen eyesight and sense of smell, it was of little wonder why the Nimrods are known for their hunting prowess. Lord Benaniah had long, black hair that he mostly kept pulled back. Nimrods did not mind too much about how they were dressed, but rather that their knives were sharp and arrows ready when called upon.

It was Lord Benaniah's guidance and direction that would lead them southeast to the Forest of Mezpha. Here, they would be able to find some food and shelter and take a short rest before heading into the lower regions of Vinyah, before finally making their way to Endorah, the last mountain peak within Lord Ekron's land. Finding food and water would not be a problem for Lord Benaniah. Besides being the most extraordinary hunter and tracker in the land, the Forest of Mezpha was generous with game and had the Podiseon River flowing through its midst. Although it had been a while since Lords Cephas and Benaniah had eaten, being the great herdsmen and hunter that they each respectfully were, they were able to divert from the growing hunger pains and stay focused on the expedition.

Every now and then, Lord Benaniah would catch some movement overhead, only to realize that it was a bird of some kind. Sckowl were abundant in this part of the land. Actually, it was a wonder that he was not seeing more sckowl. This may have been supporting evidence of Lord Augusta's assessment: that dragons had gotten as far north as the Valley of Kurdish and were even in the Plains of Elah themselves.

It is a curious thing, thought Lord Benaniah. *How did a dragon get this far north and evade Lord Ekrons hunting parties that would have undoubtedly been sent out? Normally, dragons think with their stomachs, not their brains. A Dwarf is not a delicacy in a dragon's mind, but rams and mountain goats are quite the hors d'oeuvres, and fresh mountain water is hard to pass up after the long flight over the Addalayin Depths. Also, it wasn't the scouts and border patrol that had noticed the dragon infection; rather, it was a group of mischievous boys. One would have to conclude that the dragons were trying to move stealthily, which again, is unusual. Hopefully, we can gather the information needed in order to resolve this disturbance. And hopefully the resolution will not include a barrage with our notorious foe. Hopefully.*

10

Fixing their attention on Herms, the lords swiftly came to his side.

"Herms, it is I, Lord Titus. Lord Ekron and Lord Augusta are here as well. You are safe, my friend," said Lord Titus, trying to soothe and calm down Herms, knowing that he was still much too weak and in desperate need of rest.

It was like a mother's touch when Lord Titus grasped Herms hands, for his body went from being stiff with fright to being relaxed with peace as Lord Titus gently laid him back in the bed.

In anticipation of Herms soon waking, the Lords moved their chairs to his bedside so they could start communicating with Herms as soon as he was able to do so.

It was not long afterwards that they heard Herms start smacking his lips, trying to dissipate the desert that had taken over his mouth, followed by a deep inhale. It was obvious that Herms was waking up. A curious thing then happened: while exhaling, the lords heard Herms gently say, "Finish the race." These actions made two more rounds before Herms tried opening his eyes. When he did, if you could say that they were opened at all, Herms first needed to fight through the waxy buildup that seemed to be acting as an adhesive, keeping his eye lids shut; almost as if his own body was telling him that it was not yet time for him to awake, but Herm knew otherwise. His eye lids felt like they were weighted and spring loaded, already coiled and positioned to keep his eyes shut so he could get his much-needed rest. The words *Finish the race* kept ringing in his ears, refusing to stop until he completed his task.

After a brief thought about the meaning of the words that Herms had just uttered, Lord Titus, seeing that Herms was waking up, gave him a glass of palace water. Herms was fortunate, for Lord Titus' palace was the only place in all the land that possessed water from the Tepenun Springs. This spring was located as the centerpiece of the gardens and topiary within the palace grounds. In fact, the discovery of the springs was one of the deciding factors in building the Castle Dorian in its location. The spring contained water in its purest form; thus providing rehydration, nutrition, accelerated healing, and even miraculous recoveries.

Lord Titus was careful to place the water just before Herms' lips, so that Herms would have to tilt his head, which would prevent spilling, but also so that Herms would be able to dictate how much water he took in at once. At first, when Herms saw the water just before him, survival took over as he grabbed Lord Titus' arm with both of his hands and simultaneously pulled the water forward, lifting his head in order to meet his love in a beautiful median. When Herms first pressed his lips to the glass, it was like a prolonged passionate kiss. The passion, the pleasure, the joy was insurmountable. As Herms inhaled and allowed the water to fill his mouth to capacity, a shocking truth flashed through his mind. It was this same lover, this same excitement, this same enjoyment and longing that led to his regurgitation and unconsciousness. With that in mind, Herms shut off and disconnected the flow of water as he slightly tilted his head back and swallowed.

Having to hold his breath longer than expected, Herms found himself gasping for air. After obtaining several lungfuls of much-needed oxygen, Herms once again attached himself to the aqueduct. This time, though, slow and steady won the race, as he continually drank the first, second, and a third cup of water. Feeling satisfied, refreshed, and rehydrated, it was now time for nourishment while he finished the race.

11

Lord Augusta fetched the tray of cheese, biscuits, and fruits that the lords had left untouched. It was a simple yet glorious sight as Herms sat in bed salivating in anticipation. After a few bites of biscuit, a swig of tea, and a crumb of cheese, Herms began to tell the story that the Lords had undoubtedly been waiting to hear.

"I was in the lower regions of the Forest of Mezpha, enjoying the beauty of the day. The sun was high, the air was cool, and the wind was brisk; the perfect time of year. After having a long nap, in late morning I decided, for no particular reason, to go out and enjoy the day with a nice walk. The deep reds, yellows, and oranges dressed the trees with wonder, while the soft chirp of love birds filled the air. It was a beautiful day. Already having started the day nonchalantly, I thought it a good idea to go to a nearby place of solitude and meditate. After finishing my tea and a light breakfast, I headed off into the woods."

With saying this, Herms was reminded of the spread in front of him and paused briefly for a small bite and sip.

"Yes, an afternoon surrounded by wildflowers, songbirds, and a bubbling creek was very amiable for a day like this one," continued Herms. "But that is not what fortune had in store for me. After entering some distance into the woods, I heard a ruffle up above. Looking up, I saw some birds leave their perch in a chattered commotion. I did not think this to be odd, but rather that some other kind of animal had scared them off," proceeded Herms, noticing that the lords were listening very intently.

"I brushed this instance off to the side and continued on my way. At this point, the creek was maybe a mile up ahead. As I walked, I was not thinking of any certain thing nor paying attention to any one direction, when I suddenly heard a rustle of leaves and breaking of twigs. While trying to peer though the brush from the direction the sound had come, I thought I had seen a large shadow cross my sight, from the right to the left. At this point, I was more than intrigued and cautiously headed in the direction in which I thought I saw the figurehead. I did this to satisfy my own curiosity and calm my nerves. I thought it might be a wolf or deer (hopefully a deer), but to my surprise, it was neither; although now I wish it would have been a wolf or a bear." The lords sat quietly, not interrupting, even when Herms paused briefly for a sip of tea or a bite of biscuit. They did not want to distract his thoughts, even just for a second, knowing that every little detail was imperative.

"Although there now had been many signs pointing me back to my cottage, where I could have laid blissfully ignorant of what was to come, I ignored them and continued on. As I pressed on, I began to hear some movement and what sounded like chattering from up ahead. I soon came upon a clearing in which there was a valley. Within this clearing there was a platoon of men. When I first saw them, my nerves were calmed, thinking that they were the reason for all of my anxiety, but I was wrong. After watching them for a moment, I noticed their insignia. They were Lord Titus' men. I wondered, 'What are they doing out here?' Upon further investigation, I concluded that based on the artillery they were hauling, the ranks and formation of the men, and the insignia on their uniforms, that there must have been a stray dragon in the land, for this was the dragon prevention branch.

"Realizing this struck a nerve, and all my fears and worriment came back to me in full force. If the men were stationing here, then this must be either where they have tracked the dragon to, or it was the destination on which they plan on luring it to. I knew that this was not a safe place to be. With this thought in mind, I decided that I had seen enough and that it was time to head back; out of the woods and out of harm's way. But when I turned to make my escape, I froze. There, maybe a hundred yards through the bush, was the dragon. Crouched, motionlessly staring; as if it was a lion ready to pounce on its prey.

"At first I was scared stiff, not believing what I was seeing. Then my mind started turning and I realized something. This crouched dragon that was ready to pounce was aiming in the direction of the platoon that I had just discovered. A terrible notion entered my mind; the hunters were being hunted by the huntee. Of this thought, I was not certain, so as cautiously as I could, I adjusted myself for a better observation through the thicket. By doing so I must have rustled some leaves or snapped a twig, because the dragon heard me. Without any other part of its body moving, the dragon shot its determined stare at me. Those yellow beady eyes horrified me as they fixated on their new target. I thought that I was going to die. But instead of pouncing, the dragon just sat there. Still looking ready to pounce, but continuing to stare at me. I stood stiff as a board, frozen in shock, with our eyes locked.

"During this time, something strange happened. My emotions started to change within me. I went from being fearful and scared, to feeling determined, angry, and confused. What felt like an hour was actually just a moment. I cannot fully describe what happened in that period of time, but it was almost like the dragon was allowing me to connect with it." Pausing briefly and thinking about what he just said, Herms shook the notion and continued.

"Then I heard the call, the horn of the dragon. The platoon must have spotted the dragon. At that instant, the connection was broken, and I instinctively turned my head to the sky. To my wonderment, I saw one of the biggest dragons I had ever seen. I looked back down, and to my surprise, there was still a dragon in front of me. Two dragons in the land at the same time—I had never heard or seen such a thing. My state of shock was interrupted when a tremulous roar filled the air, and in an instant, the dragon took off, sprinting for the platoon. I felt surrendered to complete dread when I did not see just the one dragon charging onto the battlefield, but two . . . three . . . four . . . five . . . SIX! There were SIX DRAGONS!

"They encircled the regiment and simultaneously breathed fire out toward the men. Some were caught in the fire and burning alive. Others tried to help put them out, but they had their own worries, as I also saw three more dragons flying in from overhead with boulders clutched in the claws for unsuspecting victims. As the wall of inferno came closing in, the men had nowhere to go. At this, I could not watch anymore. I realized the importance of what had just happened, and decided right then that this must be brought to the lords' attention immediately! So, I did the one thing that I have been doing all of my life: I ran. I ran and ran and ran. I ran from the Mezpha Forest to the Castle Dorian. Not stopping, for I did not know if any of the dragons might have been coming after me. And now, here I am."

With these final words, Herms finished his report.

12

The drumming of hooves filled their ears. The stale taste of wind coated their mouths. The sun beat relentlessly on their backs. Lords Cephas and Benaniah decided to avoid the open plains of Elah and traveled east from the Castle Dorian, pounding their way to the Forest of Mezpha, where they had been galloping along the border for some time. The lords had left the castle at the sixth hour, and now the tenth hour was upon them as they quickly and impressively approached their mark. A clear day had made it easy to search the sky for any activity. To this point, it had been unusually uneventful. Knowing that the Forest of Mezpha would soon be behind them, Lord Benaniah pulled on the reigns of his steed and brought his beast to a slow and steady halt.

"We should break soon," suggested Lord Benaniah. "Once we pass the forest, we will be in the open until we come to the Endor Mountains. If we are to take on any activity, it will likely be hereafter." Lord Cephas agreed with Lord Benaniah's words, but in his usual way, he kept his straight stone jaw still, only giving the slightest nod of agreement with Lord Benaniah's assessment.

"There is a clearing and stream not far from here, just into the woods, that will supply us with drink and meat." Lord Benaniah made this suggestion not for themselves, for they were lords and were masters of their bodies, not slaves. Many people only obey the commands that their bodies give them: to eat, to drink, or to sleep; and when these commands are not accommodated, those people then become irrational, only thinking of how to fulfill their bodily command. Not the lords. Especially given that Lord Cephas was a herdsmen and Lord Benaniah was a hunter. If one could not act rationally and think clearly during the stress of a long cattle drive or hunt, then other more suitable trades would be recommended that better fit their abilities. No, this suggestion was made for the animals. This was a hard ride for any noble stallion; thus, the Lords did not want to push their steeds too hard, in case of urgency elsewhere in the Kingdom. Thus, the lords broke from their course and headed for the place of Lord Benaniah's forethought.

It was not long before the lords approached their desired destination. Once upon the clearing, they dismounted their horses and made way toward the stream. Seeing a fallen tree, the lords decide to harness their steeds and reward them with some grain and oats for their troubles.

"I'll be back shortly," declared Lord Benaniah as he made way down toward the stream. Lord Cephas nodded as he quietly started to gather some wood for a small fire to cook the fish on. Although this break was more for the animals, it would be foolish for the lords not to take advantage of it as well. It wasn't long before Lord Cephas ignited a fire and Lord Benaniah returned to camp with four big, beautiful fish that he had collected on a single arrow.

"I know that you don't have many sea creatures in your land, so I hope you like these. This particular fish has a meaty texture and taste."

"I am sure they will be fine. Thank you," replied Lord Cephas while remaining seated at the fire. Lord Cephas was not shy to the skinning and butchering of animals, but as Lord Benaniah had declared, he was not familiar with sea creatures; so to try and be of any assistance would only be a hindrance and an insult to Lord Benaniah's hospitality.

For a master huntsman, dressing a fish was not an ordeal, nor a long process. It seemed that only a moment after Lord Benaniah's reinstatement to the camp, he had them positioned on sticks for cooking and joined Lord Cephas at the fire. There was silence between the lords as they thought about their mission. A bubbling stream, a pop of the fire, or the soft gnaw of the horses feasting on oats was the only communication between them as they watched the small fire cook their meat. Their thoughts were on the mission.

There was no doubt that Herms' sudden disruption of the Gathering of the Lords was further confirmation of Lord Ekron's reports that, not one, but multiple dragons had been seen in the land. This report was something they had not encountered before. A dragon had been known to enter into the land from time to time, but never more than one, and never traveling as far north as the Plains of Elah. There were many questions that need to be answered. Questions like, "How many dragons are in the land?" and "How did they get past Lord Ekron's lookout men at the Mountain of Endorah?" One even began to wonder if they had been able to create or find another entrance into the land. These questions, and many more, the Lords were to investigate upon arrival in Lord Ekron's land.

Pondering these things, Lord Benaniah finally addressed the obvious question that was lurking in their minds: "What kind of mobilization, infiltration, and campaign of not one, but multiple dragons, would cause Lord Ekron to lash out the way he did during the Gathering of the Lords?"

Lord Cephas only looked up at Lord Benaniah with gentle pondering eyes as he continued to cook his fish over the fire.

"We have trained battalions with proven methods in order to handle such situations. To dispatch one or two of them would be a minor thing. But yet, we are the ones riding down to investigate," continued Lord Benaniah.

Lord Cephas looked back down to watch the fire as his fish began to cook, giving off a delicious aroma. "If it is more, than we saved the lives of men who may be entering an unfamiliar situation; if it is not, then the problem is still quickly remedied," he finally replied.

At this, the conversation ended, and they enjoyed their meal with each other's company, conversing only with their thoughts.

_13_

After finishing their meal, the two lords wasted no time in readying their horses and clearing their brief campsite. Instead of mounting their steeds and racing back to their course, the lords decided to let their horses enjoy a nice walk as they strolled along the stream, knowing that it would eventually lead them out of the Forrest of Mezpha and to the Region of Vinyah, for this gentle stream would gradually turn into the mighty River Podiseon and they would be able to continue their journey without having lost much time. As the Lords enjoyed the stillness of the forest and the whispers of the river; a protruding object caught their eyes. Their leisurely stroll quickly came to an end as they approached what seemed to be a boot sticking out of the muddy banks of the stream. Upon arrival, Lord Benaniah bent down and picked up the boot, anticipating to discard it in the appropriate manner. To the lords' surprise, the boot was not without its owner. For at the moment Lord Benaniah grabbed the boot, he also felt the foot that was within it which was accompanied by a faint groan from the mud.

Taken aback for only a moment, the lords looked at each other in question about what they had just discovered, but knew what needed to be done as a second grunt protruded from the muddy pile. The lords quickly went to work in exhuming whoever maybe lying within this muddy casing. The excavation revealed that this was a citizen of Lord Titus' land. Not only that, but a military officer! Although not recognizing the person they had just unearthed, the lords did recognize that this person was badly injured, malnourished, and in need of immediate medical attention.

Ideally, Lord Benaniah and Cephas would like to take the patient back to Lord Titus' land so that his own kin would be able to dress his wounds. But to journey back was much too far for the officer, and would also put the lords a full day behind on their mission. Letting this man die was not an option, but neither was aborting their mission. After some consideration of their newfound circumstances, Lord Benaniah spoke up.

"I know of an old friend not far from this location who will be able to help this man," he said as he took lead over the situation. "Come, let us move quickly."

With that being said, Lord Cephas mounted his horse and Lord Benaniah lifted the wounded man to Lord Cephas so that he could secure him for the ride that was just further down the river.

14

It wasn't long before Lords Benaniah and Cephas came upon a wooden bridge that arched from one side to the other over the increasing might of the river. At first sight, there didn't appear to be any significance to this bridge, except that it seemingly had come out of nowhere. An old, rickety bridge that time had become acquainted with. Moss and vines made their home on this old friend, and the weather made no mistake of the years it had endured.

Here is where Benaniah stopped.

"We have to cross this bridge, and then it is not far from there."

At his word, the lords made their way toward the old creeker. As they drew closer, it became apparent that there was something carved on the post of the bridge that had grown faint with time.

"Can you read it?" Lord Cephas asked Lord Benaniah after realizing that the carving was indeed a language that was foreign to him.

"Yes, I can," replied Lord Benaniah, "but I'll need a minute," he said as he moved closer to get a better look. Whatever was written was worn and faded, like the bridge had been there for hundreds of years. Lord Benaniah ran his fingers over the post as he examined it so that he could be sure that he was interpreting the writings correctly.

"It is a riddle," announced Lord Benaniah after a moment of study. "It says, '*An inward path one must make, a solo journey one must take, faith or fear will awake, to passage through the seeker gates.*'"

"What does that mean?" asked Lord Cephas

"I am not exactly certain of the entire interpretation," Lord Benaniah replied, "but one thing I do understand about this riddle is that we are to cross one at a time."

"This brings about a curious position for our new acquaintance," responded Lord Cephas.

A moment of thought passed by as the Lords considered the current predicament. They could cross with ease, but what about their wounded friend? Being a hunter and shepherd, the lords were familiar with circumstances that required them to rely on natural surroundings as their only means of resource. After taking inventory of their current situation, Lord Benaniah made a plausible suggestion.

"Why don't we make a stretcher out of some vine, logs, and a cloth? We can secure the wounded on the stretcher and then cross the bridge one at a time, each with a vine in hand. After we have crossed, we can then use the vines to pull the soldier across."

"Would that not subject our friend to further injury?" inquired Lord Cephas.

"Yes," Benaniah answered, "that is possible, but his injuries are already terminal, and this is seemingly his only hope. If we do nothing, he will die. If we cross, he may die, but he also may live."

At this, Cephas agreed with a nod, and then they both started to put the plan into action; first by securing their horses, then by securing their materials.

"There!" said Lord Benaniah after tightening the last vine. "That should do it." It was a nice stretcher for being made in only a moment's notice. The cords were twined out of three vines and woven in and out of one of the lords' saddlebags, which was butterflied in order to give maximum length, while a couple of sturdy branches from a fallen tree made nice rails. The lords made sure to have enough slack in the vines for them to cross to the other side and then pull their comrade across. For extra precaution, a pocket was made at the head and foot of the stretcher in order to further secure the victim.

"Now all we need to do is cross the bridge one at a time and then drag our comrade over to the other side."

With that being said, Benaniah took a vine in his hand and started to cross the bridge.

Lord Cephas watched in anticipation, knowing that things are not always what they seem. As he watched, Lord Benaniah crossed the bridge. Nothing peculiar happened of note. Lord Benaniah walked up the bridge, and upon reaching the apex, stood there for a minute, then proceeded to walk down the other side. However, when he reached the opposing riverbank, he vanished.

15

Lord Benaniah walked toward the bridge not knowing what to expect, but knowing to expect something. With a deep breath, the lord started his journey across the old wooden bridge, ready for what awaited him. At the top of the bridge, he noticed that a small glimmer of light floated seamlessly above it. As it hovered in its place, golden rays came from its core with various shades of blue, red, and purple swirling around it, making each ray look like its own unique sunset. Transfixed by its beauty, Lord Benaniah curiously moved toward the floating spear without caution. Upon approaching this mysterious aberration, Lord Benaniah realized that the light was growing. As this flawless drop of the sun grew, it took on many different shapes. Lord Benaniah couldn't help but think that he saw this golden light take on shapes of the Dwarfs, the Shephen, the Fauns, the Humans, and the

Nimrods. Not just intelligent creatures, but simple creatures as well, such as a frog, a bird, and a calf. Suddenly, the light was now as big as Lord Benaniah himself, taking on the shape of a human with Faun horns protruding out of its head, clothed with a Shephen's cloth, a hunter's bow draped around his torso and a Dwarf's battle axe at the ready in his hand. These were the only details able to be ascertained, for this newly-formed creature shined liked a star, with a bright radiant center that made it hard to look upon. After a moment, Lord Benaniah heard a voice; a soft gentle voice that sounded like the words were being exhaled rather than spoken.

"Where are you coming from?" the creature asked.

"My name is Lord Benaniah, Lord of the Hunt. I am one of the five Lords of Sahleam. I have come from the Castle Dorian of Lord Titus, Lord of the Humans, on a mission to get information about a dragon report."

After a moment of silence, the creature proceeded to ask, "Where are you going?"

Not sure what to make of the situation, Lord Benaniah decided it would be best just to answer the creature's questions directly. At worst, a conflict would arise. At best, maybe the creature would allow him to pass.

"I wish to cross and go into the Calithym forest in search of the healer."

The creature just stood there as light continued to pour forth from its being, illuminating the proximity.

"What is that in your hand?" the creature finally asked, pointing down toward Lord Benaniah's hand.

Looking down, Lord Benaniah simply responded, "A rope."

He had intended to leave his answer at that, but when he looked back at the creature, it was still gazing at the vine that was in his hand. Somehow Lord Benaniah knew that the creature knew that this rope was connected to their injured fellow and that he was intending to pull him across. So the lord decided to elaborate his situation to the creature and hope for the best.

"In order to pull our dying comrade across," the lord continued.

"We have found him along our mission. He is fatally wounded and in need of the healer.

"So," the creature began softly, "this is the life of a man?" It reached down and gently lifted up the hand that was grasping the rope.

"Yes," said Lord Benaniah, not knowing what to expect. He did not fully understand the riddle, but the one thing he did understand was that only one person was able to cross the bridge at a time. Still, he pleaded, "A life that will end if not taken to the healer."

"All life is of equal value, not matter how much or how little," gently spoke the creature as its gaze went from Lord Benaniah's hand to his face.

"And it is that value," calmly claimed the lord, "that should conclude on his crossing, even though it is in need of assistance."

"Through the rope your lives are twined," replied the creature, "and the writing is clear: 'only one shall pass'."

A moment of thought besieged Lord Benaniah. If he crossed without the rope, then their Samaritan journey would come to an end. It was not only out of a great act of kindness, need, or heart that the lords needed this man's life restored, but also because he was clearly a militant and could possess valuable information regarding recent events. Then the answer came to Lord Benaniah: "If our lives are 'twined' through this rope and not just associated, then we are no longer two separate lives, but one life. Though our life force is greater than usual, we must still be considered as one, for 'No matter how much or how little, all life is of equal value'".

Lord Benaniah was not sure if using the creature's own words against it was the wisest choice he could have made, but the die had been cast.

At this, the spirit considered the lord's response, and after some thought the creature simply said, "Proceed. Continue your quest," and then vanished.

"Thank you," Lord Benaniah replied. With a sigh of relief and a grateful heart, the lord lost no time continuing across and down the other side of the bridge.

16

When Lord Cephas saw Lord Benaniah vanish, he was not taken aback, stunned, or surprised. He had been anticipating something of the sort to occur. The good news was that the rope was still taut. Therefore, Lord Benaniah was still holding onto it. Lord Cephas knew that there was no other choice. Not knowing what happened to Lord Benaniah and not sure what awaited him on the other side, Lord Cephas started across the bridge. As he reached the apex a bright light appeared to him. Upon getting closer to the light source Lord Cephas realized that it was a creature of some type.

"I wonder if Lord Benaniah ran into this being. And if he did, how did he surpass it?" Lord Cephas thought as he approached.

Now facing the being, Lord Cephas looked upon a creature of the likes which he had never seen before. A human face, Faun horns, a Sheppen's cloak, a hunter's bow, and a Dwarf's battle axe. "Is it a coincidence that this creature is a representation of each race? And if it's not a coincidence, then who conjured up such powerful magic?" the lord asked himself.

"Where are you coming from?" the creature finally asked in a soft voice.

"I am Cephas," answered the lord. "Lord of the Sheppen, of the Pastures of Jiear. I am one of the five Lords of the great land Sahleam. I am coming from the Castle Dorian of Lord Titus, Lord of the Humans, about a dragon report."

"And where," interrogated the creature, "is it, that you are going?"

"My fellow Lord, Benaniah, and I are crossing this bridge in need of a healer."

Although Lord Cephas could not see any details of the creature's body, especially his face, he could tell that it was weighing the lord's words heavily. This being was not just making polite conversation, but considering each response and the heart behind the response.

Faith or fear? thought Lord Cephas as he mused his current situation. *Hopefully the creature, or more likely a guardian, could see my words for what they are, genuine, and pure. I am not interested in finding out what fear may look like.*

"Proceed," the creature said as it stepped to the side. "Continue your journey."

"Thank you," said Lord Cephas gratefully as he wasted no time walking past the creature and down the other side of the bridge. While walking down the bridge it dawned on the lord that he was still not able to see Lord Benaniah. Lord Cephas was not alarmed by this. For in the land of Sahleam, things are not always as they seem. Lord Cephas reached the bottom of the bridge and, without hesitation, stepped over onto the other side and vanished.

17

After stepping off the bridge and onto the embankment, Lord Cephas saw Lord Benaniah sitting quietly and patiently. The lords took a moment to examine each other, looking for any kind of imperfection that may indicate that they were not who they appeared to be. After a moment of studying, both lords passed the other's eye test. They at least looked like who they were supposed to be.

"You made it," joyfully claimed Lord Benaniah as a slight smile cracked his face.

Lord Cephas only nodded as he continued to study what appeared to be Lord Benaniah.

"Well," began Lord Benaniah, "that was definitely a test that I would rather not take again," continued the lord as he got up and began walking toward Lord Cephas.

"I hope yours was not as exasperating as mine," mentioned Lord Benaniah as he continued toward Lord Cephas, grasping the vine in one hand and caressing the hilt of his blade in the other. This, of course, did not go unnoticed by Lord Cephas. But he knew what was happening and why, and began to prepare himself for what was to come.

"Unfortunately," claimed Lord Benaniah as he now grasped the hilt of his sword, "before we can continue, there is one more test we have to pass!" exclaimed the lord as he, in one poetic motion, drew his sword and brought it down to rest on Lord Cephas' neck.

Lord Cephas stood there, unhesitant, as the cold blade sliced through the air and came to a halt on his neck. Standing as still as a statue, the lord just kept his eyes locked with Lord Benaniah.

Lord Benaniah just looked back, blinked, and smiled.

"Lord Cephas," Lord Benaniah exclaimed as he lowered his sword and embraced Lord Cephas. "I apologize, old friend. I am sure you understand. I needed to make sure that it was you that came off the bridge."

After Lord Benaniah's experience with the being on the bridge, he needed to make sure that this was indeed Lord Cephas who followed him off of the bridge and not some other creature. This test proved to Lord Benaniah that this person before him was in fact Lord Cephas. For Lord Benaniah never had any intention on following through with his attack, but only came as close as possible before pulling back. If this person before him was Lord Cephas, he would not even flinch, for Lord Cephas knew that Lord Benaniah would never intentionally harm him.

"I understand." Lord Cephas answered calmly.

"Well," began Lord Benaniah, "there is no time to lose. Let us begin to pull our friend over." And with that the Lords began carefully pulling the vines in order to bring their wounded comrade across the bridge and to the other side.

18

Lying lifeless, the militant began sliding across the earth. This experience would have been painful, but his body had gone numb due to his injuries. Barely conscious, the soldier just laid there, watching the clouds in the sky. As he was being pulled, a bright light started to come into existence. Peace and comfort overtook his body as he continued to move closer to the light. Warmth and calmness grew as the light became brighter.

Being a soldier, this man knew that you do not give up under any circumstance. You are to always give your best. Pain and suffering were just temporary inconveniences that only try to hinder your mission. What happens, though, when you have willed yourself as far as you can go? When the next step that you take just might be your last? Is it time for this solider to be relieved of his mission and head home to his eternal post?

The light grew brighter as his body grew warmer.

This is it, thought the soldier, *time to let go and take that next step.* As he closed his eyes, he welcomed what was to come next.

A white light encompassed his reality as he heard the words, 'I will sustain you' softly whispered in his ear. Next, it was as if a hot coal was being pressed against his lips. The heat was intense but did not burn. It started at his lips, but then began to spread through the soldier's body. First down his throat, as if he had swallowed a hot cup of chocolate on a cold winter's night, down to his chest and then torso, melting away fear and pain. Suddenly, the sensation shot from his thorax to his outer limbs. Overcome with peace, relaxation, and joy, the soldier took one last deep breath and gave into the rest that he so eagerly desired.

19

After the lords had successfully pulled their companion across the bridge, Lord Benaniah relieved him of his harnesses as Lord Cephas collected him upon his shoulders as easily as if it were a sack of feathers. And with that, the two Lords and the soldier began due east in search of the militant's only hope for survival. Shortly after they had started their walk, Lord Benaniah suddenly stopped, looked left, looked right, looked up, and then looked at Lord Cephas.

"Where are we?" inquired Lord Benaniah.

"We are in the Calithym Forest," incredulously replied Lord Cephas.

"Oh," said Lord Benaniah with a curious look on his face as he continued looking around, trying to figure out where he was.

"And, uh, where are we going?" the lord inquired.

Lord Cephas looked at Lord Benaniah quizzically. After a moment, he answered, "In search of your friend that lives in this part of the woods."

Before Lord Cephas could add anything more to his response, Lord Benaniah quickly added, "And why are we searching for my friend?"

Now, the Sheppen are not a people who get quickly angered by nature, but Lord Cephas was starting to feel frustration rise to the surface as he carried on this conversation with Lord Benaniah. After a deep breath, Lord Cephas calmly responded, "To bring healing to this man we have found."

Looking at the man draped across Lord Cephas' shoulder, it was obvious that it was the right thing to do, to help this poor fellow. But still, Lord Benaniah could not help but to ask, "And why do we need to heal this person?"

"For any information he may have regarding the disturbance," Lord Cephas replied in a matter of fact.

Looking at Lord Cephas, Lord Benaniah asked, "What disturbance?" with all sincerity and honesty of heart.

At that, Lord Cephas just looked at him for a moment.

"I'm sorry, but I don't know anyone who lives in these parts of the woods," concluded Lord Benaniah.

Now, there is no point in arguing with someone who has made up their mind or believes otherwise than you do. You could no more change their mind than you could fit a square peg in a round hole. Lord Benaniah is a light-hearted and playful fellow, but now was not the time for any games. Therefore, without any explanation, upon hearing Lord Benaniah's last statement, Lord Cephas gathered himself and continued walking in the direction they had originally started.

Although Lord Benaniah may have forgotten where he was and what he was doing, he did not forget that Lord Cephas was a good friend and could be trusted. With that in mind, Lord Benaniah did the only logical thing he could do: he followed Lord Cephas.

As they continued to walk deeper into the woods, Lord Benaniah was falling in love with the surroundings: the chirping of the birds in the air, the crunch of leaves and twigs beneath his feet, the colors of trees, plants, and flowers that filled his eyes, and a cool crisp breeze kissing his cheeks. Just like that, as quickly as Lord Benaniah had forgotten their purpose and mission, it all came flooding back into his mind. With that, he picked up his pace, passing Lord Cephas with confidence, and once again took the lead as they headed for the healer.

It wasn't long after Lord Benaniah took the lead that he noticed that sound of Lord Cephas trailing along had diminished, and then all together stopped. At this Lord Benaniah stopped and straight away began scanning the area for any immediate danger. After a moment of evaluating the area, the Lord concluded that there was no sudden danger. Turning, Lord Benaniah saw Lord Cephas, unmoving. Gazing at Lord Cephas, Lord Benaniah remained still, waiting for some sort of communication from the other lord.

"We have to go," Lord Cephas stated flatly as he turned around and began to walk back in the direction from which they had come.

"What!" said Lord Benaniah, surprised at his partner's declaration.

"Hey!" he shouted to get Lord Cephas' attention while he made way to catch up to his friend.

"Whoa, whoa, whoa, what are you doing?" asked Lord Benaniah as he caught up to the lord and blocked his path.

"We are going the wrong way. We have to go this way in order to reach our destination," claimed Lord Cephas.

"What?" replied Lord Benaniah in confusion. "I thought you were not familiar with these parts of the woods?"

"I am not," said Lord Cephas soundly.

"Well, I have been here many times, and am very familiar with which way we should go," stated Lord Benaniah

"Then why are you leading us in the wrong direction?" calmly asked Lord Cephas.

Instead of engaging in what would be a pointless argument with his friend, Lord Benaniah decided to try and prove to him that he was indeed leading him in the right direction.

"Which direction should we be going?" asked Lord Benaniah?

"East," replied Lord Cephas.

"Well, there lies the sun as it sets," stated Lord Benaniah as he made his argument. "We know that the sun sets in the east. We also know that if we were to go west, we would be heading toward the Plains of Elah. Therefore," Lord Benaniah soundly concluded, "let us follow the sun."

With no words, Lord Cephas took a step toward the sun.

20

The Lords walked in silence for what felt like an hour, but for what was only just a couple of minutes. Knowing that they should be arriving at the healer's house soon, Lord Benaniah started to feel some worry that they might have gone the wrong way. Then, suddenly, the lord heard a shuffle of leaves. He immediately stopped, gave a signal for Lord Cephas to do likewise, and began to scan the area. After a moment of scanning, there was nothing of suspicion. After waiting one more moment, Lord Benaniah decided that there was nothing of concern and started to continue their campaign.

Before they could take another step, they heard another rustling of leaves accompanied by the howling of a mighty wind as the treetops began to sway. No sooner did the lords scan the treetops to make sure nothing was lurking above, than they heard definite movement along the ground, and a shadow of a figure moving among the treetrunks. The wind howled again, only this time it was in front of them. The leaves continued to rustle and even elevate off of the ground as two clear orbs announced their arrival, side by side, no more than twenty yards in front of them. What these orbs were, the lords did not know. The lords were only able to make them out due to the waves of energy that were coming from the orbs, making everything within an immediate radius seem wavy; like how ripples in the water do to an object's reflection. At first, they just hovered several feet off of the ground. Then they began to be tossed to and fro, from side to side in a forward motion, as if two children were tossing balls back and forth as they moved down a lane coming closer to the Lords. This happened slowly and playfully at first, but then the orbs started to move faster and with more intensity as trees swayed in their wake and leaves and other small brush were kicked up as the orbs approached the lords.

Standing fearlessly, the lords anticipated the revealing of whatever manner of creature this thing may be. As the orbs rushed closer, the lords' anticipation grew, as did the howling winds and swirling debris. Before the lords could make a move, the orbs were upon them, consuming them as the orbs spun furiously around them. The lords could not see as the raging orbs and debris encircled them. They could not hear except for the howling wind. There was no sense of direction, no sense of feeling, no sense of gravitational pull. The lords knew that all they could do now was wait; wait for this unknown magic to either wear off, or take their lives. Gritting their teeth and clinching their eyes, the lords hoped it was the former and not the latter.

As quickly as it began, it was over. When the Lords regained stability and self-awareness, something strange and magical happened. Suddenly, seemingly out of nowhere, like it had only just appeared, was a straw hut neatly placed in a clearing just ahead of them.

21

As Lord Benaniah and Lord Cephas stood there, wondering where the house had come from, a man dressed in a sky-blue robe and moon white hair came walking around from the back. At that moment Lord Benaniah remembered where they were and who this man was.

"Murlynn," exclaimed the lord gleefully with a smile and hand extended high into the air.

As the lords made their way in Murlynn's direction, one did have to wonder about the hut. Other than the structural integrity being compromised by what looked like a straw framework, it was one of the nicest huts the lords had ever seen. It was a small, circular hut complete with a door, windows, and a pointed roof.

Although it was truly a nice-looking hut, the lords could not help but think, "How did the architecture sustain rains, winds, and wild animals?"

The lord's thoughts were nothing more than just a passing question. There were more important matters to deal with, such as their comrade's life.

Murlynn stopped at Lord Benaniah's greeting and looked favorably in the lords' direction. With a smile and a nod, the lords knew that they were welcomed by this neatly-kept, homely-looking man. As the lords grew closer, Murlynn stepped out with arms extended and embraced Lord Benaniah.

"Brother!" Murlynn said with delight, "It has been a while. How are you?"

"Far too long," agreed Lord Benaniah. "I am well. Although I wish I could say the same for all of my party. There is not time for long introductions, but this is Lord Cephas of the Sheppen, and on his back is our companion, who is in need of your help."

"Greetings, my Lord," said Murlynn with a gentle bow toward Lord Cephas. Murlynn briefly looked over the man on his shoulders, and said, "I see. Come, we should go inside so I can make a diagnosis and remedy right away."

As they walked toward the hut, Lord Cephas figured it would not be more than a one-room structure. But something magical happened when the lords walked through the front door, for the inside of the hut was much bigger than the outside would lead one to believe. In the middle of the ground floor of the hut was a dining area, complete with table, chairs, and a floating chandelier. To the left was the kitchen area, with a fire, kettle, and table. To the right of that was the laboratory, with beakers, mixing burners, scales, and storage jars filled with many curious things. Next to that was the study and library, complete with a couch and coffee tables on either side. Next to the study there seemed to be a living area, which was nothing more than a chair, footrest, a coffee table covered with books, and a fire pit. If that wasn't enough, there were also stairs that seemed to lead to both an upper and lower level as well. Lord Cephas was tempted to walk outside to make sure that he had entered the correct hut, but resisted, knowing that there was some sort of magic at work.

"Lay the patient down on the couch in the study," said Murlynn upon entering the hut, and then headed straight for the laboratory.

Without hesitation, the Lord Cephas transported their friend to his final destination. As the lords were now able to fully look upon him and see the extent of his wounds, they realized how little life their friend had left, if any at all.

No sooner did the lords lay down their comrade then did Murlynn come to his side. He pulled the footstool over and sat down near his head. Without delay, Murlynn untied a leathery pouch that was in his hands, reached in, and grabbed a handful of powder. Murlynn opened his hand and gently blew the powder toward the patient's mouth and nose. At first, due to its gray and flaky nature, you may have thought that this powder was nothing more than ash from the fireplace. But when Murlynn blew upon it, the ash shimmered and gleamed as it did an aerial dance, before resting in a hovering state above the patient's face, reflecting beautiful prismatic colors that only light itself could produce. At first the ash just stayed still as the patient lay seemingly lifeless. Then the powder moved slightly, almost imperceptible. Small amounts of the powder disappeared into the patient's slightly-opened mouth. On seeing this, Murlynn exhaled in relief.

"Good," Murlynn said with a sense of satisfaction, "very Good." Standing to face the lords, Murlynn began to explain what was happening.

"Your friend is alive; barely, but alive. The prismaic medicine is entering your friend's respiratory system with each breath that he takes. No matter how small a dose, the prismaic aerotate will give back his strength. The bigger breathes he takes and the more steadily he breathes, the more energy he will receive."

"How long until he is stable?" Lord Benaniah asked.

"It may be a while," replied Murlynn. "Although the medicine works quickly, your friend was only hanging on by a thread. If you had not found him and brought him to me when you did, he would be dead," Murlynn added encouragingly. A moment of silence came over the group, not yet knowing the full importance of their actions.

"Well then," Murlynn finally said, "While we wait for the medicine to take full effect, I will put on a pot of tea."

22

"This is worse than we feared," said Lord Augusta in exasperation as he rubbed his hand on his head as though to wipe away a thought or memory.

"One dragon could be taken care of," agreed Lord Ekron as he paced the floor. "Two would be difficult, but still could be resolved . . . but nine dragons!" exclaimed the Lord as he slammed his fist down on the round marble table with a small thud of exasperation.

The three lords had since left Herms to his recovery and made their way to the War Room. This room was much like the other chambers in the castle. There were torchlit sconces on the gray stone walls, and a large fireplace— big enough to cook a whole pig on a spit—sat off to the side, trying to bring warmth to their disparaging news. A round marble table sat in the middle of the room, big enough to fit Lord Titus and his council of twelve. On the walls were paintings of great battles that took place in the land: The Fauns' victory over the Minotaurs, the Dwarfs overtaking the Azarks, the Great Siege at Hashban, and the Battle of Norfaulk were just some of the pictures that lined the walls.

"Hmmm," Lord Titus mused as he looked at a particular painting; one that had great meaning and importance to all the people of Sahleam: the great Lord King Onesomus standing valiantly in victory on a blood soaked hill after the Battle of Ezerek.

"It's a curious thing," began Lord Titus as he turned and began walking over to the war table. "Not only was there a pack of dragons in the land at the same time, but according to Herms, they showed coordination, calculation, and premeditation."

"All signs point toward this not being a small endeavor," responded Lord Augusta.

"He is right," chimed in Lord Ekron. "This is just the beginning of our troubles. We need to act now." He slammed his hand on the table again. "Before they are able to establish a base and attack us with their full strength."

"Lord Ekron is right," agreed Lord Titus. "We need to gather the troops and obtain information so we can prepare for an offensive."

"Messengers should be sent to all the kingdoms to call on their support," quickly added Lord Ekron. "This initiative affects all lands, not just ours, and they should act accordingly."

"Women and children need to find hiding and stay there until the matter has been resolved," added Lord Augusta.

"Relay stations need to be established," interjected Lord Titus thoughtfully. "Lord Ekron, your mountains would be ideal, both the interior and exterior borders, and one along the plains." Directing himself to Lord Augusta, the lord added, "All previous infiltrations have come from the south. Therefore, chances are they are going to try and make the mountains their base."

"So we are just going to give up my homeland to those beasts?" spouted Lord Ekron, as his anger quickly began to rise.

"Your men know the tunnels and those caves better than anyone or anything," Lord Titus quickly added, trying to subside Lord Ekron's anger. "Your people should be safe within the heart of your land."

"Aye," agreed Lord Ekron thoughtfully. "Our mother has always provided refuge to those who sought it."

After a moment of thought, Lord Titus declared the initiative. "Our best option is to encounter them in the plains, where there is no camouflage."

"Are we just going to set ourselves out as some sort of smorgasbord for those monsters to have at?" Lord Ekron said sarcastically.

"An attack in the open is more beneficial to us than it is to them," responded Lord Titus. "This way they do not have an area that would conceal their position. We would have clear vision of their mobilization both on the ground and in the air."

"Also, based on what Herms has said, we need our best magicians to start collaborating on some sort of new weapon that will help us defeat our foe."

Lord Ekron and Lord Augusta nodded in agreement.

With that being said, Lord Titus headed toward the door. "Brutus, Antheis, will you come join us please?"

As soon as Brutus and Antheis entered the room, Lord Titus closed the door and got right to the point.

"You have been my personal guards for a long time and have served me well. You are the bravest, most trustworthy men I know. Therefore, I have a mission for both of you that is of the upmost importance."

"Brutus," began Lord Titus as he grabbed ink, a pen, and some parchment, "I want you to ride out to the Forest of Mezpha to the Kingdom of Shaddonai and relay this urgent message to the Council of the Nimrods. We need their best troops, and they are to hide their women and children immediately until further notice. I will also need you to choose a man, one whom you look at as I do to you, and have him ride with the same urgent message to the Sheppen, who are in the Plains of Jiear, the Kingdom of Rahamah."

"Antheis," Lord Titus continued as he finished writing the declaration. "I need you also to take the message to the Plains of Elah where the Kingdom of Vatoya is and deliver it to the Council of Fauns. Choose two men whom you look at as I do you, and have them ride with haste to the Dwarfs of the Kingdom of Raphastein within the Endor Mountains with the same message. But you are to also break east after having delivered our declaration to the Fauns, and head for the Valley of Kurdish. Be sure to stay on the perimeter and use the woods to mask your presence. I need you to examine the area for any possible survivors and also gather any information you can from the battle site. Do not dally long, for we do not know where these dragons have migrated. Take three choice warriors with you as well, comrades who have served you as well as you have served me," concluded Lord Titus as he grabbed a candle, dripped wax onto the parchment, and sealed it with his signet ring before handing the letters over for delivery.

23

"If memory serves me right, there is a man in the land with great magical ability who is more familiar than perhaps anyone else in history on dragonology," quietly said Lord Augusta.

The room was silent once again. Only the crackle and pop of the fire dared to interrupt the quietness of the lord's thoughts as they sat around the great marble table, considering what actions needed to take place next.

"I believe it was he who had discovered and provided what was our initial advantage over these creatures to begin with, the carnivorous diffusion," continued Lord Augusta.

"He also provided them with food from our flocks to satisfy their hunger and an ocean of fear to quench their thirst," Lord Ekron sternly reminded.

"Not a perfect idea," meekly remarked Lord Augusta, "but, an idea."

"Humph," scoffed Lord Ekron.

"Not a perfect idea," the lord continued irritably. "Let us not forget that these creatures love to inhabit the mountainside and feed on mountain goats and rams, both of which are almost exclusive to my kingdom." Lord Ekron's tone was quickly rising from a dry sarcasm to a passionate anger, fed by the memory of what his people had to endure.

"We had to abandon our homes and hide in caves, sending hunting parties out to search for meat, not knowing who would and would not return," the lord reminded. "This was due to the same person whose passion was a blinding fixation for the beast."

"I am sorry for your troubles," said Lord Augusta sympathetically. "We all are too familiar and easily reminded of that time that seemed not that long ago," the Lord continued. "If I remember correctly, it was his potion that enabled us to drive out the beast and to keep them at bay ever since."

"And it is his potion that is currently not working," quickly rebutted Lord Ekron as his temper began to rise with annoyance of the continued suggestion. "Thus leading to this current intrusion."

"Now, Lord Ekron," said Lord Titus, calmly weighing in on the matter. "I think that we all can agree that his zealousness for dragons had blinded him to their ruthless inherent nature," first stated Lord Titus in order to help keep Lord Ekron's anger at bay. "But penitence was made, and justice dispensed. Which," Lord Titus quickly added before Lord Ekron could add in another accusation, "he willingly and peacefully accepted. And," continued Lord Titus so not to be interrupted, "it was only after accepting his judgment that the potion was made."

Lord Titus paused just briefly to see if Lord Ekron would interject. Seeing that the Dwarf lord was not going to impede his train of thought, Lord Titus finished.

"Now, although we do not forget the past," Lord Titus said in Lord Ekron's direction, "but rather learn from it, we also," continued the lord as he now directed his words toward Lord Augusta, "need to absolve those of transgressions who so willingly and so repentfully execute their sentence," finished Lord Titus.

Although logic had been dispensed and accepted, there was a thick, silent tension over the matter that was growing in the room. Knowing that this matter needed to be resolved quickly, Lord Titus made his motion, which was the last thing Lord Ekron wanted to hear at that moment or in any moment. "I suggest that we contact this man and see if there is any information or help that he is able to provide."

"And what makes you think that he is able or willing to help us?" asked Lord Ekron, annoyed with the suggestion.

"I think he may."

"And besides, right now, he is our best hope," stated Lord Titus flatly.

"Come. Let us call upon Murlynn."

24

Darkness was everywhere. The sound of marching boots filled the air, and then, silence. Clamoring of weaponry and chattering softly resonated in the background. And then, silence again. This time it seemed to go on and on. Complete nothingness. There was no light, no sound, no feeling; just complete nothingness. Then, a terrifying and ferocious roar swallowed him like a snake coming down on its prey. The ground began to shake, and his heart began to beat faster. Beads of sweat crowned his forehead. Butterflies twirled in his stomach. Cotton invaded his mouth, the all-too-familiar symptoms of battle. But before he could attack, overbearing heat consumed him. Pain, like daggers, ripped through his shoulders as his body endured a beating worse than a punching bag. Suddenly, it all dissipated, and the darkness slowly faded to light. A comforting warmth rushed through his bones like a warm fire on a frosty night. A soft whistle began ringing softly in the distance, growing louder and louder and louder until it was ear piercing and deafening. At this, he opened his eyes. He took in a deep breath and started coughing immediately.

25

Lord Benaniah sat with a deep sigh of relief as Lord Cephas gracefully took a seat next to him at the dining table. Murlynn busied himself with preparations of tea and biscuits. He was very excited to have visitors. Not many people ventured off to pay him a visit nowadays. Many years had come and gone since the dragon had escaped his possession and rained havoc on the people of the land. This was part of the punishment that he eagerly accepted—to be segregated from the people for a time. Either way, he was content with life, and happy to be making biscuits and tea for someone other than himself.

"Thank you very much for your help," said Lord Benaniah, in order to express their gratitude.

"Don't mention it," said Murlynn passingly as he continued with his preparation. "There is still a fair amount of recovery that needs to take place. Magic can only restore so much. The rest is up to him."

A moment passed as Murlynn started kneading the biscuit dough.

Lord Benaniah knew that Murlynn was a clever man and probably figured that something was wrong. It was not every day that someone dropped by unannounced, let alone two lords with a man who was near death. Before the lord could just state their purpose, he wanted to see how much Murlynn knew about what was happening.

"Are you aware of any disturbance that has taken place recently?" asked Lord Benaniah.

"No," replied Murlynn as he began rolling out his dough. "What kind of disturbance?" inquired Murlynn on second thought.

"Well," began Lord Benaniah. "We are not exactly sure yet. We don't have all the pieces."

"Huh," mumbled Murlynn as he continued cutting out his biscuits.

"We just thought, given your abilities, that you would know if anything would have happened within a reasonable distance from your home," said Lord Benaniah, trying to see whether or not Murlynn truly was ignorant of the current situation.

"No, can't say that I am aware of anything," Murlynn replied as he grabbed his cast-iron skillet.

Done playing Lord Benaniah's game, Lord Cephas finally spoke up. "Dragons are in the land again."

At this, Lord Murlynn startled, fumbling the cast-iron skillet that he was carrying.

"Dragons?" asked Murlynn sincerely. "You mean that there are more than one?"

Murlynn could not believe what he was hearing. His emotions were mixed, and his thoughts were jumbled. Even with the all the problems his dragon had caused, he still could not forget nor break the bond that was formed when the dragon was just a pup.

"Oh dear," continued Murlynn before the lords could say anything. "That's not good. Not good at all," muttered Murlynn as he collected the biscuits, placed them in the cast iron skillet, and put them over the fire into what looked like a metal box.

Murlynn was truly concerned for what this meant. A single dragon was enough to handle by itself. More than one would be menacing.

Turning from the fire, Murlynn stopped, closed his eyes, and took a deep breath. After collecting his thoughts, he joined the lords at the table for the ensuing conversation.

<u>26</u>

Antheis and his troops were riding hard. They pounded east through the Plains of Elah, as Silas and Raithyn, two of his most skilled and trusted men, road off to the Dwarfs and the Kingdom of Raphastein. Antheis and his men entered the Forest of Mezpha just north of the Valley of Kurdish. They were well aware that the Valley Kurdish was where the ambush that had started it all had taken place. Hopefully, like any good army, the dragons would not be still residing at the place of their attack. Either way, this was the most direct route from the Plains of Elah to the Forest of Mezpha.

They had already warned the Fauns of Lord Augusta, and were entering the second part of their mission: to gather intel from the battle scene. All had been quiet so far, although Antheis was not expecting much movement considering the land's new predatory inhabitants. No birds or scowl could be spotted in the air, nor were any deer seen about in the meadows. Although they were not necessarily soft footing their way through the fields, there still should have been some signs of frolicking by some animals in the distance. But there was nothing.

The woods quickly came upon Antheis and brought his concentration back to what was in front of him.

What was in front of him? At first, Antheis thought he had seen a figure at the forest's tree line ahead. Dismissing the image as a figment of his imagination, Antheis and his company rode through the mouth of the forest and into its belly.

Antheis had ridden through these woods many times, but never before had an eeriness come over him like this. Silence crept through his bones. Thoughts of the trees trying to snatch him from his horse projected themselves from his mind. A chill bit his nose and watered his eyes.

Then, out of the corner of his eye, he saw a flock of birds hurry away from their perched concealment, flapping over one another, trying to escape whatever danger may befall them. At this, Antheis pulled his reigns hard. His horse whined and erected itself onto its hind legs so as not to have its neck broken by the sudden pull and jerk of the reigns. His comrades followed suit. There was a loud commotion as dirt and leaves filled the air, concealing them in a cloud of dust and debris. Antheis didn't pay this any bother.

His senses were on full alert, like a deer that suddenly knew that all was not right. Scanning the area, jaw tight and eyes keen, Antheis looked for any sign of danger as his men armed themselves, arrows and swords ready at the hilt. Antheis jumped when he heard a rustle of leaves from behind. Turning, ready to die for his country, he saw a red fox trot out of the bush. Before there came a sigh of relief, unclenched jaw, or untensed muscle, a bloodcurdling roar filled the air.

27

"We don't mean to impose, suspect, or interrogate you on the matter," started Lord Benaniah as Murlynn had joined himself and Lord Cephas at the table. "We are just trying to collect information. We ourselves were journeying to the spot Herms had indicated to try and discover more information when we came across the gentleman who is now lying on your couch, for whom we are most grateful for your assistance. It just so happened that when we discovered our friend, we knew that his only hope was you. Since we are here, we figured we would inquire about any information you may have."

"Rightly so," began Murlynn, his eyes and head looking down at the table, seemingly still uncomfortable with the actions he had committed that led him to this current situation. "Given my previous involvement with the last dragon incident—" said Murlynn in choked voice, pausing briedly to collect himself. He removed his spectacles with one hand, rubbing his eyes with the other. He took a deep breath, placed his glasses back on again, and cleared his throat. "I suppose it was only a matter of time before my presence was requested."

Looking fully upon Lord Benaniah, Murlynn found the strength to properly state his plight. "Unfortunately, there is nothing that I know that will help you in your quest, for I was ignorant of the situation until you just now presented it to me. Of course, if there is anything I can do to help, all you have to do is ask."

The lords did not reply at that moment of any needs, although they had many, for they were fixed on Murlynn and what he had to say.

"May I ask," continued Murlynn, after he had given a moment for the lords' reply, "what exactly is this disturbance that you speak of?"

"We are not exactly sure yet. All we know is that Herms had witnessed some type of coordinated attack of dragons that dismantled a dragon retaliation platoon. Fortunately, Herms was able to escape and make it to the castle, informing us of the events."

"What!" replied Murlynn softly. "Were the soldiers not armed with the carnivorous diffusion?"

"Yes," emphatically responded Lord Benaniah. "Indeed they were. It seemed to have no effect on the dragons, thus making the attack futile and leaving the men helpless."

"Did you say, 'a coordinated attack of dragons,' plural, as in more than one dragon?" asked Murlynn incredulously.

"Yes."

"But these things cannot be," insisted Murlynn as he rose from his seated position and began to pace the floor. "Dragons are extremely territorial. The males are Alpha driven, and the females only tolerate the males when they are in heat . . ."

Murlynn paused both in sentence and in stride as he stood with mouth agape, head shaking slightly, eyes bouncing back and forth as he tried to connect the dots to a formula that had come to an impenetrable point. Then all at once he stopped, looking up in horror as if solving a problem whose answer was trying to remain concealed, but ultimately failed. The undoubted reality was then unwantedly but fully embraced.

"If what you say is true," stated Murlynn, "then I am afraid a war is coming unlike anything we have ever seen."

28

No sooner did Antheis and his platoon hear the roar than they saw the trees shake. No sooner did they see the trees shake than three dragons were upon them. One soldier was able to fire off a potion-enhanced arrow which diverted one of the beasts to the air. To Antheis' horror, the other two men were pounced on like helpless does, unaware that the attack was ever coming. One of the men was bitten in half with such force that you would have thought there was no bone or muscle to account for. The other was ravaged by the monster's powerful and sharp hind claws, the back claw sticking him right through his abdomen while the two front claws easily crushed his shoulders down to his hind quarters. With two beasts claiming their kills and the other one in flight, Antheis knew that 'fight' was impossible and immediately took to 'flight'.

With a kick and a whip, Antheis and his companion were off, riding for their lives. Their only hope was to find some thick brush that the dragons would not be able to follow them into and hopefully lose them in the thicket. Antheis' heart was pounding so hard and fast that he could feel each beat climb up in his throat. Nervous sweat gathered on his brow as they rode into the wind, praying for a miracle. Either out of curiosity or the desire to build hope onto their current situation, Antheis looked back to see how much distance they had gained from their pursuer. This grave mistake filled him with horror, for when Antheis looked back, what he saw was the beast diving in through the trees, coming down upon them like a missile of death. With all his might Antheis yelled "Ya!" and spurred his horse on, racing for his life. The monster was successful in its dive as it grabbed Antheis' last comrade and lifted him and his horse up above the tree line, only to fire them back down. As one, they hit a thick oak tree like a cannon hitting the mast of a ship. Not much damage was done to the tree, although the tree did splinter, but the loud thud from the impact combined with the breaking of bone would have made one believe that there was a barrage of cannonade falling upon them. No sooner did Antheis see his partner fired through the air than he was upon him, looking at his broken body, alive and in torturous pain. He wanted to end his fellow soldier's life for him out of mercy, but knew that any hesitation would cost him his own. So with a stony face and compassion in his eyes, Antheis rode on.

It wasn't long before the dragon had caught back up to him and decided to go in for a second assault; apparently its first kill of horse and rider was not enough to satisfy its bloodthirst. The shadow outlining his demise above grew larger as it swooped down to claim its prey. Antheis did not give up. He beat his horse harder than any man or rider would dare imagine, but this meant life or death. He truly felt sorry for the steed, but knew that if it could understand his reasons, the horse would not only welcome each blow gratefully, but would encourage more severity with each strike as well.

Alas! Although both horse and rider were giving everything they had, it was not enough. The shadow grew continually, consuming them like darkness upon the land. No sun, no moon, no stars to give them even a glimmer of hope. All was gone, and now the dragon was finally upon them, digging its hind claws into the rear of the steed. With a loud whine, Antheis felt them both begin to take flight.

No, no, no! he thought. *This cannot be it! This is not how it's going to end for me!*

Out of sheer will, or maybe luck, the steed was being lifted with its rear end up. As they tilted forward, getting last chance to feel the comfort of solid ground, Antheis freed his feet from his straps and leaped forward toward the earth. A tuck and roll may have helped alleviate the landing, but it was by no means comfortable or soft. Putting pain and injury to the side, Antheis got up and sprinted. There was no time or need to evaluate the situation or formulate a plan. There was only one thing to do: run and pray. Run, and maybe find a thicket the dragon would not be able to enter. Pray, and maybe he could miraculously survive. The pounding of the earth suddenly dissipated, and

Antheis found himself falling, again, toward the earth. The slope was not long, but he felt like the fall took an hour, feeling every rock, every branch, every thud, every tumble, every turn, very aware of each new injury that occurred along the way. Up was down, down was right, right was left, and left was up, until he came to a sudden stop with a thud. Lying helpless at the base of the slope with all of his energy beaten out of him, Antheis closed his eyes and waited for his fate as a loud roar lulled him off to sleep.

29

Tension grew thick as Murlynn's words of caution and warning proceeded out of his mouth and entered the timeless void of eternity, never again to be taken back and forever vibrating within the cosmic hum of the universe. Before the lords could make any further inquiry, a hoarse cough erupted from the living area, drawing the party from their translucent thoughts and back to the reality that was before them. At this signal, Murlynn decided to revisit his patient and assess his current state after the first application of medicine had been received.

He grabbed a potion from his laboratory while on his way over to the living area. Pouring the potion into a bowl, Murlynn dipped his hands into the metallic blue liquid and gave them a gentle scrub. A soft glow resonated from his hands, like a dim candle flickering in the night.

Murlynn approached his patient, keeping his hand up and in front of him to be sure that nothing would touch them. Kneeling at his side, Murlynn began to murmur a soft chant as he slowly moved his hands from the top of the patient's head to the bottom of his feet. The lords could not help but to remember all the times they had spent at the altars, reverently and fervently praying on their knees for guidance, wisdom, and hope as they prepared to lead their people. It takes a great man to lead a people, but it takes a greater man to lead a people by trusting in and following the example of someone, or something, greater than themselves.

As Murlynn hovered his hands up and down the militant's body, many wounds began to reveal themselves in a soft blue radiant light. These wounds were not external and able to be diagnosed by mere observation. Rather, the wounds that were being announced were of internal ailments, such as organs, contusions, bones, and any other parts of his anatomy that was not in the right state.

"Oh dear," mumbled Murlynn as more injuries continued to declare themselves. "Oh dear, indeed."

The lords just watched; patiently, quietly, closely.

"Well," said Murlynn as he turned toward the lords in order to give them a report of his assessment. "Your friend has suffered wounds unlike any I have seen in a long time."

The lords just listened.

"But I do have remedies for a quick and full recovery," continued Murlynn as he got up off of the floor. "And when I say 'quick,' I do mean in comparison to an unaided or normal recovery time. It will still take some time for complete restoration."

"I see," replied Lord Benaniah. "Do as you must."

Murlynn gently bowed and headed toward his laboratory. At that moment, Lord Benaniah remembered, although he could not believe that he had forgotten, that he had a skin filled with water from the Tepenun Springs.

"Would it be okay," implored Lord Benaniah, "if I were to give him some water from the Tepenun Springs?"

"Oh yes," said Murlynn excitedly. "That would be most helpful; although he may need some assistance in getting it down."

"No problem," replied the lord as he eagerly approached their companion.

"Here," said Lord Benaniah after filling a cup with the contents of the skin. "This is fresh water from the Tepenun Springs from the kingdom of Ev'ron. It has nutrition and revitalizing properties."

Having just come back to consciousness, the militant was not sure what was going on or who the people were. There was one thing he did know, though: that he should be dead. Whoever these people were must have played a part in his survival. Therefore, the contents of this cup were likely exactly what this person is claiming it to be. What sense would it make to revive someone from near death just to give them a cup of poison? With that thought, the militant opened his mouth for a drink. Lord Benaniah, seeing this act of acceptance, gently lifted his head and tilted the cup so he could drink.

<u>30</u>

Deep blues and purples fused with the dark night. The stars and moon shone brightly, singing praises and shouting "Glory!" Their exaltation was accompanied by the strings of the crickets and the percussion of the crackling fire. An intoxicating aroma of roasted pork seasoned with fennel and rosemary paired with apple and cranberry stuffing delighted Herms' taste buds as the smell of hot cider and cinnamon filled his nose. Each bite of succulent pig had released some stress and anxiety of the day and replaced it with satisfaction and relief, to the point where, if possible, Herms would have completely forgotten the events that had occurred just earlier that morning. The palace chef had really out done himself this time, far beyond any meal he has had of late. If the entree wasn't enough, there was a piping hot blueberry pie that was bursting with filling, waiting for when he had finished. Herms ate in silence as he took in all the smells, tastes, sights, and sounds that filled his room that night. It is amazing the pace of recovery one can have when at the hands of the palace healers mixed with the waters of Tepenun Springs. With the warmth of the fire filling the room and a crisp, cool breeze fighting its way through the window, Herms knew that even these simple delights were going to be hard to come by in the near future.

Knock, knock, knock, came the timely intrusion of Herms' solidary moment.

"Come in," gently invited Herms, although his initial thoughts didn't agree with his verbalization.

Unsurprisingly, it was Lord Titus, still dressed in his royal garb from when he and Herms first conversed earlier that morning.

"My Lord," immediately stated Herms as he rose from his chair and bowed to greet his king.

"Please, Herms," replied Lord Titus caringly. "Do not get up. Please continue," said the lord as he gestured toward the dining area, heading to the table himself to accompany Herms.

"I trust your accommodations have been satisfactory?" asked the lord as he now somewhat casually leaned against a dining chair.

"Exceedingly!" replied Herms after he had chewed the large portion of pork and stuffing that he had decided to indulge in, seemingly at the same time that Lord Titus addressed him.

"Smells exquisite," said Lord Titus as he caught a whiff of the intoxicating perfume.

"And tastes even better," added Herms as he eyed another forkful of food.

"Do you mind?" asked Lord Titus as he gestured toward the dinner rolls.

A grunt of approval was all the lord got in return from Herms, for he had synchronized another mouthful with the lord's question.

"I am quite famished," said Lord Titus casually. "It has been a busy day." He grabbed a roll and walked over to the window. Gazing out at the stars, enjoying the simplistic beauty of creation, Lord Titus almost regretted the business that he had brought to Herms' room.

"Do you remember when we were kids, when father was alive, long before the split had occurred, the nights that we would spend by the lake?"

"Swimming," continued the Lord as he simply stared at the stars, "fishing, hunting, racing, building fires, lying out under the stars . . .humph," exhaled the lord as he smiled, reminiscing the thought.

Walking back over to the table, refilling Herms' drink and pouring his own, the lord mused, "We were simple kids, in simple days, in a simple time."

"I still cherish the memories of our youth," Herms declared.

"As do I," responded Lord Titus as he took a seat at the table. "But to yearn for what was, will prevent you from making the best out of what is or what will be. Times come and go, and it is those times that we cherish, that help us get through the times that we would sooner forget," finished Lord Titus as he finally took a bite of his roll followed by a sampling of wine.

"Titus," started Herms, trying to make the lord feel more comfortable, knowing that he was talking to a friend, "What is it? What's on your mind?"

Hesitantly, the lord decided to share his worriment and his requisition. After all, this was the purpose of his visitation. "I fear that the report that you gave me is only the beginning."

Herms stopped chewing his last piece of succulent pig that he had been savoring and swallowed. Putting his utensils down, Herms locked eyes with the lord and gave him his full, undivided attention.

"A war is coming," stated Lord Titus plainly. "A war that we are not currently prepared for. Messengers have been sent in haste to the other lords' kingdoms, calling their best men to arms. But that will not be enough. According to your report, our current method of immobilizing and disarming the beast with the carnivorous diffusion has been thwarted. If we cannot neutralize the battlefield, then I'm afraid, any offensive would be impractical."

Like a determined athlete focused on the task at hand, Herms' expression did not change. He just continued to stare intently at the lord.

Being forthright, the lord put it simply: "We need to be able to take down the dragons, or else all of our efforts will be in vain."

The lord did not want to, but knew that he had to finally propose his request. "I know that you have already been through a lot," sympathized the lord, "but I need you to go call on someone for me."

Focused on the conversation, Herms could not tell if the lord did or did not hear his answer. He himself heard the word "Who?" softly whispered as he slightly opened his mouth, but to the lord, it might have been nothing more than a brief pause.

"I need you to call on Murlynn," continued the Lord. "If I recall correctly, you two were friends. I believe you have continued in good standing with him after all this time. He should listen to you."

Herms had experienced a great recovery at the royal physicians' hands, but he knew he was not one hundred percent yet. This was of no consequence, though. The lord's request wasn't a matter of being, state, or even national significance, but one of historical implications.

"Of course," Herms replied without hesitation. Nervous anticipation grew within him as he recalled what he had seen in the early morning of that very same day. His stomach began to turn, and his heart began to beat like a drum. Images crept out of the storage banks of his memory and came back to life within his eyes while the words "finish the race" echoed within his mind.

"When do I ride?"

"Immediately," said the lord flatly.

31

Even after just one cup of water from the Tepenun Springs, the lords could see rejuvenation and stability come upon their recovering friend. Although great progress had been made in such a short period of time, the wounded soldier was still a long way from a full recovery, but was now perfectly capable of recalling his accounts and sharing how he came to be in this current state.

Feeling that there was no need to wait any longer, Lord Benaniah skipped over formalities and pleasantries and got straight to the heart of the matter.

"I am Lord Benaniah of the Hunt," the Lord began, "and this is Lord Cephas of the Sheppen. We found you along the riverbank not too far from here. You were near death, and would have died if we had not retrieved you and brought you to where you are currently. Now, please, given the circumstances that have occurred, we implore you to tell us of your tale of how you came to be in this state."

"My lords," said the man as he gently closed his eyes and nodded his head. "My name is Surgyn of Ev'ron, Captain of the Dragon Prevention Branch. Upon the orders of Lord Titus himself, I was to take our best platoon, the Flaming Arrows, and resolve a dragon sighting that was reported by the Fauns of Lord Augusta. Here is my account.

"After I was given my objective, I went straightway and gathered my men for what I thought would be a typical mission. I must say, though, I was not surprised to hear of a dragon in the land, although it had been some time since the last sighting, but I was surprised to hear that the sighting was as far north as the Plains of Elah; far be it for me to dishonor my lord and question his resources. Instead, knowing the intense and immediate action required, I gathered my men, took up arms, and sought after my duty."

Lord Benaniah and Lord Cephas sat intently around Captain Surgyn's bedside. Murlynn joined them as he brought over some bread, cheese, and grapes for the captain to aid in replenishing his strength. They sat and waited for the captain to continue with what would definitely be critical information in regards to further action.

Ripping off a piece of bread and grabbing some fruit, the captain continued, "The southern land of Elah is a half day's march. Knowing that we would want to get into position by the new day, I rounded up my men at the sixth of the night, and marched straight through the heart of the night. By the time we got to the southern regions of Elah, the sun was beginning to kiss the horizon. Knowing that we would have a better chance of engaging a dragon near a watering source, I decided to make camp in the Valley of Kurdish."

At this, the captain paused briefly for a crumb of bread and a couple grapes before continuing.

"After having marched for a half of the night, we finally settled in a patch of open field within the valley that was boarding the Mezpha Forest. After positioning our artillery, we formulated our battle strategies over a hot breakfast. Lord knows that after a half the night march my men were not in position to encounter a dragon. As soon as we were done, we let out the goats at the west point of our camp, knowing that their bleating cries would drawl in our foe.

"And draw them in it did," remarked the captain as he reached for his cup of the Tepenun Spring water. "In all my years of military service, I never experienced anything like what happened next."

The lords continued to patiently sit and listen.

"It was not long after we had released the goats that their luring bleats had successfully pulled in the dragon. We heard a roar from the east, which was unusual because dragons are not known to inhabit in the forest, but we made no concern of it. Within seconds, we saw a monstrous beast fly over us, just above the tree line. It must have been over thirty feet long, with a wingspan twice as wide. When it flew over us, it was like a dark storm cloud blotting out the sun. Stunned at first by the enormity of the beast, my archers were not able to take aim upon the monster. Being men of courage and honor, they did not let their intimidation overtake them for long. When the beast made a second pass to claim its prey, my archers were ready and took fire upon the creature. It seemed to me that their aim was true, but their arrows did nothing more than deter the beast, as they bounced off its under-belly like a rubber ball. Now, I know that these are the best archers in the land, but I wrote off their unsuccessful assault to nerves. I myself had gotten butterflies upon the first appearance of the monster. When the dragon was ready to make a third pass, I knew that we must not falter, for the beast surely would not relent without claiming the life of a goat. My archers were ready; being sure to cover their arrow heads with the carnivorous diffusion, they took their aim. It seemed that luck was on our side when the beast made such a low pass that even a novice would have been sure to hit the mark. Their aim was true, and their arrows flew swift and straight. But alas, the results were the same as before, as their arrows bounced off the monster's underbelly. This time the dragon was not to be deterred, and it swooped by and claimed its prey."

The captain stopped and let out a deep sigh. His eyes began to fill with remorse and sorrow as he recalled from his memory those events which he hoped that he would never have to revisit again. The memories that would haunt his dreams, make him uncomfortable when he was alone, and uneasy to be in any place without a light.

Seeing Surgyn struggle to vocalize the rest of the events, Murlynn tried to bring comfort by placing a friendly hand on the captain's shoulder.

"After having collected its prey, the dragon perched itself on a small hill no more than 200 yards away," Captain Surgyn finally continued. "Strangely enough, the beast stayed fixated on me and my men as it held the goat down with its front legs and mercilessly bit off its head. Never losing sight of my men, the beast let out a ferocious roar. This was the beginning of the end for us."

Tears began to swell in the captain's hazel eyes as he continued his account. Upon seeing this, Murlynn offered him a handkerchief that he had brought over with the spread of food. After a quick dab of his eyes, which Surgyn felt embarrassed about—he was a military man, and death is an inevitability of those who serve—the captain took a sip of Tepenun spring water and continued.

"If this beast's initial roar wasn't enough to strike fear in our hearts and stir up the nerves of my men, then the response to the dragon's declaration would have been," stated the captain, after having finished the contents of his cup. "The responding roar felt all-encompassing as it beat our ears and shook the very ground we were stood upon. Before we had time to process what had happened, we heard the breaking of tree limbs and the pounding drums of our enemies charge as they advanced upon us."

At this, the lords leaned in with their interest piqued, taking in and weighing every word that the captain gave account for.

"Before we knew it, the dragons were upon us and had us surrounded. It would seem that I had led my men straight into an ambush," remorsefully stated Captain Surgyn as he fought back his emotions. "I never have seen so many dragons at once, and seemingly working together for a solitary cause. To the best of my knowledge, dragons are isolated creatures that hunt and live in seclusion except when they are in heat. Yet I found myself in a perfectly-executed ambush that was concocted by the very same beast."

The captain paused for just a moment to allow his company to interject and clarify his understanding of the dragons' actions. After realizing that no one was going to bring understanding to his confusion, Surgyn continued. "Seeing that survival was unlikely at best, let alone a victory, I knew that our greatest chance was to stay together and attempt a counter assault. I called the platoon to form ranks and to press together. Any kind of heavy artillery would be useless in close-range combat, so we readied ourselves for the oncoming assault with bows and arrows, long swords, and long spears. As I looked on at our enemy, I knew that the grave was eagerly waiting to greet me, for it was death himself who was staring back at me.

"I mustered all the bravery that I could, and encouraged my men to take heart and fight not only for their own lives, but for the lives of their loved ones and the life of their country. The men found hope in my words, but it did not change the inevitable.

"Soon after my words faded off into history, the dragons made their charge. I told the archers to fire at will upon any dragon that came within range. This, our first and only assault, was fruitless. As the dragons moved within range, any arrows that managed to hit them fell to the ground with no effect. It seemed that the carnivorous diffusion and tactics that had worked for so long were no longer penetrable. We grabbed our spears and drew our swords, ready for short range combat. But the dragon on the ground never got close enough to engage. They stopped about thirty yards off and got ready for their own assault: a wall of fire.

"As the dragons began to press this inferno toward us, it was all we could do to stay tight and try to keep the beast at bay as best we could. The platoon name, the 'Flaming Arrows,' took on a whole new meaning when we realized that they could still harm the monster by shooting arrows and throwing spears and other objects into the mouths of the dragons just before they unleashed their fiery furry or immediately after they paused to get ready for another breath. This counterattack seemed to bring some hope to the men, as the dragons were kept at bay and were no longer able to spew their flames at us in unison."

Captain Surgyn spoke with all the pride that he could muster as he recalled the rest of the events. His platoon fought with bravery and honor, not backing down from an overwhelming enemy, and sacrificing their lives for the people and country that they loved. Although the captain could not have been prouder, it was all he could do not to let his emotions get the best of him as fresh images of the event replayed themselves over again in his mind.

"Yet again," continued the captain sorrowfully, "any hope that was found was soon to be lost when we looked to the sky and saw aerial reinforcements quickly approaching. Three more dragons made a pass and dropped boulders down upon us. Having been successfully divided with two opposing assaults, it would only be a matter of time before we were conquered. Now that the last shred of hope had withered away, fear gripped our hearts and burned in our eyes. Primal instinct took over, and survival became the only course of action. If any were to survive, there was only one way out: through the walls of fire. When the dragons on the ground stopped their blaze to drawl breath, some men decided to try to make a run for it. It was not the best of ideas, but it was an idea. It did not present us with a great chance of success, but it provided a chance. Most who attempted this act of desperation were not able to get outside of the range of the next fiery blast. Those who did make it out of their range were snagged by the dragons patrolling from the air. These dragons would swoop down and snatch up the men who tried to escape and use them as arsenal by dropping them onto us. My own men were being used as weaponry against us. It was the most horrific and vicious assault that I have ever been a part of. I knew that we all were going to die."

Captain Surgyn's demeanor went from pride to shame as he tried to work up the courage to confess his act of abandonment.

"With that in mind," Surgyn continued ashamedly, "I decided to take my chances and see if I could escape the fiery fate and make it into the woods."

This time tears swelled in his eyes. There was no hiding it, knowing that the last time he saw his men was when their own captain was fleeing his post, leaving them to their fate.

"I know that I should have died with my men," repented Surgyn, "but I also know that someone needed to try and make it out of our situation to alert the lords of what had happened. Every able-bodied man needed to take their chances and see if they could escape the clutches of death."

Although Surgyn's rationalization was plausible, he knew that he would not be able to live with what he had done, no matter how honorable his intentions were.

"When the dragon that was closest to the Mezpha Forest had paused from its fiery assault, I decided to take my chances and make a run for it," continued Surgyn. "To my surprise, I had made it pass the blaze of their inferno and was quickly approaching the woods until what felt like knives pierced through my shoulders. In one fell swoop, a dragon had captured me; digging its claws deep into my flesh, we quickly made our ascent up and over the tree line of the forest. I knew what its plan was for me, as the dragon was preparing to make a turn and take me back as ammunition. But that was not my fate; that was not how the end was going to come for me. So, in an act of desperation, I grabbed the dagger from the heel of my boot, and with everything that I had within me, I stabbed the beast in its ankle, sinking the blade into its joint and sinews. With a thunderous roar, the dragon opened its claws and released me. Thankfully, we were not too far above the trees, as I hit some branches that helped break my fall, resulting in a minimal-impact landing. I willed myself up against my body's resolve for restoration and continued to head further into the forest. This is when I came upon a hidden embankment; falling down the slope as if I was falling into an open grave. The last of my strength had left me, and pain covered me like a warm blanket as I lay at the bottom of the bank. Realizing that I could no longer go on, I closed my eyes and accepted the inevitable.

"My next act of consciousness was waking up here, in this room."

"Thank you for your report my friend," expressed Lord Benaniah, "and for your bravery and loyalty to your king. You have been through much, but do not fret: you are in the company of friends. Get some rest."

With that, the captain relaxed his body and sunk back into the sofa. With a deep sigh, the captain closed his eyes and was fast asleep.

32

A small fire crackled in the kitchen as Lord Benaniah and Lord Cephas sat with Murlynn at the dining table with a spread of biscuits, cheese, fruit, and nuts before them. Tea warmed their bellies as they had a cold conversation about Surgyn's account. They all knew the implications, and did not spend much time discussing them; for truly, there was not much to discuss. If the dragons were communicating and working together, then they must treat them like a militant threat advancing with purpose and not just a lost creature that got turned around along the way. If the dragons were organized and formulating a strategy, then they must treat them like an intellectual threat and not just a ravage beast loose in the land. If the carnivorous diffusion was not working, then there had to be some type of antidote given or immunity developed, which put all of Sahleam at a great disadvantage.

Not much dialogue was needed to come to these conclusions. Although a more opposing question would be, what would be their retaliation to this new information? Surely the land of Sahleam would need to pull together; no one kingdom would be able to overcome such a foe alone. Also, another potion or mixture of some sort would need to be created to help neutralize the dragon's offensive. With their ability to fly, razor-sharp teeth and claws, their sheer size and strength, and the capacity to breathe fire, the dragons were nearly an invincible enemy. It seemed that the only advantage that the people had was their intellect, knowledge of the land, and overwhelming numbers. If planned properly, they may be able to repel this invasion.

Again, not much conversation was needed to formulate these conclusions. Murlynn and the lords found themselves sitting in silence, mulling over the matters at hand. Although their conversation was silent and their bodies were tired, their minds raced over the information and thoughts of what may need to happen next.

Lord Benaniah broke the silent tension and started a more casual dialogue. At first, he started some small talk by thanking Murlynn for his hospitality and how delicious the spread of food was. This quickly trailed off to the art of cooking and which foods were everyone's favorites. Of course, with Lord Benaniah, when one talks about food they have to talk about the means in which the food was obtained:

hunting. On this subject, Lord Benaniah continued to drive and dominate the conversation as he shared his most recent hunting adventure and big game kill. He then shared an anecdote of late-night pranks that had become tradition among his hunting party, especially to those on their first hunt, and it brought such delight that even Lord Cephas cracked a smile and may have even given a faint chuckle.

They all knew the importance of the account given to them by their recovering friend, and the immediate action that needed to be taken. But a moment was needed to refresh and refuel their bodies and spirits, especially after such a day that the lords have had, even if it was only a moment.

Now that the tea had warmed their hearts, food sat in their stomachs, and laughter refreshed their spirits, the decision needed to be made in regards to the matter at hand.

"Thank you for your hospitality, my friend," began Lord Benaniah, "but I am afraid that time has run out on our visit, and both Lord Cephas and I must be off. The other lords need to be informed of what we have learned so that we can start formulating a counterattack before anything more disastrous happens."

"Far be it from me to advise my lords on how to rule the land, but please listen to me," humbly requested Murlynn.

The lords gave him their attention.

"At night, the woods are dangerous enough by themselves. Having to constantly be on alert for wolves, mountain lions, and other predators would make for a tireless night. Not to mention any bandits or thieves that may be foolish enough to attack one of the five lords. These are normal dangers, not including an apparent dragon attack, and that there is no way to track them as they hunt you in the dead of night," stated Murlynn. "Please spend the night under my roof. There is food, tea, protection, and means of refreshment. What you have learned will be of no help if you are too tired to be aware of your surroundings, too weak to defend yourselves, or if a calamity befalls and you are not able to deliver your report."

The lords silently contemplated Murlynn's plea.

"Please, just for tonight. You can leave at first light."

"Okay," agreed Lord Benaniah. "But just for tonight, and we leave at first light."

This delighted Murlynn, even with the given circumstances, for he had never had anybody stay the night before.

He took Lord Benaniah and Lord Cephas upstairs and showed them to their rooms. Murlynn showed Lord Benaniah to the guest room and Lord Cephas to the master bedroom. After he made sure the lords had everything they needed, Murlynn made his way back downstairs. For although the lords needed to rest in order to carry out the next part of their mission, Murlynn needed to start his new mission immediately: devising a new potion to replace the carnivorous diffusion.

33

Riding in the night is not an easy task. Normally, one would stay in open lands in order to use the moon and stars to help guide them on their journey. And although it may be the quickest route, for Herms, the open fields would not be the best path for travel given the presence of dragons in the land. A dragon already had a great advantage during the day hours, but during the night hours, what little chance you did have would be eradicated. They had the ears of a deer and the eyes of an owl, which helped them stalk their victim under the cloak of night undetected. In either case, Herms' journey to call on Murlynn would only have a brief stint in the fields if Herms would choose to take it. When riding into the woods, dragons were not the only predator that one had to worry about. Between making sure that you were not being hunted and the needed awareness to not run into a tree, Herms had plenty on his mind to keep him alert. But no matter how hard Herms tried to focus, there was a mental game of tug of war between the mission at hand and the attack that he had witnessed.

Images of the forest betrayed his mind into recalling images from the awful attack. A cluster of leaves on a branch would recall an image from the attack, or a group of bushes would remind him of what he had seen. Even the clouds betrayed him, soaring in the night, clustered together into what might have been a dragon flying overhead. It seemed that the harder Herms tried not to think about it, the more he was reminded about what had happened in the early hours of the day.

Dragons are truly vicious and unruly creatures, but then what about that brief moment beforehand, where he actually made eye contact with the beast? He felt like there was some type of connection. Although he felt anger and vengeance, he also felt confusion and regret. In that moment, the beast didn't look like a fierce monster, but rather a poor creature that was alone, scared, and had lost its way. Those aged, tiresome eyes that were full of years and experience were also the eyes that pierced through the heart of its victim and brought fear and death to those who were foolish enough to stare back.

"What are you thinking, Herms?" he said out loud to himself. "Are you actually feeling sympathy for these creatures?"

Herms knew that there was no one in earshot except his horse, and no magic had been invented to allow animals to communicate with humans; at least, not yet anyway. But with the night growing darker and the ride taking its toll on Herms' recovering body, perhaps a brief stop for some rest would be in order.

"How could anyone show sympathy to such vile creatures?" Herms continued to think to himself. "Those men had loved ones that they will never get to greet again. No longer can they laugh with their friends. No longer can they embrace their children. No longer can they kiss their wives. From that day forward, they will only be kept alive in the memory of the hearts of those they have touched and shared their life with."

No matter how disgusted Herms was with everything that had transpired, no matter how alert Herms kept himself as he rode through the woods, his mind kept going back to that moment where he looked deep into those yellow eyes.

It was almost as if they were reaching out to him.

"Was it also this beast that had told me to run?" Herms asked himself as he continued thinking about the matter. "Was the dragon actually warning me about the ensuing attack? Surely survivors or witness were not a part of the plan," he rationalized, trying to make sense of his unique encounter.

"No. NO!" he quickly resolved. "Don't be a fool. Running is what you do. It is natural. It is instinctive. It has been my way of survival for years. It is who I am and what I do."

But that eye. What am I to make of that eye?

"That's it," Herms claimed aloud as he pulled on the reins of the horse. "I cannot focus. My body is beaten and my mind is wandering," Herms persuaded himself. "The ride has been long, the hour is late, and the night is deep and dark. Perhaps it is time to find some rest and gather my wits about me and regain some strength before collecting Murlynn and heading back to Lord Titus.

2

DAY 2 | ASSEMBLE

34

W ithin the darkness there was silence, and within the silence there was nothing. Pure nothingness; no thought, no feeling, no emotion, no senses—a timeless void of emptiness, drifting through the black rivers of annihilation. Then again, who is to say that you are not floating, or soaring, or racing, or staying completely still? For there is only nothingness.

Is this death? Is this all life amounts to; all the kindness, the joy, the love, all the selfishness, the greed, the hate? Do all accumulative accreditations of such actions receive the same approval and are deposited into the same account?

This cannot be it. There has to be more to life; meaning, purpose, or even . . . a small . . . light? Yes, a star sparkling in the dark of night. A small flame in the distance, penetrating the dark void; bringing hope, faith, and belief to the lonely traveler who gazes upon it, crushing despair and disabling defeat.

As this trio of life grows, a newfound inspiration ignites, revitalizing and invigorating the mind and body once again. What seemed impossible now is easily achieved. Redemption overtakes this other-

wise doomed situation. Where nothingness lurked and annihilation waited in the shadows, now there comes a new creation, bursting forth with potential and possibility.

A sudden burst of wind. The light: no longer a small object of hope in the distance, but a growing beacon of salvation. Its rays confirm its reality as they melt away this icy gloom that burdened the soul. As the light grows, so does determination, purpose, and hope, like a cup being refilled again and again under crashing waves of the mighty waterfall. With no sign of stopping, waves continually freefall from their unknown source, until . . .

Birds chirping, the smell of mud and river, and the sound of leaves crunching. Pain quickly brings me back to my senses and reminds me of the events that have taken place. A groan escapes my body. As I open my eyes and become aware of my surroundings: the river, the forest, the bridge, the . . . man?

Yes, a man standing in front of an old wooden bridge, wearing only a hood as dark as the night. Who is this person and where had they come from, I do not know. What I do know is that they are my best hope and chance of living to see tomorrow. As I lay there, I try to scream or yell to call his attention, but with a dried, hoarse voice, the only noises I am able to make are grunts and groans. This figure, unable to hear my cry, steps onto the bridge and walks up to the keystone. Pausing briefly, I think this person somehow did hear me and is coming to my aid. I muster up another groan to reaffirm his attention, but to no avail. The figure continues their descent to the other side. When he steps upon the opposing side of the riverbank, he disappears.

35

To Herms, the woods was like a second home (his first home being whatever route he is running on). When he was young, there would always be a big yearly camping trip that his parents would orchestrate. Hunting for food, fishing, games, and laughter made these trips some of his fondest memories. This was where he also developed his love for the stars. In Shalom, the stars filled the sky like sand on the seashore; a canopy of glittering lights giving off hope, guidance, and life to those beneath them. As he settled down for a brief rest, he could not help but to look up and wonder at what was above.

"How did they get there? Why are they there? What purpose do they serve to those who are seemingly so far away?" These were some of the questions that went through Herms' mind as he laid under their ambiance.

"How did they get there?" is easily answered, thought Herms as he folded his hand behind his head and sank into his restful state. *If I found a sword in the woods it would only be logical to assume someone had left it there. To think that the sword would have somehow been formed by chance or randomness is ridiculous.*

But what about their purpose? pondered Herms. *Why are they there?*

Well, ever since I was a little boy I was taught how to navigate according to the constellations. They also give off light while the sun is away. These simple yet satisfying answers pleased Herms as his eyes grew heavy with sleep.

Before he could continue his thought or make any further deduction on the purpose of stars, Herms noticed something out of the corner of his eye that startled him, breaking his concentration. A creature of some sort had just made cover in the bushes straight ahead. Now, Herms was not one to be considered adventurous, brave, or daring, but in this instance he was, for some reason, extremely curious. Getting up and drawing his sword, he approached the brush very carefully so as not to frighten the creature. Being as close as he desired, Herms used his sword to move some of the brush around in order to gaze upon the animal. To his surprise, it was a rather larger snake that shot out of the bottom of the bush and slithered off into a clearing.

Again, Herms was not the bravest or most adventurous of fellows, but he could not help but to be very curious when he saw a small fire ablaze in this clearing, and that the snake seemingly slithered into it. Standing only on the other side of the brush, Herms suddenly saw a man walk out of the fire, or from behind the fire, he could not tell which. With a loose dark cloak covering his body and a hood over his head, the only distinction that Herms could make out of this person was their square jaw. The darkness of the night and the fire being at the man's side did Herms no favors for determining the rest of his features.

At first, this person just stood there in the firelight with his arms at his sides, facing towards Herms, which made him wonder if he had been noticed. Then Herms heard a whisper as the man's head turned from side to side. Suddenly, all at once, huge winged creatures filled the air, overtaking the stars and challenging the moon. There had to be at least half a dozen to a dozen creatures taking flight into the dark of night.

While fixated on the launch of these huge beasts, Herms again heard a whisper, but this time it was his name that was being softly spoken. Having been distracted from the flight of these animals, Herms looked down to see what had broken his attention. Although he was still unable to see the hooded person's facial features, there was no doubt that the hooded figure was looking directly at him. Herms was not quite sure, but he thought that he could see what appeared to be two yellow eyes hiding in the dark shadows of the hood. As the eyes glowed, they pierced Herms, making him grow with fear and anxiety. Herms tried to take a step back, but found that his feet felt like they were cemented into the earth. Herms, perplexed but undeterred, tried again to make way from the brush, but the harder he tried, the heavier his feet became. Fear and anxiety quickly turned into panic as he saw a rather large emerald green snake come out of the fire and head straight towards him. Panic was now desperation as the snake quickly slithered upon him. He desperately pulled at his feet, but they still did not budge. As Herms looked up to see the snake's progress, the creature was now only about five yards away. Ready to strike, it curled back, reared its large fangs, and launched itself at Herms. With the serpent's fangs dripping with venom and a small ball of fire billowing in the back of its throat, Herms squeezed his eyes closed, dreading in antici-pation what was coming upon him. When he opened his eyes, he found himself lying awake, once again under the morning sky.

36

Has the pain interfered with my senses, or did a man just vanish?
thought Antheis. *Surely Sahleam is a magical place, but people
normally just don't dematerialize into nothing.*

As Antheis lay there, he knew that he could not stay where he was.
Trying to sit up, he was quickly reminded of the injuries that he had
sustained. Lying back down, he knew that to stay in his current position was not an option. Antheis may have gotten lucky this time, as the
hooded figure obviously did not take notice of him, but the next patrol
may discover his whereabouts.

Surely that ambush was meant to have no survivors.

Before he could get back up, Antheis had a sudden feeling that
someone was watching him. Pausing and surveying the immediate
area, Antheis did not see anyone, or even anything, for that matter. Yet
he still felt as if he was not alone. Worriment and anxiety quickly crept
upon him as the feeling that something bad was going to happen
started to grow in his stomach. While still unsure about what to do
next, something caught Antheis' attention. He began to hear sounds,
what seemed to be voices faintly in the distance.

Antheis froze like a deer. Stiff as a board, he concentrated on the
voices to see if he could tell who or what may be coming his way. As
he listened, the voices got louder and clearer until he was able to make
out what they were. The voices were not of travelers, villagers, or even
soldiers. Instead, Antheis heard a compilation of men and women,
young and old, screaming, crying, and making pleas. Just as an
orchestra has four major divisions, and each division has an array of
instruments that come together to make one sound, so it was with what
Antheis was hearing. There were screams of horror, screams of pain,
and screams of fear. There were cries of grief, sadness, and depression.
There were pleas for mercy, pleas for help, and pleas for relief. They
came from all directions, and all conducted in unison to orchestrate one
sound.

Disturbed with what he was hearing, Antheis' attention was
diverted by an orb that appeared across the river. Surrounded by black

mist, the orb gave off a purple radiance that swirled within the mist like a fine slab of marble. To Antheis' dismay, the orb was not stationary, but was making its way across the river, heading directly toward him.

As it drew closer, so did his fear. Panic took a hold of Antheis as he lay there, unable to do anything. The closer the orb grew, the more his fears took hold of him, but the screams, cries, and pleas never grew louder. Coming across the river, then over the riverbank, the orb eventually came to a halt and hovered over Antheis' abdomen as he lay paralyzed in fear. Then two rods protruded from the orb and struck Antheis just below the ribs. It felt like two swords had run him through. Antheis let out a deafening scream. As he opened his eyes, Antheis saw the rods moving upon him like bolts of lightning dancing upon the earth. Some type of black substance, not from the mist or from the orb, but from Antheis' body, was being collected through the rods and deposited into the orb. Although it felt like shards of metal were being dislodged and removed from Antheis' body, he was mesmerized by what was happening. To Antheis, the orb's procedure seemed to take an extended period of time, but in reality not much time had passed at all. When the last of the blackness was extracted from Antheis' body, the orb retracted its arms, and with a puff of smoke, it was gone.

At that point, despite all the pain and horror that Antheis had felt, he now realized that whatever that thing was, whatever it had done, and wherever it had come from, it had healed him of all his injuries. Although Antheis felt refreshed, he still took his time getting up, just in case he still had any other injuries that he was unaware of. After he had gotten up and come to realize that he was indeed fully well, he was dumbfounded at this amazing feat. What could it be accounted as but nothing more than sheer luck? Antheis was left unsure of what exactly he should do next, until he heard the commotion of two nearby horses that were tied to a branch.

What fortune! thought Antheis. *I escaped the attack, received a mysterious healing, and now these horses are here to aid me.*

Without any delay, Antheis untied one of the horses, subsequently releasing the other in the process, which had taken the opportunity to gallop away, making haste for the castle.

37

No sooner did Lord Cephas fall asleep than he woke up. Being a shepherd, sleeping in a bed was not his custom. Nor did it help that he was about a foot taller than his host. Instead of trying to make himself comfortable on a piece of furniture that was undersized and unfamiliar to him, the lord made his bed on the floor next to the open window. The cool air and starry night reminded him of his homeland and the many nights he had spent with his sheep. Now, instead of protecting his sheep, he needed to protect his people. Instead of the enemy being a lion or a wolf, it is a savage, blood thirsty dragon. But wisdom was found in the council of many. He would be of no use being exhausted and famished. With his heart crying out for his people and his mind still processing the new information, Lord Cephas eventually got what sleep he could.

. . . .

At the crack of dawn, Lord Cephas awoke from what little rest he was able to get. Folding his blanket and grabbing his staff, he headed downstairs. The smell of a delightful breakfast filled the air as he walked into the kitchen. Lord Benaniah was already at the table enjoying the meal.

"Good morning, Lord Cephas," greeted Lord Benaniah after swallowing a large portion of food that he was working on. "Were you able to find some rest last night?"

"Some," replied Lord Cephas as he walked over to the kitchen to find the source of the different delicious smells that were enticing him.

"Murlynn has been good enough to make us breakfast before our journey this morning. Please have some and join me before we part ways," encouraged Lord Benaniah.

Before we part ways? That is an interesting thing to say, thought Lord Cephas as he grabbed a plate and bowl from the table and made his way to the fire pit, where the porridge was bubbling and the bacon was sizzling. A pan of eggs sat covered aside the heat to stay warm. After filling his bowl and plate, Lord Cephas made his way back to Lord Benaniah's side, where a bowl of mixed berries, freshly squeezed juice, and a hot loaf of bread adorned the table. After taking his place, Lord Cephas gave thanks for the food that had been provided and began to eat.

They both sat and enjoyed the feast that was laid before them. No one felt the need to say anything; rather, they just enjoyed each other's company and the meal in which they were partaking. After several minutes, Lord Benaniah was the first to finish his meal. Being fully satisfied, he sat back in the full comfort of his chair and began to discuss their plan of action.

"So, I was thinking that I would head north for the kingdom of Shaddonai, gather the troops, and head back to the Castle Dorian."

Lord Cephas just looked on in confirmation as he chewed his food.

"And I thought that it may be best if you rode straight to the Castle Dorian to relay the information we have gathered from our journey," continued Lord Benaniah.

He did pause briefly here to allow Lord Cephas to interject if he would like, but the lord only took another bite of his eggs.

"But what about our original mission that Lord Titus had sent us on? Should I take some men and march toward the Endor Mountains while the rest of the men march back to the Castle Dorian to meet you and the other lords?"

After finishing a sip of juice, Lord Cephas simply replied, "No."

Lord Benaniah was surprised at such a flat statement.

Lord Cephas continued after wiping his mouth, "If the dragons have made it as far north as the Plains of Elah, then the kingdom of Raphastien would have already been compromised. With their new ability to communicate and organize attacks, you would be marching to your death, especially with the carnivorous diffusion being null and void."

"But should I not at least go with a couple of my best men to see if there are any survivors . . . anybody who might have been able to escape if the dragons did indeed attack Endorah?"

"If there are any who have managed to escape, they would be heading north to reconvene at the Castle Dorian," replied Lord Cephas.

After a moment of silence, he continued, "If you want to send some of your best men to try and find any survivors, then do as you wish. It will not be easy, though. They will be moving in the shadows, and there is a lot of land to cover between the Endor Mountains and the Castle Dorian."

"But you," continued Lord Cephas before Lord Benaniah could boast about his knowledge of the trials throughout the land, "should head back to the castle. Your knowledge of hunting, tracking, and strategizing would be much better used to help organize an offensive rather than being out on a search party."

Although Lord Benaniah did not like this suggestion, he did see the wisdom in it. "You are right. I will head back to Shaddonai, gather the troops and head toward the castle. I will select a few of my best men and have them go and try to find any survivors from Raphastien. They are to take no more than four days to report back to me. One day to travel there; two days for searching; and one day to travel back."

Lord Cephas nodded in agreement.

At that moment, the entrance door creaked open and a hooded figure in a black robe walked into the hut.

38

After Antheis had delivered the message to the Fauns in the Kingdom of Vatoya, he then sent Silas and Raithyn off to Mount Endor to deliver the same to the dwarfs, as he and some men road to the Valley Kurdish.

Silas and Raithyn were highly skilled and trusted, having come through the ranks quickly and received high marks at a young age.

All had been quiet on their journey so far, nothing worth reporting. The beauty of the morning sky made them forget for a moment why they were racing toward Endorah, the capital city of the Kingdom of Raphastien. As they rode into a sea of golds, blues, and pinks, Silas and Raithyn felt as though they were riding from this earthly kingdom into the one that awaits all men when they pass from here to eternity. Only when the mighty Mountain of Endor broke through the horizon and pierced the sky did they realize that the Dwarf city was upon them.

As they approached the city, they could see how the houses, aqueducts, and places of business where carved into the mountainside. The living quarters were pressed together and stacked on top of one another to accommodate for their population. The houses were of simple design; square frames with flat roofs and plenty of windows. Stairs and tunnels ran up and down and in and out of the mountain, from one street level to the next, and deep into the heart of Endor, for easy accessibility to work, shops, and homes.

Dwarfs were a simple race. They took enjoyment in their work, pleasure in life, and always defended what is true. They did not care much for outward appearances or material possession. To them, what mattered most was the love of a family; except when it came to matters of heritage, which was a completely different issue. For matters of heritage, there were fountains and exquisite statues made in honor of great kings, heroic men, philosophers, and engineers; anybody who played a significant role in preserving or advancing the Dwarf lineage. These depictions of battles and defining moments of the Dwarfs' history were stationed throughout the city so that the dwarfs would always be reminded of where they came from.

As Silas and Raithyn approached the great city, they quickly found themselves at the great wall and gates at the mountain's base. Guarding the city gates were two enormous Dwarf warrior statues, one on either side, stationed with their armor on and their battle axe ready in case of any impeding danger. By the time that Silas and Raithyn got to the gates, the sun had already started the adventure of the new day. The letter sealed with the king's signet ring gave them no issues gaining entry into the city, and an immediate audience with Lord Ekron's council. A simple spread of meat, bread with jams and butter, and wine was put out for them as the council convened over the request.

The council convened in a room that had no walls, for it was not merely the thought and opinions of those within the council that should be considered, but how each decision will affect all those within the land. Instead of walls, the room was surrounded by pillars that were inscribed with their law and significant moments of their past that lead them to where they are today. No decision was to be made without thought of what it had taken for them to be where they were at that moment, and all decisions were to be weighed against the laws that helped them govern their land. There was no ceiling, because no decision was to be made without prayers of wisdom, knowledge, and guidance from their 'mother' (the earth). They sat at a white and blue marble table that reminded them that although they had a king, no decision is to be dictated to them. Just as the marble colors were intertwined, so were the lives of all those within the kingdom. Therefore, no decision would be made only to benefit one person or people group, but for the best interest of the whole kingdom, for all are connected and affected by each other's actions. This is what the council was to consider as they heard the request of the kings, even their king, Lord Ekron. The letter read as follows:

To the most honorable Dwarfs, whose strength and bravery is legend among all manner of peoples; greetings from the Lord King Titus of the land of Sahleam, King Augusta of Vatoya, and your King Ekron of Raphastien. We send you this letter in urgency; dragons are in the land! We request the immediate need of your best men. Send them at once to the Castle Dorian to convene with the rest of the troops that are being gathered from all the kingdoms within Sahleam. As for you and your kin, you should find immediate hiding and resources in order to survive the coming times. We are at war.

The dragons are strategically infiltrating the land. If you have not yet faced opposition, I fear that you soon will. Do not hesitate; rather, make haste so that we can engage and defeat this rising foe.

Signed, the Lord King Titus, King Augusta, King Ekron.

"If a war is upon us, and they are anticipating an attack upon the city, then it would be foolish to send all of our best men to the lords," stated Eibner after hearing the letter read. "Who would be here to help defend us?"

"They are not asking for all of our troops, just our 'best men'. There will be a number of brave and courageous men left here to fight," AcKrin said in response to Eibner's question. Although they seem to be opposing thoughts, in reality these two suggestions were of the same heart, but of different expressions, much like Eibner and AcKrin. Eibner had an oversized, fat crooked nose and thick red hair and beard, while AcKrin had a very circular nose with round checks and a stringy dark brown beard, his hair pulled back into a bun. Both had noses, hair, and a beard, but expressed differently.

"By sending our best men, we might as well send all of our men. Quality is not in quantity. Sheer numbers will not help us overcome one stray dragon, let alone a coordinated attack of dragons. We need men with specific skills and knowledge on how to work specific weaponry. These men are some of our best men, who will not be here to help defend the city when the attack comes," Eibner rebutted AcKrin's counterargument. He was feeling good about the reception of his advice, as other members of the council nodded along with what he was proposing. With that, Eibner also added, "Who would take charge and lead our men into battle if all of our war heroes and generals are not here to aid those who need guidance?"

AcKrin would normally agree with Eibner, but the request was not the most logical course of action if they were to be preparing for some type of assault. But no matter how illogical the request may have seemed, AcKrin knew that it was what was best for the land. "I know that it seems like we are putting ourselves in a peculiar position, but I do not doubt that this course of action is what's best for Sahleam. Brothers of the council, look at it like this: just as we make our decisions with the whole of the people in mind, so this request was made with the whole of the land in mind. This war is not just on Raphastien, but on the whole land of Sahleam itself. Therefore we must act accordingly. Our decision must be for the good of the land of Sahleam, not just for the good of the dwarfs."

At this, the council began to murmur with consideration for AcKrin's argument. Seeing this, AcKrin finished his statement, "We must oblige. This letter was sent by the Lord King Titus and our own King Ekron. Their seals prove its authenticity. To hold back our men would be treason. We must do as requested and send out our men at once."

Seeing AcKrin's persuasiveness, Eibner decided to switch from the logical debate to one of emotion that was rooted in his character. "We are the country's crest. We are the only line of defense from any foe who dares cross the waters and enter into our beloved land. Where is the honor, where is the courage if we cowardly surrender our beloved Endorah and flee from our enemy without making a stand?"

"The letter does not tell us to abandon our mother," AcKrin firmly interjected. "It actually says the opposite; that we are to take refuge in her."

"But without a fight?" Eibner now interjected. It was obvious that this debate was quickly growing into a heated argument. Eibner believed that anything other than defending their kingdom, even in the eyes of certain death, would bring into question the dwarfs' bravery and honor. "Why should we do such a thing? Endorah has been our home for many ages. We have seen much in the ways of war, advancements, and progress. We have not only endured but developed alongside of our fellow country people, both weeping and celebrating along the way. Not once have we ever surrendered our position before engaging with the enemy."

Seeing that Eibner was full of conviction and convinced of his words, AcKrin switched the topic from 'should we fulfill the request' to 'whose signatures were on the request'. "Were we not already aware of the possibility of a dragon infiltration? Was it not one of the topics that our beloved king was going to bring up for discussion at the Gathering of the Lords? When King Ekron left, did he not decree any such action or implement even a suggestion that such a course should be taken or prepared for beside the continuation of our daily lives? This letter is confirmation of what our lord and king feared when he had left us, and it only affirms what he had suggested to do in the pending circumstance. Let us not look past the signatures on this parchment and the seal that bound it shut. Brothers, let us not waste any more time and do what our king has required of us."

"Thank you, brothers," interjected Sorth before Eibner could start his rebuttal. "Both sides have been well made and established, and are both good courses of action, but either motion requires immediate action. I do not believe that there is any reason to delay any further. As you know, neither action is one for a single man to make. An agreed motion from the council will decide which path we will follow. Our laws state: 'Out of the council of many, the heart of the people will rise'."

"Should we then bring in Silas and Raithyn so they can share with us their report that we may make such a decision?" requested Eibner.

Not that Sorth was the head of the council, for they all had equal yet different roles to fulfill, but the rubies and gems from deep within Endor that were throughout his long, snow-white hair and thick white beard witnessed to his wisdom and experience. "That will not be necessary," Sorth said in finality. "Our King's request alone is enough for us to weigh the importance of the matter. At this juncture, we now need to simply make a decision. Will we send our best men to the Castle Dorian to join the armies of Sahleam, or will we keep them here in order to help stave off whatever danger is coming for us?"

Sorth did have a way of putting things simply.

"Now, let us not tarry any longer. What say you, Eibner? Do you wish to send our men or have them stay behind?"

"Ahh, I see you already enjoyed your breakfast," commented Murlynn as he took off his hooded robe and hung it next to the door. "How was it? Did you sleep well last night?" he continued, losing no time and heading straight toward his laboratory.

"The food was very good, and yes, Lord Cephas and I were quite comfortable last night. Thank you," replied Lord Benaniah. "Your hospitality has been very generous, but now it is time for us to be going."

"Yes, right, of course," agreed Murlynn absently as he took some roots and herbs that he had collected from his garden and put them in a mortar and pestle to be briefly ground before adding them to the potion that he was brewing.

"But before you leave, I must insist that you take these," added Murlynn as he carefully poured a substance from a hot beaker into two vials and plugged them with a cork. It was hard to tell what this substance was due to its unique composition, for it was sort of clear, almost looking as if it were a liquid glass.

Along with the two vials, Murlynn also grabbed what looked like two small river stones that were no bigger than his palm. "These stones may look ordinary," began Murlynn after having made his was over to the kitchen, "but I have enchanted them so that they will let you know when dragons are nearby."

At this, Lords Cephas and Benaniah excused themselves from the kitchen table and examined the stones; surely enough, they did look like ordinary river stones.

"These stones can detect a dragon from over two hundred yards away," Murlynn continued. "When a dragon is within range, the stones will get hot, not enough to burn you, but hot enough to get your attention. Not only will the stones get hot, but they will let off a sulfur and brimstone smell as well, just in case the stones are in a place where you will be unable to detect their heat. When the rocks do these things, you know that a dragon will soon be upon you, but it does not tell you what direction that they are coming from or if they are approaching by land or by air. At any rate, at least you will know when a dragon is close and hopefully avoid another ambush.

"Now," continued Murlynn after handing the lords each their own river stone, not allowing them any time to express gratitude, "this is a very special formula that I have just concocted. It may look like nothing more than ordinary, but this silvery liquid is an advanced form of communication that will allow you to converse over a great distance of land."

Handing the vials to the lords, they examined the substance curiously as Murlynn further explained the procedure in which the substance worked. "All you have to do is pour some, not much, mind you, of this potion onto a smooth surface, and say 'hear me know or hear me later, live or stored in thy communicator'. With these words, you will activate both the speaker's and the receiver's potion. You will know the potions have been activated when they give off a light blue glow and begin to hum for about thirty seconds. The reason for this delay is to notify the receiver that you are trying to contact them so that they can activate their potion, if they are able to, and thus you will be able to communicate with each other in real time."

Lord Cephas and Lord Benaniah were not sure what to make of what they were hearing, but Murlynn just continued nonchalantly, not allowing them room for questioning. "If you are not able to communicate in real time, just speak your message and your message will be stored in the potion until the other person is able to listen to it. You will know that a message has been stored because the liquid will have a continuous blue glow until the message is received. When you are done communicating, say, 'With this having been said, I am finished' to end the enchantment. Use this potion wisely. Once it has been activated, you will not be able to activate that portion of the potion again."

The lords stood in virtual disbelief. They knew Murlynn was a great alchemist, but such a potion had never been dreamed of before, let alone attempted and accomplished. Being able to communicate over great distance of land would be a great advantage. If there was any doubt or reserve, the lords did not show or express it. Instead they only shared their gratitude as they secured Murlynn's gift for their travels.

"Thank you, my friend. You have truly outdone yourself," expressed Lord Benaniah as he put a friendly hand on Murlynn's shoulder. "These new acquisitions will surely be of much help in the days to come."

"Where are you going?" asked Murlynn.

"We have decided that it would be best if Lord Cephas headed back to the Castle Dorian. We left our steeds down at the river, by an old wooden bridge. Lord Cephas will make his way toward them, and if fortune finds us, he will race back to the castle and be there by the sixth hour."

"And what about you?"

"I will head back to my kingdom. Warriors will be needed for this great battle that awaits us, and none are mightier than the Nimrods," answered Lord Benaniah with a hint of pride in his voice.

"Very good," agreed Murlynn. "Very good. Well then, I do not wish to prolong the task, but if I may suggest a point of order for your journeys:

"Lord Cephas, your journey is easy, head due west. As long as the sun is in front of you, it will guide you to back to the bridge you had crossed and your horses."

"Lord Benaniah, you will want to go due north. As you know, the Podiseon River flows into the Mezpha Forest from the southwest and works its way through the forest before making its exit in the northeast. Heading north is the quickest way for you to meet the river and allow it to guide you back to your home.

"But," continued Murlynn, "As you go, make sure to follow the river and the sun. Do not turn from them. Fight any urge or questioning you may have within yourself about what direction you are going or why you are going in that direction. If these urges come upon you, just remember the words 'guide straight and true' and you will be sure to find your destination."

Lords Cephas and Benaniah found the last bit of information to be a little peculiar, but they did not want to inquire about it for they really must be going.

Goodbyes were given and gratitude expressed, and the lords made their way from Murlynn's hut and onto the next part of their journey.

Surgyn remained on Murlynn's couch in a deep sleep as the potions continued to help his body make a full recovery.

Murlynn watched as his guests went out the door and headed due west and due north toward whatever fate may have for them. Murlynn watched and thought about everything that had transpired throughout the previous night, what it meant for the upcoming days, and the impact it would have on all of Sahleam.

Lord Benaniah and Cephas marched on; true heroes, true men of valor—men who loved their land and the people within it. Men who were willing to march straight into the clutches of death and offer their own lives so that the many would be spared.

These thoughts filled Murlynn's mind as tears filled his eyes and sorrow filled his heart. Death and sorrow were coming to the land of Sahleam, and although it was not his fault, Murlynn could not help but think that he might have had something to do with it all those years ago.

As Murlynn watched Lord Cephas and Lord Benaniah take one more step, they disappeared, and in so doing, Murlynn withdrew and headed back into his hut.

40

"So, the votes are in," stated Sorth after what was a rather quick vote. "We will honor our lord and send our best fighting men to rally at the Castle Dorian in a collaborated assault against our enemy.

"Gurther, gather our best men, save half a dozen, and tell them that they are ordered to go directly to Castle Dorian to rendezvous with the Lord King Titus and the gathering armies of the nations of the land. They are not to turn from this order, no matter what. If they do, it will be counted as treason." Sorth said this as he wrote out official orders, sealing them with wax and pressing his sign, an owl perched on tree branch, onto the parchment with his signet ring. "Also, when they arrive, have them give King Ekron a full report of our state, that we are prepared to defend our beloved mother at all cost."

Handing the orders to Gurther, who was the administrative assistant to the king's council, Sorth gave one last order, "The half a dozen that are to fall behind are to report here to the council immediately."

....

"I don't understand what is taking them so long," said Silas as he paced along the floor.

"There is not even a decision to make. Every minute they spend debating what they should do puts the whole country in danger."

"You know the Dwarfs," said Raithyn calmly as he lounged on a couch with his eyes closed and hands behind his head. "To enrage their anger could cost you their friendship, and . . ." not seeing any reason to finish his initial thought, Raithyn decided to say something a little more constructive instead. "They will make the right decision; you just need to let them come to the conclusion in their own way."

Silas had stopped his pacing and just stared at Raithyn, not sure why he wasn't more anxious or impatient about gathering the men and heading back to Lord Titus. At that moment, a Dwarf made his way into their chambers.

"The council will see you now," stated the assistant flatly.

....

"After discussion upon the pending request, the convening council has decided to meet our lord's request and has sent our best fighting men to rendezvous at the Castle Dorian. They are leaving even now."

Relief and surprise came over Silas and Raithyn at once. They were relieved that the dwarfs finally made a decision and were sending men to meet with Lord Titus, but they were surprised because they had thought that they themselves were going to be escorting the men back to the castle.

"Since we have obliged the request of our king," continued Sorth, "we have also decided that you two should fall back and organize our men for any onslaught the enemy may be preparing for us." Before Silas and Raithyn gave an answer, Sorth gave their reasoning for the decision that was made. "We have sent our best men, captains, and generals to go and fulfill this request that you have brought to us. Such a request leaves us unorganized and ill-prepared for any attack that may come upon our people. We must be able to defend our city and the people who reside in it." Sorth's case was more than compelling. To lose Endorah would be to give the enemy a great stronghold that would not be easily taken back. Furthermore, it would give the enemy access and control over obtaining reinforcements as they saw fit.

"What do you say?" asked Sorth, looking at the men sternly. The love for his city and its people shone through his strong gentle emerald eyes.

Looking at each other, Silas and Raithyn knew that they really did not have any other choice but to accept the Dwarf's request. Sorth was right; sending their best men would disrupt the hierarchy of the chain-of-command. Silas and Raithyn could help bring orders to the ranks. They were the people who brought this request to the drawfs, and lastly, but probably most importantly, the dwarfs would probably see the rejection of their request as treason. Bowing slightly, Silas and Raithyn accepted Sorth's request. They knew that this was more of an order than a request, but could see the love for his people in Sorth's eyes.

"Good," replied Sorth with a sense of relief. "Leave here and go to the city square and meet up the leaders that we have elected to stay behind. They will inform you of our arms, men, and fortifications we have for any pending attack."

With another slight bow, Silas and Raithyn were off to their new mission.

41

Sitting at the kitchen table, Murlynn tried to eat some of the leftover spread that he had put out for the lords, but found himself unable to do so. His mind was distracted, as it had been ever since hearing Surgyn's story about the dragons. The pieces to the puzzle did not fit. Something was missing. The cornerstone, in which all of this would come together, had yet to be revealed. No matter how hard or long Murlynn tried to fit everything together or tried to discover the missing link, he was unable to. Finally, giving up on the biscuit, he put it back on the serving saucer and leaned back into his chair, trying to relieve his mind from the mental stress of categorizing and chronicling all the current information.

As he leaned back, Murlynn's attention was brought to the small fire that was still burning in the kitchen hearth. The glow of the embers seemed to rise and fall with each breath that the fire produced. The flames performed a hypnotic dance to the rhythm of life that was beating within its essence. While transfixed on the flames, they brought back to mind a memory of long ago, but not since forgotten, of Murlynn's youth. He remembered it as if it was yesterday. The day when, while he was working in the fields, he stumbled across an egg.

It was rather a peculiar egg in color and size, one that Murlynn hadn't come across before. Now granted, he was just a lad, no more than sixteen years of age, but he had already had his share of expeditions into the woods, up trees, down caves, and into lakes and streams. Young Murlynn was curious and had a thirst for the world; how it worked and the things in it. So when he came across an egg bigger than his head and as brightly-colored as the coral reef off of the shores of the forest of Mezpha, it was only natural for him to want to examine it. Now, Murlynn was not a thief, nor was he trying to disrupt nature. No, he would always do his studies and research in the natural habitat. This egg, however, was stumbled across while Murlynn was out walking and working in the field. From what he could tell there was no apparent nest nearby, nor any trace of its mother. Furthermore, Murlynn had been working in this section of the fields all day, and had not seen this egg before. It was almost as if the egg had just appeared. Not wanting any danger to befall the offspring within this egg, Murlynn decided to take it back to his home and care for it until it hatched, or he could locate its nest and its parents.

Over the next couple of days, Murlynn found no sign of the egg's nest or mother. He had gone back many times and inspected the work field where he had found the egg and could not find any track marks, animal shedding, droppings, or any other indications of an animal living, nesting, or even having been in the area where he had discovered the egg. Murlynn also asked the other workers if they had seen anything while out in the fields, but besides the normal wildlife activity that keeps to brush and tree line, there were no reports that could possibly be a match for this egg.

A couple of weeks had passed when it happened. Murlynn was sleeping in his bed, dreaming a dream that he had never dreamt before. He was dreaming that he was flying high in the heavens, soaring across the land. It was a wonderful feeling to be gliding so freely, high above the world. The view was magnificent! He could see for miles on end. The mighty mountains of Endor that stood so high and proud looked as if Murlynn could easily pick them up and move them if he wished. Murlynn could see the Podiseon River flowing from the Endor Mountains, through the region of Vinyah, and into the Mezpah forest as it broke off into streams, creeks, and channels which gave life to the inhabitants of the land. And this was the view from beneath the clouds. When Murlynn climbed higher still, what he found was breathtaking. The blue of the sky was so vibrant that no emerald could ever match its brilliance. The clouds looked like a heard of sheep, grazing freely upon the land without bother or concern. The sun sat just above the clouds, shining with brilliance, keeping watch over its flock, extending comforting rays of light and warmth. It all felt so very real to Murlynn as he took in each new view and experience. He could soar high above the clouds or dive low into the fields. The adventure lasted much longer than any dream would have. So much so that, for a time, Murlynn believed his dream to be his new reality and his other state of being to be a form of subconsciousness. It was the most magnificent feeling he had ever had. Life was very good until, while he was flying, he spotted a group of armed men in a field just ahead. As he approached, he could see the men get into a sudden frenzy as they scurried around their campsite. This was curious to Murlynn, so he had swooped down to get a better look. But when he did, the group of men formed ranks and started firing arrows at him. In a panic, Murlynn stopped mid-flight and tried to pull up so not to get hit, but it was too late; there were arrows whizzing by him. One scraped his leg, another pierced his wing, and one final arrow was on a trajectory to sink into his heart.

Murlynn woke up in a sweat, but before he had a chance to think too much about his dream, he heard a crack. The egg he had found was hatching! Murlynn sat up and watched with fascination. At first, he thought maybe it was some type of lizard when he thought he saw a tail. Then he thought maybe some type of bird when he saw a wing. His anticipation blew into full excitement when he saw that out of the egg came a dragon!

Due to its sea-green skin and its brightly colored egg, Murlynn decided to call the little dragon Korel. Murlynn never had any aspirations to keep the creature that was within the egg. His desire was always to keep it safe until it hatched and then release the animal back into the wild. With a dragon, though, this complicated things. If you released a dragon into the wild, you would eventually have an untamed free-reigning dragon on your hands. This would likely escalate into a problem for villages and farmers. Another option was to hand her over to the authorities. Then again, the authorities would more likely use her for examination and experimentation for anti-dragon weaponry or just plain execute her. There was little doubt that the authorities would not spend time and resources safely exporting the dragon, given the fact that she could always make her way back into the land. With these options in mind, there seemed to be only one that made the most sense to Murlynn: he himself would keep and wean Korel until she was developed enough to survive on her own and then safely deport her out of the country. This idea pleased Murlynn as he began to coo and coddle Korel. *Also,* thought Murlynn, *this may afford me the opportunity to prove that dragons can be domesticated and docile.*

Weeks had gone by, and everything was going well. Murlynn was giving her plenty of care, exercise, and food. Korel also had been doing well with Murlynn as her caretaker. But soon, sneaking kitchen scraps and playing different games and exercises wasn't enough. Korel was growing too rapidly, and needed a place to run, fly, and hunt. And what an excellent hunter she was. Rats, rodents, pigeons, and the like were no longer any problem. With razor-sharp claws, quick reflexes, and keen eyesight, there were few animals that were able to escape Korel. Yes, taking her out for her daily activities was working well, but Murlynn needed to find a more permanent residence for Korel, for she was becoming too big even for the barn, and was discovering that she had the ability to breathe fire.

Korel was not able to breathe fire at birth. It was something that came upon her when she matured from a childlike state to more of an adolescent state. The first time she breathed fire, she accidently set a section of Murlynn's mother's flowers a blaze. Fortunately, there was a pail of water right there that Murlynn was able to extinguish the flame with. This was also the first time that he felt a deep connection with Korel. It was hard to explain. Kind of like a man and his dog, but more than that, but not as much as a man and his friend. When Murlynn looked into Korel's eyes and scolded her for what she had done, he saw disappointment and regret.

It is easy to tame and conceal an animal when it is little, but as Korel grew, she became more unpredictable and was pushing the boundaries and testing the limits. At last, Murlynn had to release her into the wild. He knew that he would need to eventually take her to the shore and encourage her to fly away to her new home. But Murlynn was not yet sure on how he was going to be able to convince Korel to willingly leave, especially with their unexpected relational development of caretaker and child. So, until that time came, Murlynn took her to a nice cave that was within the woods and far from any village. Before letting her go, Murlynn told her that he would come visit her and that she could do what she wanted, as long as she hunted in the woods, stayed out of sight, and did not cause any fires to the village. Korel seemed to understand, for when Murlynn left she did not chase after him.

That night, Murlynn had a dream that he was a dragon again. This kind of dream would frequent Murlynn after his departure from Korel in the woods. The dreams were mainly the same; Murlynn was a dragon, and he was either flying, hunting, or perched on a high place. They were nice dreams, and made him miss Korel all the more, but Murlynn knew that taking her to the woods was what was best and he would venture out to call upon her every day that he was able to.

Shortly after Murlynn had left Korel in the woods, he was out in the yard experimenting with some different herbs that he had found when he got an unexpected visit from King Titus. Even as a young king, Titus was discreet and used wisdom in all that he did. On this occasion, he had come alone on a horse and was covered with a cloak. For King Titus knew Murlynn and that he was brilliant, and did not want to make any decisions without first confirming and understanding Murlynn's reasoning for his actions.

As the king approached Murlynn, he did not recognize him, and thought that he was just a peddler or farmer from the village. After King Titus revealed himself, Murlynn and the king went inside so they could speak more privately and openly. After they had gone inside, King Titus got straight to the point of the matter. His visit was about Korel.

He had come to discover her when he was resting from a hunt that had proved unsuccessful and heard the commotion of a large creature and a voice talking nearby. Figuring that it was someone who was on a hunt as well, King Titus thought that he might lend his assistance with dressing or removing the carcass from the woods. To his surprise, when he was finally able to make visual contact with the source of the commotion, King Titus saw that it was a human talking to a dragon. And not any person for that matter, but the young genius, Murlynn. If it had been anyone else, King Titus would have taken the proper precautions and measures that were customary for such a discovery. But since it was Murlynn, and he seemed to have some sort of connection with the beast, King Titus wanted to hear his reasoning and explanation for concealing such a creature. Therefore, Murlynn told King Titus his story of how he had discovered the egg and took care of it until it hatched. His intention was to release the animal back into the wild, but when a dragon came forth from the egg, he decided that releasing her was not the best option. He did consider handing Korel over to the authorities, but thought that keeping her with him would be the best for learning about dragon development, behavior, and experimentation. Murlynn further explained that it was his desire to take her from the land so that she could live with her kind, but until then, he was no longer able to conceal her at his home due to her size. King Titus listened patiently to Murlynn's story and could hear Murlynn's passion in his voice, and could see the bond that had developed for Korel in his eyes. Against King Titus' better discretion, he said that he would not take down the beast unless he was given reason to, and that Murlynn was to evacuate her from the land as soon as he was able to.

Murlynn tried to find different accommodations in order to release Korel, but every arranged attempt would seem to fall through one way or another. The fact that the Addalayin depths were enchanted did not make the situation any easier. With every missed opportunity to remove Korel from Sahleam, the harder it became for Murlynn to make another arrangement. For the longer Murlynn cared for Korel, the stronger and deeper their relationship became. This was not necessarily an issue at first for no one knew of her existence besides Murlynn and King Titus, for she wasn't given anyone a reason to suspect her existence. But as Korel grew, her appetite grew as well. The small game of the woods were becoming scarce, and stags were hard to come by in that area of the forest. Murlynn knew that he had to consider moving her when the farmers started complaining about missing cattle and sheep from their herds. At first, they thought that maybe a common predator had stumbled upon the village, but it was uncommonly avoiding the traps that had worked so well in the past.

Also, the amount of each herd that went missing in a short period of time made the farmers conclude that this was a substantial beast.

Then, early one morning, it happened. A group of farmers stayed up all night to see if they could encounter and resolve their current predator situation, but they got more than they bargained for when Korel finally arrived in the late of the night hours. She did not just swoop down and take her pick of the litter, but gently descended and landed in a clearing where the moonlight showed what a glorious and splendid beast she was. The farmers, after being awestricken at first, worked up their courage and made their attack on Korel. These farmers had faced many large animals before, so their engagement with Korel would be similar, but modified. They attacked from all angles so as to confuse her and not allow her to focus on a solitary person. They had a weighted net that could be used to immobilize her wings and keep her on the ground. The farmers also had rope that could be used on her legs and a muzzle for her mouth. Since they had the element of surprise, and Korel had never encountered a hostile human, victory over their new enemy came with only a few causalities.

Having heard the commotion from his home, Murlynn decided to head over to see what was going on. When he got there, Murlynn saw the farmers celebrating their truly great victory. Murlynn stayed hidden, not knowing yet what he should do. Then he heard the farmers ponder the question of what they were going to do with Korel. The discussion did not take long, nor was there any debate over the answer to their situation; Korel was to be executed immediately.

"She is too dangerous, and she would just keep coming back to feast on the herds," the farmers concluded.

Upon hearing this, Murlynn's heart broke. He could not allow them to just slaughter his beloved Korel. Not sure what to do, Murlynn snuck over to Korel. He could tell when he first saw her that she was relieved to see him. Korel was confused about the whole situation. Her only dealing with human interaction had been with Murlynn, which was positive to say the least. These people were acting out of anger, and showed nothing but hostility toward Korel. Fear had crept upon her as she lay patiently in defeat awaiting her fate. Sneaking up to her with his finger over his mouth, Murlynn looked in her eyes and could feel her dread of what was to come next. He could not let this happen to her!

"Shhh," Murlynn whispered as he stroked her neck, trying to bring some sort of relief to the situation. "I'm going to get you out of here."

Before he knew what he was doing, Murlynn found himself working to get the weighted net off of Korel's back. Since she was lying on the ground, this wasn't too difficult; he just needed to be careful not to get it further tangled in her wings. As Murlynn worked, he kept an eye on the farmers, but they were so jovial in their celebration that they were paying no mind to Korel. You would think that they would have had someone stand guard over such a magnificent creature to make sure that their entrapments kept her secure. But they were so busy boasting and celebrating their great accomplishment that Murlynn could have paraded himself to Korel while declaring his intentions, and no one would have still paid him any mind. In either case, Murlynn still needed to move quickly and get out of there before their predicament became worse than what it was. After a moment or two, Murlynn was finally able to remove the net, and Korel let him know with no uncertain terms that she was ready to depart by spreading her wings and arching her back and head to the stars.

"I know. Be patient. I have to get your feet loose first," Murlynn told her as he rubbed her side, trying to bring some relief to Korel's anxiety.

Pulling out his knife, Murlynn started feverishly cutting the bonds around Korel's feet. Although this too took longer than he anticipated, the farmers came no closer to noticing this heroic rescue than to throw away some bottles and other trash from their celebration.

As soon as Murlynn cut her feet free, Korel began to squirm, ready to be relieved of the situation. But Murlynn knew that she would only starve to death or die of dehydration if he was not able to get her muzzle off. This proved difficult with all of her jostling. As Murlynn tried to keep Korel calm so that he could remove her muzzle, he saw her tail swing into a horse-drawn plow, knocking it over. As Murlynn watched the plow fall in slow motion he knew that there was nothing he could do to stop the large hunk of metal from crashing into the earth. When the plow hit the ground, it made such a great noise that it would have woken up the farmers if they were not already outside celebrating. Finally becoming aware of Korel's escape, the farmers immediately stopped their celebration, grabbed their arms, and quickly headed in Murlynn's direction.

The bang had also gotten Korel to pause. When Murlynn saw this, he jumped up and grabbed her by the muzzle and started to cut furiously.

Murlynn's ploy was up, as the farmers undoubtedly discovered his foiled rescue.

"Stop. Step away!" they cried, amongst some other more unfriendly phrases as they ran down and encircled Korel and Murlynn. Not giving up on his task, Murlynn continued to cut the muzzle until one brave soul rushed in and pulled Murlynn away. Although not succeeding in removing the muzzle, Murlynn was able to cut through the material enough so that Korel's powerful jaws were able to finish the job and snap the muzzle off.

Murlynn looked into her eyes and no longer saw fear and defeat, but anger and rage. Korel swiped her tail in order to keep the farmers at bay. Now understanding how to use her body to combat those opposing her, Korel now had the upper hand and could have retreated, especially since many of them were injured due to her mighty tail swipe. Fear and dread now lived in the eyes of the farmers.

"Enough, Korel. Fly away!" Murlynn encouraged her. But she did not listen. With another swipe, Korel was able to knock a man away from the group of farmers. Laying on his back, this poor soul was completely defeated. Murlynn pleaded for Korel to stop and just leave, but Korel ignored his pleas and did the unthinkable. She looked at Murlynn, and then took a deep breath, turned upon her victim, and unleashed such a terrible blast of fire that it would have melted the finest armor. Everyone watched in horror as the blaze not only engulfed its terrified victim, but also spread to the crops and even reached the house. Awestricken at this dreadful sight, Murlynn looked at Korel, who seemed to be surprised at the amount of damage that her one fearsome blow had done.

Murlynn was only trying to understand dragons better. The farmers were only trying to protect their livelihood. And Korel was only looking for a nighttime meal. No one was expecting what had happened that night, and it would change how dragons were viewed and treated from there on out. As for Murlynn, he would have to live with what he did, what he saw, and the decisions he had made for the rest of his life.

42

The city square wasn't a square at all, for how could there be a square in a city that was carved into a mountainside? Rather, the city square was a place where daily trading occurred and the latest gossip could be heard. It was also marked with a beautiful marble statue. At the base of the statue was a clover-shaped basin filled with water. In the middle of the basin was a Dwarf who was standing with one foot on a rock and the other in the water. The rock was half a slap of quarry stone and the other half was a cluster of diamonds. In one hand, the Dwarf was holding a pickaxe that was resting on his shoulder, while the other hand was cradling artistic artifacts like a toy horse, an ornamental Dwarf soldier, and a paintbrush. This was where Silas and Raithyn were to meet up with Master Sergeant Xoarah.

"You must be Xoarah," Silas declared as they approached the statue. Silas and Raithyn really had no idea who they were looking for, but seeing that this young man was the only person in uniform, they figured it was a safe bet.

Xoarah was a younger-looking man, whose skin had not been aged with war or battles, whose hands had not yet adapted to their work, and whose beard was not fully grown in yet.

"Yes, and you must be Silas and Raithyn," said Xoarah, reaffirming their intuition.

Silas and Raithyn were not much older that Xoarah, but their rough skin and battle scars showed that experience was on their side.

Silas was shorter than Raithyn, with blond hair and blue eyes. Unlike many other men in Lord Titus' army, Silas was beardless. Not that he did not want to grow a beard, but rather that the ability to do so eluded him. He did not have the chin for a mustache, and when Silas did try to grow a beard, everyone called him "Patches".

Raithyn, on the other hand, did not have a beard, but preferred the stubble look with his long black hair.

"Are you in charge?" asked Silas point blank. Silas and Raithyn had gotten in trouble before by making assumptions due to one's outward appearance. How one looks is not a good determining factor for their knowledge, courage, or heart. Xoarah may have looked young and inexperienced, but he was a Master Sergeant for a reason.

"Yes," answered Xoarah with a lack of confidence in his new position. "I was given the promotion to Master Sergeant just this morning."

Silas and Raithyn did not like the sound of that. If Xoarah was the man they promoted and left in charge, then what did that say about the infantry?

"You are aware of the situation?" asked Raithyn, wondering if Xoarah knew why he was promoted and what he would possibly be going up against.

"Yes," answered Xoarah with a boast of confidence. "And don't let my youth discourage you. We are all well-trained in dragon disturbances. It is the first thing that is required of all incoming recruits."

"And what of your fortifications?"

"We have heavy artillery crossbows stationed on high points throughout the city for long-range assaults. We also have catapults capable for throwing heavy boulders, nets, fireballs, or anything else we want to arm them with," stated Xoarah with reassurance. "We also have nets, ropes, muzzles, long spears, and ground troops stationed at posts throughout the city as well," he added before they could ask any other questions.

Before Master Sergeant Xoarah could go over any tactical information or what the plan was for Silas and Raithyn, he quickly noticed that he had lost their attention, as they were now focused on the sky.

"You said that all your men go through a dragon disturbance training upon first entering your army?" asked Raithyn while still peering up at the sky.

"Yeah," replied Xoarah mindlessly as he still had not caught sight of what Silas and Raithyn were looking at.

"Good. That's good, because here comes a whole mess of dragons heading straight for us," calmly stated Raithyn, never taking his eyes off the sky as he pointed out the small batlike figures that were quickly approaching in the distance. With that being said, the warning horn sounded loud and fierce, sending the whole city into a frenzy.

Everyone immediately stopped what they were doing. Women and children ran for shelter, while the remaining troops armed themselves and got to their post as quickly as they could. Master Sergeant gave orders as best as he could based on the emergency drills they had gone over with him during his promotion. Communication throughout the whole city was a difficult task, but being located at the southernmost edge of Sahleam, the dwarfs had successfully developed attack plans for when dealing with air raids. Tunnels within the city and mountain-side allowed for quick mobilization and effective communication throughout the city. Although the dwarfs had successfully strategized attack methods for such a situation, two unsuspected facts revealed themselves as the dragons flew in closer. First, they were flying in from the north, which meant that they would have already came up out of the southern land and passed over the city undetected. Second, this was the largest fleet of dragons the city had ever seen.

It was impressive to see how quickly the men got to their stations and had their long range weapons and heavy artillery locked and loaded. Now the only thing that they could do was wait. Even with their long range weapons; the dragons were still out of range. As the dwarfs waited, the small bat like figures grew into what could be described as massive ships sailing through the sky. The anticipation and calm that had taken over the bustling city left an eerie lump in the back of their throats. As the beasts drew closer, they climbed higher in altitude, still out of range for any assault, and spread themselves out methodically over the city.

"I have never seen this before," Xoarah said to Silas and Raithyn as he continued to watch their military tactics in amazement.

"Many people have been saying that lately," remarked Silas, who was more concerned with what he was seeing rather than impressed.

"Well, don't get too excited. The only thing we can do at this point is wait for them to dive," added Raithyn.

As everyone waited, they were not sure what they were waiting for. The dragons' altitude was just out of artillery range, and they were not showing any signs of starting their assault as they just hovered in the sky. This was the calm before the storm that was about to enrage. After a moment that felt like a lifetime, the squall of fury hit; not from above, were everyone's attention was directed, but from the south gate.

The dragons attacked with ferocity and rage. For so long, they had been shunned out of Sahleam. For so long, every time they entered the land they had been met with arrows, nets, and potions that would lead to their death, capture, or retreat; but not this time. This time the dragons would have retribution. This time, the dragons would not be pushed out. This time the dragons would finally show what kind of creatures they were and what they were capable of.

The attack started with two dragons that were undetected until they overtook the south gate with ease. Perched on top of the two great Dwarf statues that served as gate posts and symbols of their strength and protection, the dragons let out a thunderous roar signaling their advancement, followed by a blaze of fire that engulfed the nearby homes and shops. For that brief second, while everyone's attention was diverted to the destruction of the southern end, the aerial assault began.

The dive bombers made a b-line straight for the heavy artillery. Before the dwarfs knew what happened, the dragons were upon them. Not bothering with fire, the dragons swooped in and grabbed the soldiers and artillery, ripping it from its mounts and carrying it as if it was no more than a stag or goat, but with a more vicious intent. The weaponry became airborne missiles that the dragons would use to dismantle other artillery stations. Soldiers, crossbows, catapult launchers, statues, and other objects that made a decent projectile missile were used in the assault against the city. Homes, shops, public monuments, even sacred places were all part of the dragon's raid. This was not just an attack on the standing army, but the complete destruction of an entire city.

With nowhere to hide, the women and children ran frantically in the streets, trying to avoid the fury of the dragons as the soldiers tried to keep the dragons at bay. Realizing that their once-reliable defense tactic was now useless against their familiar enemy, the Master Sergeant decided that the best decision was to abandon the city to its capture and get to the safe room. The safe room was a big room that was built within the mountain that could house most, if not all of the city's residents. With thick steel doors and walls, the safe room was their best option to protect the civilians of this lost city. With a broken heart, Xoarah gave the order for the retreat horn to be blown. Immediately the people stopped scurrying about the city and headed for the tunnels. Out of all the places the tunneling system could lead you within the city, the one place they had never hoped to use was the safe room. Now it looked like this safe room would be the means of their salvation.

43

Lord Cephas kept west, which was easy because all he needed to do was keep the sun in front of him. As he kept true to his course, Lord Cephas mulled over the information that he had collected over the past day in order to give a descriptive report of the accounts and some sort of resolution for the events that had expired.

"Straight and true," he repeated to himself as he walked briskly toward the creek, remembering what Herms had said.

Suddenly, Lord Cephas stopped, pondering for a second where he was, and where he was going. Befuddled he turned around expecting to see a hut of sorts, but instead all he saw were woods. Staring blankly, Lord Cephas tried to recall the hut and persons he had spent that past day with, but could not. As he tried to recall the course of events, he suddenly realized where he was. Remembering the words "straight and true," Lord Cephas turned around to continue on his trek through the woods, but instead found himself standing on the banks of the river, looking at the bridge that was not there just a moment ago. At once, Lord Cephas recognized the bridge and quickly crossed it, hoping to find his and Lord Benaniah's horse where they had left them, but they were gone.

After briefly examining the area, it was easily concluded that someone had come up from the south and taken one of the horses north, while releasing the other one from its constraints as well. From the tracks it was easily deducted that the horse that was left behind went to the river, probably for a drink of water, and then started its way north as well. In this scenario, Lord Cephas would have to conclude that the animal followed its primal instinct and started making its way back to the Castle Dorian. In either case, the lord figured it would be worth giving a whistle, for if the horse was still nearby, maybe it would come back. Time was of the essence, and with a horse, Lord Cephas could be back to the castle this day, but it would be a challenge to get back by the night on by foot. After giving a whistle, Lord Cephas waited only a moment before deciding to start his journey back to the castle. Also, it would not be the best idea to make such a public decla-ration of his presence in the current circumstance and remain in the same place for any length of time. As he headed north, Lord Cephas did decide that it would be good to periodically give a whistle in case the steed may be nearby.

44

"We cannot let these beasts intimidate or bully us with size and strength," stated Lord Ekron in a frustrated tone. He was not frustrated with Lord Augusta or the Lord King Titus, but with their recent events.

"We might not have a special potion to aid us in this fight, but we still have courage, heart, and our wit," he continued.

Sleep did not come to any of the lords' eyes the night before, although they had tried. One by one all the lords ended up in the same place they were when they were first made aware of the invasion: the council chamber. This room was only used for two reasons. First, when the yearly gathering of the lords occurred, and second, whenever a situation arose that would require a strategic planning session with Lord Titus and his high-ranking officers. When the doors to this chamber were shut, no one was to enter or leave without granted permission on the pain of punishment. Across from the entrance were three stain glass windows that allowed light into the room. Torchlit sconces decorated the walls as well, providing light when the session went from the day into the night. A couple of paintings were hung on either side of the doors, with a map of the lands directly across the fireplace which sat off to the left of the entrance. A circular table with five chairs was placed in the middle of the room. Only two chairs and scraps of food were left at the table as the three lords huddled around the dying fire. Their focus and attention was so intense that they did not realize the time of day it was. With their backs to the rays of light beaming through the windows, the dark stones and the worn sconces gave little confirmation to the correct time of day.

"I have no doubt that any one of us would run recklessly into the very mouths that spout the flames of hell if it meant the safety and salvation of our people," encouraged Lord Titus, "but what about our men?" he asked concerningly.

With a glaring look from Lord Ekron, Lord Titus knew that he needed to add meaning to his statement.

"Please, Lord Ekron, hear what I am saying. We have never faced opposition like this before. Yes, we have faced dragons, and yes, these are the best men that our land and kingdoms have to offer, but will their courage stay strong when they see a fleet of dragons approaching?" asked Lord Titus, pausing briefly for emphasis. "Will their heart and love for their country be able to keep pressing onward, even into billowing fire?" Lord Titus paused again. "When new challenges and enemies arise that are unlike anything we have ever seen, I wonder if our courage and hearts will sustain us to victory."

The lords were silent while the gravity of what Lord Titus said was considered. Fear and intimidation are crippling allies that their enemies will surely try to oppose onto them. The men needed something to give them hope. Something that they believed that would assure them victory.

"They do not know that the carnivorous diffusion is ineffective," Lord Ekron finally stated. "For their sake, and ours, I think we should keep it that way. This battle is challenging enough; there is no need to unnecessarily lessen their confidence any more than what it already may be."

"Are you suggesting that we lie to the men who are going to pay with their blood the price that has been put on this land?" chimed Lord Augusta in disbelief.

"No. We should not lie to our men," interjected Lord Titus, agreeing with Lord Augusta. "But I do agree with Lord Ekron. This information does not need to be made public, either. Both of you speak the truth. We will not lie to the men who are going to pay dearly with their lives, nor are we going to take away any hope that these men might have in winning this fight. I believe that we need to be honest with our troops, but not all information is pertinent among the ranks. Those who need to know will know."

"This is all well and good, but it does not help us pluck a dragon from the sky, nor shield us from being burned alive. We need a strategy that will help neutralize our enemy, and even the battlefield," bolstered Lord Ekron.

"You commonly deal with dragons," piped Lord Augusta, "what are some proven tactics you have used that might be able to help us?"

"Those tactics are useless to us," said Lord Ekron in a deflated tone as he shrugged off Lord Augusta's suggestion. "The mountains brought us within close range; we normally only had one dragon at a time to deal with, and we had an effective carnivorous diffusion. None of these benefits will be with us for this attack."

Silence hovered over the room as the three lords sat and watched the embers dance in the smoldered fireplace. How could they overcome this seemingly impossible task? How could they neutralize the enemy? The land of Sahleam herself was being challenged, and the inhabitants must come together to defend her. For it is better to die for what you love and what you believe in than to run and hide and die a coward. But you must be tactical, for it is stupid, not heroic, to willing run into the jaws of death.

"Their biggest threats are their ability to fly and breathe fire," whispered Lord Augusta to himself as he was thinking aloud. "If we could neutralize that, then the dragons become nothing more than a lion or a bear."

For some reason, this comment of Lord Augusta's brought back a distant memory of Lord Titus; a memory of one of the very first instances of when a dragon terrorized a group of local farmers. "Well, according to our records, a group of farmers was able to capture a dragon once with a net and a muzzle," thoughtfully added Lord Titus. "It was a long time ago, and it was only one dragon, but maybe the same principle can apply," suggested Lord Titus as he was starting to believe in what he was saying.

"I do remember that account as well," recalled Lord Augusta, "but how are we to get close enough to demobilize the beast when they are hundreds of feet in the air and dive faster than bolts of lightning when they are attacking?"

Without moving his focus from the dying embers, Lord Ekron made the only plausible suggestion, the suggestion that he had been trying to avoid all night long.

"We bait 'em."

Lord August and Titus' attention arose as they gave Lord Ekron their attention and waited for further explanation of his statement.

"Few things in life are more thrilling than an exciting hunt: suspenseful anticipation, an exhilarating chase, and a worthy death of a noble animal," started Lord Ekron. "But if your family is starving because they haven't eaten in days, then the sport of the hunt is no longer the goal, but rather the provision for your family."

"Although it might not be as invigorating or honorable as a proper hunt, some apple cores and corn can lead the animal right to you instead of having to go out and look for it," concluded Lord Ekron.

"We are already the huntees Lord Ekron," began an already annoyed and exhausted Lord Augusta. "What are you suggesting we do that will not only bait the dragons, but will switch the roles and have us become the hunters as well?"

"The oldest trick in the book," Lord Ekron retorted, "divide and conquer."

"They know that they are a superior foe and that our potions are impenetrable, but they are not aware that we are knowledgeable of this information, so let's lead them to believe that we are still ignorant of the matter."

"We can position our battle lines in the same manor that we normally do, but we will have our archers take aim specifically at the dragon's wings. The heavy assault arrows and catapults will accompany the battalions as normal to keep the beast at bay. We will also have net launchers among the ranks to try and ground the beast."

"After the assault has begun, we will unsuspectedly flank the beast. All ground troops will concentrate on the grounded dragons, focusing specifically on slashing their wings so that they can no longer take flight, netting their bodies to immobilize them, and muzzling the beast so we can neutralize the fire. A simple weight spell on the nets and muzzles will ensure that they stay contained."

"To ask our men to engage in hand-to-hand combat with a dragon is to sign their death certificate," protested Lord Augusta.

Pausing for a minute, Lord Augusta considered the plan. No other plan had been formulated within the entire night that had a notion of success like this one. Lord Augusta was a passionate man who loved deeply, especially for the people. At this point, with this foe, and the current circumstance, Lord Augusta finally reconciled within himself that rivers of tears would flow, and the symphony of disparaging grief would have to ring through the land if they were to have even a notion of victory.

"And what do we do with the beast if we succeed?" asked Lord Augusta as he unwillingly had to come to grips and accept the fact that many lives would have to be lost.

"Use your imagination," said Lord Ekron with a twisted grin.

"Lord Ekron is right," chimed in Lord Titus resolutely. "Our strength is in our numbers. A frontal assault would never be expected, nor would such guerrilla tactics. Men will die, good men for sure. But in their sacrifice, the land of Sahleam will live on."

At that moment, a knock came at the door. After being granted entry, one of the guards stationed outside the chamber came in with an announcement. "My lords, word has just been delivered from a carrier that Lord Cephas' men will be arriving before the first hour of the night."

Having delivered his message, the guard bowed and dismissed himself back to his post.

After the previous day and long night, the lords were feeling satisfied with their decision and that the armies from the other kingdoms were already starting to arrive. Confidence was rising in the lords as seeds of hope and belief were planted deep within their hearts. But any measurable amount of optimism that the lords did experience did not last long, for no sooner did they get the chance to take satisfaction in their plan, than did Antheis come bursting into the room; ragged, famished, and with bad news.

45

The statue that once ordained the town square, demonstrating the Dwarf's craftsmanship with remarkable beauty, declaring their paradoxical nature of having a rugged attitude and caring spirit that was bound together by the trust they had in their "mother earth", now laid in ruins. Many soldiers laid dead or dying, having been either used as live artillery or struck down during the attack. The buildings were either collapsed or barely remained standing. This was truly a statement attack that left Endorah in ruins.

As the evacuation horns continued to blow, Master Sergeant Xoarah continued to give orders to help the remaining civilians into the tunneling system. There was no way to tell if every abled person made it out of the city, but with the dragon's attack raging, Silas and Raithyn convinced Xoarah that he had done the best he could and now needed to go into the mountain so that he could lead the remainder of his people.

As they ran down in the dark, damp tunnels, they could hear the crumbling of buildings, the thudding of the massive beast, and the roar of victory that was ensuing up above. There was little light to see where they were going, but this was not a problem, for the Dwarf's eyes had acclimated to having only minimal amounts of light from time spent daily deep in the mines.

With hundreds of people bottle-necked into the tunnels, one would expect congestion of pace, but the dwarfs moved fluidly like a river until they reached their haven.

Silas and Raithyn felt as though they were caught within white river rapids as the flow of dwarfs traveled along the current to their destination. Their eyes had no such acclimation to the deep darkness, so they had to let the torrent of the dwarfs guide them along the winding path. It wasn't long before Silas and Raithyn were able to see a set of doors in the distance. The tight winding pathway led into a large open receiving area that looked similar to a cathedral with its high ceiling and torchlit walls. After running in almost near darkness with the raging torrent of dwarfs, Silas and Raithyn were able to see over the sea of people and catch a glimpse of the huge iron doors that were opened with light flooding out of them. Relief came upon them as they knew that they would soon have a moment to take stock of their current situation and evaluate what needed to be done next.

While Silas, Raithyn, and Xoarah were driving in the last of the dwarfs into the safe room, a dragon busted through the wall like a cannon ball, forcing its way through the starboard side of a ship. It was a large, deathly-looking thing. If the shock of a dragon having discovered what was to be their safe haven did not overtake them, then the fear and death emanating from this monster's pores would have frozen you stiff. It was a terrifying sight; it had a large, spade-shaped head, horns fanning its cheek bones, a long smoking snout, and green, snake-like eyes that gripped at your heart and would squeeze your very life out of it. Intimidation was not the only weapon that this beast had;

razor sharp claws, dagger teeth, and a club-like tail penetrated with bones would make it a fierce competitor against any of its contemporaries. Surely, death was inevitable.

Silas and Raithyn knew the importance that Xoarah was to his people, so without delay they implored him to quickly get into the safe room and shut the doors as they distracted this deliverer of death.

Trying to sound brave, Xoarah protested their urgency. "I will not leave you out here to die for a people that is not your own."

As noble a rebuttal as Xoarah had, Raithyn knew that his people could not be left leaderless. This was not a time to argue over principles or formalities, so Raithyn gave Xoarah a very clear and very damning ultimatum: "Go, or I'll kill you before the dragon gets a chance to!" as he drew his sword from its scabbard and pressed the point into Xoarah's throat.

Xoarah, being young and inexperienced, was really just being cordial. So, without delay, he took up their offer and made way for the safe room, leaving Silas and Raithyn to try and figure out how to defeat death.

If death remained undefeated, then why would one want to try and fight it? Why not join the others in the safe room? Well, two reasons: first, you did not know if the dragon would be able to break down the door as it did the cave wall. Second, if the beast was left to its own devices, it may go back and get reinforcements to lay siege on their heaven. No, to take down the beast or to drive it away was the best option.

Two soldiers with only swords, no matter their experience, were not much of a match for a full-grown dragon, but they knew that in this setting, their strengths would play right into the dragon's weakness. The dragon's size would make it hard for agile movements, even though the room was quite large for people standards. Also, the room was too small for the beast to use its best weapon, fire, without more likely inflicting pain on itself as well.

With this in mind, Silas and Raithyn agreed that death by a thousand cuts would be their best tactic. Duck, dodge, and slice was their strategy as they stayed light on their feet, slashing at the monster's underbelly while being keenly aware of the different armaments the dragon could end them with.

They were valiant in their efforts, and even succeeded in diverting the beast, so that the remaining dwarfs could get into the safe room and out of harm's way. It was like watching someone go spear fishing for the first time. When light hits water, refraction occurs, bending the light. This makes something like a fish appear to be in one spot when it is really in another spot altogether. Even if you were fast enough, you would not be able to spear the fish without knowing this. In the same way, the dragon could not land a single blow on Silas and Raithyn. But also, like in spear fishing, if you stay with it long enough you will learn this principle and be able to adapt to it. Silas and Raithyn knew this, and knew that it was only a matter of time before the beast would start anticipating their movements no matter how random they tried to make them.

In fact, it was shortly after everyone was in the safe room that the dragon caught Silas on the back of his head with the broad side of his tail, knocking him down and causing a concussion-like state. Raithyn was not as fortunate. The beast caught Raithyn with a monstrous backhand that sent him flying into the tunnel wall. Raithyn hit the wall hard; breaking his lower back and fracturing his ribs. He knew that it was over. Even if he was somehow able to escape the dragon that was before him, death would still come through his injuries. The dragon knew it was over for Raithyn as well. With a sinister grin, the beast made its way over to its victim, licking its chops in anticipation. There was nothing Silas could do but watch, as he felt like he was in a dream like state due to the blow the he himself had absorbed.

Seeing that the dragon was coming to claim its prey, Raithyn reached out and grabbed his sword. It would not be long before he would meet his maker. At the very least, if this beast was going to finish him, then Raithyn was going to fight until his final breath.

The dragon came over and picked up Raithyn. With a tight grip around his waist, the dragon held up Raithyn and looked into his eyes. For a second, Raithyn could feel immense hatred and anger pouring forth from the dragon. Preparing himself for what was to come next,

Raithyn grasped his sword with both hands as tight as he could, knowing that he only had one chance to bring down this monster. As the dragon put Raithyn in his mouth and bit down hard, Raithyn thrust his sword with all of his might up into the roof of the monster's mouth, causing it to fall lifeless to the ground.

46

Herms was closing in on Murlynn's hut. He knew that it would not be much longer, and frankly, he was rather excited to have someone else to converse with instead of being left to his own thoughts in his head. No matter what he did, no matter how hard he tried, Herms could not stop thinking about the visions that he had been having.

What do these dreams mean? What is the connection?

The snake; the emerald green snake like dragon thing has appeared in both my dreams, but why?

Although Herms made camp for the night, he did not sleep long. And after his dream about the shadowy figure and the dragons, it was hard for him to get any more sleep thereafter. On the other hand, he was making really good time and should be at Murlynn's hut well before the middle of the day. He had come down from the north as directed by Lord Titus, keeping the sun at his right as he rode "straight and true". Lord Titus told him to remember these directions and even to say them out loud if he became unsure which way to go.

As Herms was mulling over his thought, this very thing happened. It is best described like riders hypnosis. This is when you are riding and become so engaged with your thoughts that your subconscious takes over steering the steed until you reengage with reality. When you finally do leave your thoughts and focus back on reality, you are not exactly sure where you are or how you got there. This is what Herms was feeling. Thankfully, his horse kept pressing onward, for if Herms was on foot, he might have abandoned his path for a course that was more familiar.

As the steed kept pressing on, Herms finally remembered where he was and where he was going. With a kick and *"Hiyah*!" Herms spurred on the horse to make hast. As soon as the horse picked up pace Herms felt that he was going the wrong way and was sure that he needed to turn around, but before he could pull the reigns to redirect his path, Herms remembered what Lord Titus had said to him just before leaving the stable, "straight and true". The words came to him like a whisper in his ear. With that encouragement, Herms continued onward.

Immediately after the desire to change direction had left him, leaves began to rustle on either side of him, coming together to form two wave-like barriers that raced him through the woods. Suddenly, the leaves sprinted ahead of him and came together directly in his path, forming a figure that seemed to be a person holding up their hand for Herms to stop. Not that Herms is the type of person to challenge mystical figures that randomly form in the wood, but before he could react to the apparition's warning, he slammed into the specter, plowing through the figure as easily as one jumping into a large pile of leaves on a cool autumn day. After bursting through the leafed figure Herms saw a straw hut coming up fast. Herms pulled on the reigns hard so that he didn't crash through this straw figure as well. Luckily, he was able to stop just before the hut without even trampling any of the flowers and herbs that were planted around the hut. Taking a moment to collect himself, Herms dismounted and started to approach the hut, knowing that this must be Murlynn's place.

. . . .

Murlynn was in his laboratory hard at work, for he knew that they needed some sort of spell, potion, or enchantment in order to help overcome the dragons, but he just wasn't sure of what. Obviously flying and fire breathing were their two biggest advantages, besides their armor like scales and sheer size. The problem was that you would need to make some sort of physical contact in order to immobilize a physical feature. And according to the captain, any physical contact would need to be close range for their long-range tactics are no longer viable. Direct penetration into their blood stream would be their best option at this point, but would also be extremely dangerous. Before resulting to something that would be a one-way mission, Murlynn had to try and find some other practical solution to their predicament.

"Well they really don't have a weakness that can be exploited," mumbled Murlynn to himself as he continuously flipped through a pile of books that were before him.

"What about their animal instincts? Is there something that I can draw on that might make them revert back?"

"No, no," agreed a frustrated Murlynn.

"They have shown signs of extreme intelligence and communication. I am sure that given time, I may find something, but time is not something I have. Nor would it be guaranteed that they would give into the lure of temptation that I would lay before them."

"What if I am looking at this all wrong?" said Murlynn with excitement.

"Instead of trying to make the dragons vulnerable, why don't I focus on creating an offensive way of leveling the playing field? Being able to fly, fire protection, or some sort of piercing enchantment for our weapons?"

"Ugh. No." groaned Murlynn after little thought. "I cannot see a way where any of their hexes would be able to give us total advantage over these demons. We would still be vulnerable to their overall size and strength, and would still need to come within close range in order to secure any type of victory."

Frustrated, Murlynn finally gave in to what he knew needed to be done, but before he could get to work a knock came at his door. Curious as to who this could be since he wasn't expecting anyone, and normally never is, Murlynn stopped his work to greet his new guest.

. . . .

Herms waited anxiously for Murlynn to open the door. What was only a minute felt like an hour. Impatience grew as he was tempted to barge into this shabby hut when suddenly the door swung open and there stood Murlynn looking back at him. Now, Herms knew that he was going to collect Murlynn, so him being there on the other side of the doorway was not a surprise. But he still couldn't believe that he was standing there looking at him. It's been a long time since Herms had seen Murlynn face to face.

Herms could not hold back his emotion and gave Murlynn a long-awaited hug.

"Uff," grunted Murlynn from the unexpected hug. "Oh, hello. While yes," agreed Murlynn. "Um . . . may I ask, what brings you here my boy?"

Pulling back, Herms wasted no time, for he knew that there was none to waste, and got straight to the point of the matter.

"There has been a dragon attack in the land. It turns out that they have formed an alliance with each other and are attacking the land with coordinated precise military strikes. A gathering of arms has been called throughout the land. We need to make a unified offensive strike. But there is a problem; the potion that you have given us is no longer effective. We need you to come at once to the Castle Dorian to help with preparing and making another potion or weapon so that we can oppose our enemy."

"Awe yes" said Murlynn to Herms surprise as he turned and started walking to his laboratory. "I was most expecting someone to come and fetch me from the king's court, but I didn't think it would be you, Herms."

Herms stood in the entrance puzzled.

"You see," Murlynn continued as he gathered some things into a bag, "yesterday I was visited by the Lord Benaniah and Lord Cephas. They had come with this gentleman, who was on the brink of death," said Murlynn as he pointed to the captain who was in a sleep like state as he continued his recovery process. At that moment, Herms stood in unbelief as he recognized who the man was from the previous day. Unable to say anything from the shock of the this revelation, Murlynn kept on with his soliloquy, "After I had healed him he revealed to us that he is Surgyn, Captain of the King's Dragon Prevention Branch, and told us that a rouge dragon mission had turned out to be a calculated ambush. Barely escaping with his life, the lords found him and brought him here."

Herms was intrigued both with the information that was being presented and with Murlynn's bag. Murlynn had already put a sufficient amount stuff into the bag to fill it, but he just kept putting more and more things into it. The stranger part was that the bag looked half empty and Murlynn was carrying it as if it had not weight at all.

"He's alright now, poor chap," Murlynn continued, not leaving much time for Herms to interject, "but he will need to stay here and rest and continue to take some medicine in order to get a full recovery."

Herms continued to just stand there, taken aback about the whole situation. His mind raced as he considered and questioned all that was happening. How was Murlynn's house so big on the inside compared to the outside? What was he to do with the unexpected information about Lord Cephas and Lord Benaniah's visitation? How was Murlynn able to continue to fill his bag that seemed to never be full? What would become of the captain lying on the couch, whose appearance seemed gravely? Why did Murlynn not seem bothersome in his mood about the current situation?

"Okay, that should do it." mentioned Murlynn. Swinging his bag onto his back, he also grabbed a couple bottles of potions, mixed them together and then poured the new concoction into a bowl. He set the bowl on a table next to the captain with a note informing him that he had gone away, but would be back soon, and that he was to take the medicine in the bowl after it solidified.

"Are you ready?" asked Herms as he was still waiting in the entrance way trying to process everything that had just taken place over this short period of time.

"Yes, we can; oh wait a minute," exclaimed Murlynn as he shot over towards the kitchen! "I haven't had breakfast and would faint by the time we got back to the castle. Would you like something to eat as well?" Murlynn asked as he put some hard-boiled eggs, biscuits, and bacon in a bowl? Murlynn's question was more rhetorical than anything, for he did not even listen for Herms reply and made sure to bring enough along for the both of them.

"Ok," Murlynn said smiling, "now we can go."

With that, Herms did not want to give Murlynn a chance to remember something else that he might have forgotten, and made straightaway for his horse.

After they had walked out the door and mounted Herms horse, Murlynn stopped Herms once again before he could take off, "Oh, one more moment please."

Turning toward the hut, Murlynn lifted his hands and chanted an incantation. A white ball formed on top of the hut and burst out forming a bright white ring that fell down and consumed the hut.

"A protection spell for the captain," answered Murlynn before Herms could ask. "Given everything that has happened, we wouldn't want anyone to stumble across my hut who should not be there, now do we?"

Herms just looked back in astonishment.

"Shall we go?" suggested Murlynn.

Without any further to-do, off they went, racing back toward the Castle Dorian.

47

"Antheis. What happened? Are you alright?" questioned the lords as they clamored to get him to a seat.

"Ambush!" began Antheis in an exhausted tone. He had been riding in hast since the first hour of the day in order to get to Lord Titus with the news of what had happened.

"There was an ambush. North of the Valley of Kurdish. My men and I had successfully delivered your message to the Fauns. We then decided to ride into the Forest of Mezpha in order to circle around to the battle scene under the cover of the trees, for we know that dragons did not inhabit the woods, or at least that is what was known to be true.

Having been escorted and seated in Lord Titus' chair, Antheis continued. "No sooner did we enter the forest than did those monsters attack us. It was horrifying, to see my men dismembered and impaled right before me. I knew I did not stand a chance, so I fled. I fled like a coward. I fled for the love of my own life, terrified of what those beasts had just done to my men."

Food and drink were brought to him as the lords listened intently to Antheis' experience.

"As I rode, Cassious was propelled at me; missing me by sheer luck, for it seemed that luck was on my side," continued Antheis as he took a sip of drink and bit of jammed toast. "The beast was not done with me, for it came back for another assault, this time grabbing my horse by its rear and started to lift us into the air. Somehow, I was able to dismount the horse. Although I hit the ground hard, I knew that I must keep going if I wanted to somehow escape. So I got up and continued running until I found myself falling down a cliff that left me lying on the banks of a river."

While Antheis continued his report, he continued to take nibbles of food and sips of drink for he was truly famished. The lords paid no mind and stayed fixed on all the information that Antheis was providing them with.

"How did you survive?" asked Lord Augusta concerningly.

"That is the strange part, and is still a mystery to me," answered Antheis with a quizzical look. "I thought for sure that dragon would have pursed me, but it did not. To my surprise I found myself waking up earlier this day writhing in pain only to see a hooded man disappear across a bridge. Not long after he disappeared an orb appeared across the river and made its way over to me. Rods like lightening probed my body and then it disappeared as well. Although shocked by all that had taken placed, I was quick to realize that I was healed. By some good fortune, I was well, and quickly realized that there was a horse nearby. So I took it, and now here I am."

"Thank you for this report." encouraged Lord Titus kindly. "You are more brave than you think. And now, you must get some rest," he continued succinctly as he waved over the guard who was still standing in the entrance, "for you have hardly eaten and barely sleep. Apollos here will take you to your chambers where you will wash, eat, and sleep, for you have done your fair share of work for this day."

With that, Apollos escorted Antheis out of the chambers.

. . . .

"What a story," cried Lord Ekron. "Do you believe 'em?"

"What other choice do we have?" answered Lord Augusta

"Well, if it is true, then I have a couple of questions. First, how is it that he was the only one to survive this dragon ambush? And second, not only did he survive, but a mysterious hooded figure just happened to be nearby and shows him mercy and compassion by healing him?"

"I can not blame him for wanting to have some camouflage." started Lord Augusta in Antheis' defense, "It would not have added much more time to circle around and approach the Valley of Kurdish from the east. I suppose that if there were any survivors, they probably would have headed east into the forest. He was pretty fortunate to have someone with healing abilities nearby." Lord Augusta paused briefly. "Do you think that this person was Murlynn?" Lord Augusta proposed.

"I do not think so." started Lord Titus. "Herms should have collected him by that time. Also, Antheis said that the hooded person crossed over the bridge into the woods. If that were true, how would have Murlynn gotten across the bridge in the first place? No, I do not think it could have been Murlynn."

"Then there is another powerful wizard in the land," chimed Lord Ekron. "One who may be more powerful than Murlynn."

"But who and why?" asked Lord Augusta musing to himself. "This would explain why Murlynns potion is not working and how the dragons are able to strategize and coordinate unified attacks."

"It does seem to be the missing piece that would make all the recent events make a little more sense, but it also opens up many questions about this hooded figure. Like: why would they heal Antheis, and why would they team up with the dragons, and how are they able to get them to work together?"

"All these questions will be answered in due time," assured Lord Titus, "but for now we need to continue to gather arms and prepare for battle. For it seems that the dragons have made an alliance."

Their thoughts were interrupted by a brief knock on the door. Having been granted entry, a guard announced that Lord Augusta's men started arriving and that a massager of the Nimrod's from the kingdom of Shaddonai had arrived as well with news that Brutus had made it to Lord Benaniah's land and that they are acquiring arms and will be arriving at the Castle Dorian by the beginning of the next day.

Being thanked and dismissed, the lord's began to ponder a new thought about the news they just received.

"How is it that these large groups of men from the north and east are able to make it to the castle without any incident, yet Atheis and Captain Surgyn both walked straight into an ambush?" asked Lord Augusta.

"It looks like the dragons are occupying a specific part of the land . . . Lord Ekrons portion of the land."

"Endorah is the southernmost city. The dragons could easily control their supplies and reinforcements without us ever knowing."

"Dear mother," stated Lord Ekron in shock, knowing that the implications of such tactics would mean that Endorah would most likely be, and already was, defeated. Tears began to trickle down his face as the thought of the loss of the city took hold of his mind

"I am sorry my friend," stated Lord Augusta, as he and Lord Titus tried to console Lord Ekron.

"I guess there is one thing that the dragons do not know," began Lord Ekron and his sadness turned to anger, "never give reason to a Dwarf to become your enemy!"

48

Fighting through pain and unawareness, Silas pulled himself off of the floor in order to make his way over to Raithyn. Was his longtime friend and military partner dead? Silas, afraid to confirm the reality of what he had just seen, still needed to behold the ultimate sacrifice that his dear friend had paid for these people.

Upon approaching the dragon, he could see its head lying lifeless on the ground. Raithyn's lower abdomen had been run through by the dragon's razor-sharp teeth. Looking at the scene Silas knew exactly what had happened. Raithyn's injuries were fatal. So in his death, he took the beast with him. When the dragon had put Raithyn in his mouth and bit down, Raithyn used whatever stregth he had left, combined with the force of the dragon's bite, and drove his sword through the roof of the beast mouth and into its brain.

Although the monster had died instantly, Raithyn was still lying there dying, impailed by the dragon's teeth, inside of its jaws.

Silas did all he could to hold himself together as he witnessed the last moments of his friend's life on this earth.

Raithyn did not express any fear of dying, nor begged to be saved, nor wished that it would have ended in any other way, but rather collected himself enough to reach his hand out to Silas so that he would not be alone as he passed from this life to the next.

As Silas took his hand, he could no longer restrain himself as a whimper and tears started to flow freely down his face. But in this moment, when Raithyn had expressed so much honor, so much courage, and so much nobility, Silas knew that he could not let his emotions get the best of him. So, in order to soothe their souls in this situation, Silas reminded Raithyn of a memory that was dear to both of their hearts.

"When we were young you were the strong, brave, and resound one and I was the outgoing, crazy, and misguided one. I remember that I use to make fun of you, thinking that you were missing out on life, that you were not experiencing all the pleasures that life had to offer. But that night, when I had far too much ale and stumbled into a bull's pen after a party, it was you who had saved my life. I will always remember what you had said, 'That this life is a gift. A gift that we are not to use on ourselves, but a gift we are to give to others. And although we can have self gratifying moments, those moments will always be fleeting and we will always wake up the next morning just as empty as we were the night before.' You told me that, 'we can either spend our life trying to find menial ways that will only temporarily fill our emptiness or we can accept the fact that we are not our own and allow our maker to fill that emptiness.' Those words have always stuck with me and I hope that I was able to live them out before you. Now, as you go to meet your maker, go knowing that you lived a selfless life. Not only did you help me and many others to realize the truth, but you gave your life to save a people you do not know. I know that your maker is well pleased and will accept you with open arms."

With these last words spoken, Raithyn passed from this life to the next.

Raithyn was dead.

In his death Silas took a moment to say a prayer and to collect himself before letting go of Raithyn's hand. It would not be right to leave someone like Raithyn, who paid a heavy price, lying in the jaws of the one he defeated. Therefore, Silas took it upon himself to remove Raithyn from the jaws of the enemy and carried him off to the safe room, all the time thinking, "This was a great sacrifice for a lost city."

. . . .

The safe room was filled with many emotions as Silas walked past the gates with Raithyn's lifeless body. There was great fear for all that had taken place since the beginning of the day. There was relief that the dragon that had found them was dead. And there was sadness, not only for the one who gave his life for their survival, but for all of those who returned to their mother earth that morning. As Silas walked through the crowd of dwarfs, they parted for him and his fallen friend as they made their way to Master Sergeant Xoarah. The dwarfs could not be more honored and grateful for the sacrifice that these men had paid. Stopping before him, Silas just stood there looking at the Master Sergeant with his lifeless friend in his arms. With tears in his eyes and emotions swirling within him, Silas was unable to articulate the words that he wanted to say, knowing that at this moment if he were to open his mouth the only thing that would come out were wails and sobs over the loss of his dear friend.

"We are all very grateful for what you have done for us here today," Xoarah began. "If it were not for you, not only would our city be in ruins, but we would be lying with it. You helped not only save a person, but an entire people; a people who are unlike your own, who are unfamiliar to you, and of whom you do not call friend or acquaintance. What you did here today was not out of order, command, or obligation, but out of love, respect, and decency for the fellow being. A life; no matter how old or young, accomplished or inexperienced, wealthy or poor, is the ultimate sacrifice that one can make. This sacrifice is one that can never be taken back or made amends. For once a life is taken it can never be given back. A life given so a stranger may live runs deep out of the wells of selflessness and love. We did not know Raithyn or his kin, but we do know that he will be honored through song, craftsmanship, and records from this day forth about the heroic deed he has done."

After Xoarah had finished his words, Silas was overwhelmed with emotion from the respect and honor the dwarfs gave to his fallen brother.

"Is there anything we can do for you," asked Xoarah?

Barely able to talk, Silas found the strength to reply, "I want to bury him properly."

"Indeed he will be. With full honors in accordance to what he has done," bellowed Xoarah so that all could hear. "We are not able to bury him here and now, but we will take his body with us, and guard it with our lives until we are able to give him the burial that he deserves."

With that Xoarah started a chant "To Raithyn," that all the other dwarfs quickly followed suite. The chant grew so loud that the walls and roof began to shake.

49

Walking through the woods he knew what needed to be done. If victory was to be assured, then there could be no interference and no surprises. The last thing they needed was something unexpected to come up and deter them of everything that they have worked so hard for. There was truly only one person who could put a damper on their plans. The only way to prevent any interference was to remove the player from the game.

With those thoughts he came upon a shabby straw hut in the middle of the woods.

…………………..

Captain Surgyn was lying on the couch when he awoke. All was quite; there was no commotion, chatter, or bodies moving about. He was in fact alone. This was not a surprise or concern to him. Not knowing how long he was asleep for, he did not expect to have someone babysitting him while he slept. He saw that the medicine that was hovering just above his mouth was almost gone. Out of the corner of his eye he saw a bowl and piece of parchment on the end table next to him. He rolled over to grab the note. When he did, he realized how much pain his body was still in. Although the medicine had no doubt healed his insides, there was still pain and soreness from the injuries.

After he got done reading the note, Surgyn felt a slight tremor of rumbling and then heard a sound that was hard to explain except that it sounded like a splash of water. After which it felt like time itself had stopped. Fires where no longer flickering, water was no longer boiling, and birds were no longer chirping as Surgyn saw black smoke billow through the cracks of the door. Still paralyzed with pain, Surgyn was forced to remain bed ridden as he watched a tall shadowed figure walk through the door.

Surgyn surmised this figure to be something of a phantom, for it walked through the door like a ghost or some sort of specter. This thing was almost seven feet tall, for if it was any taller it would have had to duck under the door way, with a silky black hooded cloth hanging from it body as if there were nothing more than a skeleton holding it up from within. Surgyn was unable to see its face for the hood hung low and created such a shadow that any facial features would be indistinguishable. As this apparition seemingly glided across the floor into the kitchen, Surgyn laid stiff with fear.

Given the cold food on the table and the protection spell on the house, the figure quickly realized that Murlynn was not here. Grabbing a biscuit, the intruder concluded that if he could not kill Murlynn, then maybe he would be able to figure out what he was up to. With that thought, he made his way over to the laboratory to see if there were any clues as to what Murlynn was working on or where he went off to.

There, he found a book that was left open: "The Ancient Art of Healing Internal Wounds".

"Is Murlynn hurt? Or is he healing someone? Or is he brushing up on his healing magic for the upcoming battle? If he is preparing himself, then how does he know about our invasion? And if he knows about the invasion, then who else knows about the invasion?"

The element of surprise has been foiled! Now he must prepare for a full out war.

The figure sniffed the mortar and pestle and put his finger in to it and tasted what had been concocted to see if would give him a clue as to what Murlynn was working on. To no avail, for they were ingredients used for a healing potion.

"If he concocted a healing potion of this potency, then whoever he concocted it for should still be nearby."

At that moment he turned his head over his shoulder and looked directly at Surgyn. Flashing his yellow eyes, this dark stranger made his way over to his next victim.

…………

As the Captain laid there, he knew that his time had come when the figure flashed its yellow, snake like eyes. Too injured to fight or take flight, the Captain stayed still awaiting his fate, knowing that he must die to fulfill his last mission: keep the note that Murlynn had left from this figure. For this note contained information about where Murlynn is heading and his thoughts about how they may be able to overcome the dragons.

The figure glided over to the couch. It looked down and saw the healing potion that no doubt Murlynn had drawn up for this poor fellow. The phantom chuckled to itself about the irony of the situation as he collected the medicine on the table and the remaining prismatic aerotate.

"If you want to live another day," slowly spoke the phantom, its voice like a soft whisper that seduced the mind, "you will tell me where Murlynn is and what he is up to."

Captain Surgyn did not as much as blink as he looked into the eyes of death.

"I know you helped him. I know you survived. Do not let that be for naught."

Captain Surgyn continued to lie still, having found his courage and accepted the fate that he eluded him only the day before.

"If you are not for me, then you are against me. If you are against me, then you must die," said the specter in its usual seductive whisper.

As it lifted its hand up, Captain Surgyn grasped tight the note that remained clutched in his hand, safely hidden from this darkness. This time the Captain did not run, did not cower, did not only think of himself, but welcomed his fate gladly knowing that it comes with honor, respect, and for the good of his country.

50

Seeing that the sun was around mid day, Lord Benaniah continued to walk toward his kingdom, consumed with thoughts of actions that needed to take place upon his arrival.

Thus being distracted, Lord Benaniah did not realize he had headed straight into a camouflaged trap and was quickly covered by a huge net.

No sooner than the net had dropped on him, a guard came out of his concealment to procure the trespasser.

Amongst the all the excitement, the guard did not realize who had been detained or he would had been a bit more accommodating in removing the nets.

"Nappitt. Is that you?" inquired Lord Benaniah after collecting himself.

Shocked and embarrassed, Nappitt quickly lowered his spear and proclaimed, "My Lord," as he gave a Nimian Bow, which consisted of bending one knee slightly and bowing one's forehead into their elbow. This is a formal greeting within the Nimrods to someone of a superior rank.

"I am so sorry. I did not know that it was you. I thought you were still at the Castle Dorian. Are you alright?"

"No I am not, I am here, safely secured under your net," answered Lord Benaniah jovially.

"Oh, right. Sorry," said Nappitt as he snapped into action and released Lord Benaniah from the net.

"I do not remember this trap being here? Did you set this?"

"No my lord, this trap was not set upon your departure. And yes, I did set it. Under the order of Commander Gilliyad, new traps were to be set due to the dragons that are in the land."

"How did you come to know about the dragons that are in the land?" inquired his lordship.

"Chief Brutus from Lord Titus' private guard came to us at the beginning of the day with a sealed letter informing us that there are dragons in the land and that we need to send men to the Castle Dorian at once to build a cohesive army to launch an attack," informed Nappitt.

"Really?" responded Lord Benaniah, glad to hear to the good news. "That is good. I must meet Brutus at once to further discuss our plan of action."

"By the way, nice job on setting this trap," complimented his lordship.

It was not much further of a walk before they got to the Kingdom of Shaddonai. Unlike the other kingdoms, Shaddonai was the only one that had been fortified high in the Mamer Trees of Mezpha. Mamer trees were huge in height and width, growing over 150 feet high and up to 10 feet in diameter. The villages utilized the natural surroundings, using vines and wood to make balconies, walk ways, and bridges to help the Nimrods get around the kingdom. Elevators, stairs, and tarzan ropes also made quick forms of transportation when scaling up and down the trees. Tiki torches were lit around the clock, for the tree canopy did not let in much light. The houses were carved into the trunks of the trees. They were nothing glamorous, and did not need to be, for they were rarely used for more than to rest. The Nimrods would much rather be outside. In fact, much of their daily activities where done on the ground level during the day. The higher levels were mainly used for the night hours, so that they did not have to concern them-selves as much with predators or enemy attacks.

Upon Lord Benaniah's arrival, he saw that the men wasted no time preparing for their departure. There were men talking with their loved ones, making sure their weapons were in good order, packing supplies, and others who where already in ranks marching as they were preparing for the upcoming battle. The men were so focused on their task that they barley recognized that their king was among them, but those who did bowed their head in respect as he past them by.

In the middle of all the preparation was Brutus and commander Gillyad.

"My Lord," proclaimed Gillyad when Lord Benaniah came upon them as he gave a Nimian bow.

Chief Brutus followed suit as Lord Benaniah quickly engaged himself into the matter.

"Good day Commander Gilliyad, Chief Brutus. Nappidd has told me that you have been informed of the invasion and that Brutus has come with a sealed letter requesting our best men prepare for a counter attack."

"Yes my Lord," confirmed Gilliyad. As you can see we are preparing to leave before the fourth quarter of the day and march through the night in order to arrive at the Castle Dorian by the next day hereafter."

"We have already sent a messenger to the Castle Dorian to inform them of our arrival and have also made instructions for those who are staying behind; including what posts, traps, and stations are to be occupied" continued Gilliyad. "And what the emergency plans are if, for some unfortunate reason the battle were to come to here."

"You have done well. I am proud of you Commander Gilliyad, Chief Brutus. I am assured that no matter what happens, there will be a remnant of our kin that will survive"

"My Lord" chimed in Brutus "after you left, the lords were able to gather a report from Herms. It is worse than we feared. The carnivorous diffusion no longer works and the dragons are attacking the land with military tactics. Upon learning this knowledge Lords Titus, Augusta, and Ekron decided to mobilize the armies of Sahleam in a united counter attack. The Lords believe that a quick and decisive counter attack in the Southern Plains of Elah, beneath the Kingdom of Vatoya, would be unexpected and give us a slight advantage. In making such a decision, the Lord King Titus put Antheis and myself in charge of making sure that the messages where delivered and responded to as quickly as possible."

Lord Benaniah took in what Brutus was saying without any wavering for he had already known of this report from Captain Surgyn and thought that the same response was required. Although, Lord Benaniah could not help but wonder about Endorah. If the dragons are truly acting in a tactical manner, then it would make sense for them to establish a base. What better place to establish yourself than in the mountains of Endor? The mountains would be the obvious choice if they wanted to overtake the city. Having Endorah as a stronghold would allow mobilization of supplies and reinforcements without interference, and, to top it all, it would be an act of revenge for the dragons, for it was the dwarfs who had kept the dragons out of the Sahleam for so many years.

Although Chief Brutus had reported that Antheis was sent to the city of Endorah with the same urgent message, Lord Benaniah could not fight the urge to find out what had become of Endorah, for either information about the city would be critical.

"Chief Brutus," Lord Benaniah began after a moment of thought, "you have done an excellent job in fulfilling your duty to your King and to the Sahleam. But I must ask a request of you."

"Of course, my Lord."

"Lead my men back to the Castle Dorian."

Brutus was not shy in showing that this request was confusing to him.

"I cannot shake the feeling of needing to know what happened to the city of Endorah," pleaded Lord Benaniah. "I know that you said Antheis had been sent there, but I fear he might have arrived too late. The dragons need a place to establish themselves and the mountains of Endor would be perfect for their cause."

"I understand my lord, but your men also need you. You are an inspiration, not only to your men, but to the land itself. To know that the Nimrods are here to fight will inspire all the armies, but even more to see all the lords together fighting in one accord. This will give more hope than any strategy or weaponry that we may obtain."

Before Lord Benaniah could respond Brutus offered his services as a way of compromise, "Let me go. My men and I will be more than honored to take this burden off your shoulders."

"Now I see why the Lord King Titus has named you chief of his most regarded men. There is wisdom in your consul and honor in your heart. Do as you said but please take these for your journey," said Lord Benaniah as he poured half of the communication potion into a container. "This is a communication spell Murlynn made for Lord Cephas and myself. With it, you will be able to report to me as soon as you know what has become of Endorah. And this," continued the lord as he handed Brutus a smooth river stone, "will let you know if a dragon is nearby becoming hot and letting of a sulfuric order."

"Even in the face of death, I will make sure to complete my mission," replied Brutus as he took the items, gave a Nimian bow, and was on his way.

Lord Benaniah was grateful for Brutus and his bravery. But he could not help to wonder what type of dangers Brutus might run into. This was no easy task; one that may require the ultimate sacrifice. But Brutus was right, Lord Benaniah was needed with his men, leading the charge into battle.

"Come Gilliyad, there is no time to lose."

And off Gilliyad went with Lord Benaniah to continue making preparation for their march to the Castle Dorian.

51

The chanting had stopped. Hunger had since kicked in. Murmuring had begun among the people. It had been more no than a couple of hours, but to a young adolescent or a growing baby, a day or two might as well have passed. Infant cries started to fill the room while patient mothers tried to lovingly sooth them. The young children brought a constant reminder of "I'm hungry" and "When are we going to eat?" to their fathers, even though their fathers reassured them that "as soon as things get situated, we will eat." The teens no longer had their tools, trinkets, or games to keep them occupied and were becoming restless and bored. The room was hot and the air thin and the Master Sergeant Xoarah had yet to make a decision about what to do next.

If the morning events were not enough for one day, the emotional events they endured since entering the safe room had been enough to sap the energy out of the most optimistic person. First, the dwarfs that were able to escape the city had to run terrified past the biggest dragon they ever seen. Then they all cheered triumphantly for Silas and Raithyn as they took down the dragon that had found the safe room. Next, they mourned over the death of Raithyn, the destruction of their city, and for all of those who had died during the attack. Now, only shortly after a time of grieving had passed, the children are beginning to complain about their current circumstances. Although they might not fully grasp the gravity of what had just taken place, they are none-theless adding to the situation with the constant reminder of their needs of basic wants and necessities.

Having realized this growing matter, while trying to consul some people, Master Sergeant Xoarah decided to gather a small council of people who had wisdom in military matters, knowledge of the mine, and who were of high regard within the Dwarf community. There was Kithorah, who was a rugged little Dwarf with long frayed hair that always looked like it needed a brush. Kithorah was an inspector of mine regulations and safety. Mendull was a bright and lively fellow that could make conversation with a complete stranger about the fly on the wall if he wanted to. Mendull was engineer of mine infrastructure and support. Next was Gurther. Gurther was well aged compared to the rest and had experienced much in his length of years. He was the administrative assistant to the Dwarf council, and a rock of support to Lord Ekron and the kingdom of Raphastien. Finally, of course, there was Silas the dragon slayer from King Titus' royal guard and Master Sergeant Xoarah, the newly appointed commander of the Dwarf army.

"Brothers and man, thank you for convening with me," began Xoarah as he addressed his newly formed committee. "You know that our situation is dyer. I do not need to recount why we are here. Now that we are safe from danger, we find ourselves in another predica-ment; what do we do next? To stay where we are may mean starvation and a slow death. To leave the room may result in a painful death by the dragons. I have asked you to meet with me because you know the secrets of these mines and the hidden treasures of our great city better than any of those among you. So I ask you, what are our best options for what to do next?"

No one responded at first. This was an unfamiliar situation for everybody. Never before had they lost their city and were forced to find shelter in the safe room.

"I personally don't know much about this room, except that it was built for this very purpose." Mendull said, being the first to speak up. "It doesn't seem to make sense that a room be built in case of invasion and not have any type of supply chamber."

"You're right," agreed Xoarah as everyone else nodded in confirmation. Mendull's logic was obvious. How can it be that such experienced miners like themselves could seemingly forget one of the basic rules and principles of mining? "There should be an armory, pantry, or even a secondary route out of the mines."

This statement of fact raised their hopes, for it would be a silly thing just to build a safe room without any of these additions. For without them it becomes nothing more than a chamber of death.

With a new hope, the committee decided to examine the walls to see if they could find any indication of anything more than just this brick, stone, and dirt. After a quick scan of the walls, the council came up empty, deflating their recently raised hopes. There is no evidence within the mountain rock and soil of any type of passage or room contained within its hearth.

"Figures that there would be a safe room that was either left unfinished or would lead us to our demise," retorted Kithorah. For most people, when asked if the glass is half empty or half full, they would optimistically say half full. Well, Kithorah would not only answer that the glass is half-empty, but would assume that the glass was completely full at one point and someone drank the other portion of the beverage. This attitude is not because he is negative and had a poor outlook on life, but that he is overly critical of every situation and circumstance.

"Don't be so foolish youngling," began Gurther, "the elders of Endorah were very wise in forging this great city. The eyes can be deceived."

"That's great," responded Kithorah sarcastically. "Are we to sit around and wait for a rescuer or continue to examine the walls for a hidden entrance, which according to you, we cannot see anyway, while starvation begins with our young and eventually captivating our women and men?"

"Are you questioning whether or not our great mother will provide for her children?" questioned Gurther.

"No!" responded Kithorah sounding more like an annoyed teenager than a high ranking official. "I am questioning if looking for invisible clues or just sitting here is the best options."

Kithorah knew that arguing with a man solidified in his faith like Gurther would be a waste of time. There is no way that Gurther would be able to take his "faith glasses" off and look at the situation through more reasonable lenses. With that, Kithorah turned to Xoarah.

"Look, Xoarah, you are the leader of the people now. We can only sit around for so long before the people start murmuring. If progress is not made, the people will rise up against you. Not because of you, but because of themselves and the fear of their own lives. I do believe that our mother will provide. But she works in mysterious ways. Maybe her way of providing is by rallying the people out of the city?"

Xoarah was torn. He was very dedicated to the practices of following his mother, but following Her does not necessarily mean just sitting around and waiting for Her to do something. There has been many times in Xoarah's life already where his Mother has shown her provision and affirmation in the decisions that he had made. After all, if you are truly seeking her and what she wants you to do in your life, doesn't it make sense that she can lead you through your decision making process?

Looking at Gurther, Xoarah agreed that the elders must have provided more that just this room, but he could not help but to heed Kithorah's wise council either. Going against his heart, Xoarah asks Kithorah, "What do you think our best options are?"

With excitement, Kithorah grinned and began, "First we need to move the people to the sides, away from the opening of the doors, for if there is a dragon out there, it will probably unleash a hellish blast as soon as they open. We also need to have an initial group of men who can distract the beast, if there is one, as Silas and Raithyn did, so that the rest of the people can run by. Straight ahead there is a central hub system that has at least half a dozen tunnels that lead throughout the city. Upon reaching the hub, the people should be further split into groups, each with armed men who can distract any further dragons they may come across while the women and children escape. Whoever is able to make it out of the city should meet at the Podiseon River in the Region of Vinyah."

"That's it? That's your plan?" Mendull critiqued no sooner than Kithorah had finished.

"Do you have anything better?!" retorted Kithorah heatedly.

"We would be better chancing a mutiny than to risk so many men"

"It's not a bad plan," chimed in Silas. He did not necessarily think it was a "good" plan either, but given their situation there were few options to choose from. "To risk the mutiny only brings division and may only delay the execution of an escape plan. Many lives will be lost, but a remnant will be spared to preserve your line and to start rebuilding the great kingdom of Dwarfdom."

Looking Master Sergeant Xoarah in the eye without an ounce of fear Silas declaired, "I will lead the charge of men against the first dragon that may be waiting outside these doors if the Master Sergeant will allow me the honor."

Xoarah did not know what to say to such a brave and honorable request, so he nodded in affirmation.

With that, Mendull stepped out and offered to co-lead the charge as well, "It is going to take more than just one experienced warrior to distract the dragon long enough for the people to get by."

"Are you sure?" questioned Silas as they clasped forearms. "This may mean your life."

"I have served my time in the ranks and am still quite familiar with my axe."

Looking into Mendull's eyes, Silas knew that no other words were needed and grinned as he was reminded of times when Raithyn and himself would run off into the fray.

It was settled. Silas and Mendull would lead a charge against whatever may be waiting for them on the other side of these doors, while the rest of the people tried to make their way out of the city using the mine tunnels. If all goes well, they would meet up at the Podiseon River and head north from there.

Master Sergeant Xoarah addressed the assembly and divided everyone into their groups and had them press against the walls as best they could. Seeing the faith and wisdom that exuberated from Gurther, Xoarah thought that it would be a good idea to let such a respected elder of the community to lead in an invocation before the execution of the plan.

Although Gurther was not in favor of the plan, he knew that Xoarah his new leader and would not disrespect him. Obliging to his request, Gurther looked out among all the faces that were before him. Seeing the downcast, trodden, disheartened looks on their face, Gurther knew that a prayer of encouragement and hope would be good for them.

"Our mother, who knows all, sees all, and is in all places. You have seen the tragic execution of your city. You witnessed the displacement of your children. Even now, the few who are left look to you to preserve a remnant of your children, so that we can carry on your name and proclaim your strength and might to all the nations. May our feet be swift, may our swords be sharp, and may you guide us back into the safety of your loving arms."

When Gurther had concluded, the people looked up and saw something that they had not noticed before: there were actually two doors in the safe room. One in the front of the room, which they always knew was there, and now one in the back of the room. This new door lined up directly across from the other and was identical to it. At this Grrther smiled softly, looked up and whispered a "thank you" to his mother.

You may think that in this situation that it would be best to run to the new found door and open it, but let me tell you that such foolishness may be your undoing, for you do not know what lies behind the door. Examination must be the first step, and that is exactly the approach the committee took. At first they thought that the big red iron clad door was indistinguishable to its predecessor. But upon further examination there was a difference. On top of the new door lie an ancient inscription. As fortune would have it, Gurther's position had given him access to the ancient archives. The history of the dwarfs and their first language was a passion of Gurthers, and one that he spent much time in. Therefore, when no one else was able to make out what the ancient lettering meant, Gurther was to provide an interpretation.

"If a baby cries and a mother hears, she will offer help. If you ask, you will receive, safety from what was dealt."

"What in the world is that suppose to mean?" complained Kithorah

"Isn't it obvious?" snide Mendull, "The key to opening this door is to cry out to our mother for help, just as a child would cry out to their mother when they needed help."

After having just been embarrassed for his lack of faith, Kithorah did not find it appropriate to make any grounds for argument in this instance.

Xoarah could not think of another person to whom such a request would be appropriate. "Gurther, you stood strong in your love for mother in the midst of adversity and when others were wavering. With that, I think it is only appropriate for you, who has the most childlike faith, to call out to our mother in this time of desperation."

Such an admission brought a smile to Gurther's face and joy to his heart. Without any doubt or consideration of the impossibilities of the request, Gurther closed his eyes and lifted his hands as he made his plea.

"Oh mother hear your children's cry. A great terror has invaded your land and murdered your people. We are all who is left and face certain death. Spare your children from affliction and agony and help us in our great hour of need."

As soon as Gurther finished his supplication something wonderful happened. An intense beam of light flooded the bottom seal of the door. Standing in awe, everyone watched as the light expanded up the middle of the door. Then upon reaching the top it broke into two equal lights that arched around the top and continued to outline the door back down the bottom. The door was flooded with light that was growing with intensity until it was so bright that one had to shield their eyes and look away. And just as the light came, it all at once vanished without trace or warning. Everything seemed as it was previously. Slightly dumbfounded by their experience and not sure what to do next, Kithorah did the only obvious thing. Not because he thought the door would be opened or that their Mother had just supernaturally intervened, but because he wanted to be able to move onto whatever it was that they were to do next. Kithorah reached out and pulled on the knocker, and to his surprise, it opened.

52

With the sun setting, the end of the day was upon Lord Cephas and the night would have its turn to rule the sky. Lord Cephas had yet to cease walking north near the edge of the Forest of Mezpha, for running was not something that the Sheppen were particularly known for. Not familiar with the land, he followed the streams and creeks that broke off of the Podiseon River, knowing that they would take him on the path of least resistance while keeping him on course. Luckily, there had not been any encounters with dragons or predatory animals thus far. With being in a foreign part of the land, and knowing that he was not the dominate species on the food chain, Lord Cephas understood the importance of gathering some food and shelter and laying low for the first part of the night before continuing his journey. Many animals come out to do their hunting when the moon first breaks into the sky, trying to find an unsuspecting victim who had wondered off or stayed out too late. Attacking a herd or a family of animals is only a move of desperation, but to find an animal alone, unprotected, and defenseless is a predator's specialty. With that in mind, Lord Cephas began looking for a place that would make a good shelter as he continued his journey north.

When it comes to articulating ones thoughts, there are two kinds of people. There are people like Lord Benaniah who say whatever comes to mind without much consideration of what is being said, to whom it's being said, and where it is being said. Then there are people like Lord Cephas who enjoy their thoughts and like to contemplate and articulate every thing he says. There are many years of experience that reside in Lord Cephas, for he is easily the oldest of the lords, and he is also full of wisdom and discernment. At this particular time Lord Cephas was mulling over their current paradox of, "how to stop a juggernaut?" For this is what a dragon is, a juggernaut. They do not have a particular weakness that has been discovered, but rather become vulnerable when specific abilities are taken away. Their whole scheme on how to beat a dragon has been based on the idea of taking away key components that make a dragon a unique and unstoppable force. With all things considered, their only options are to either find another way to disarm them, discover a weakness that has been overlooked, or devise a plan to beat them as they are.

"What about using their natural animal instincts against them", thought Lord Cephas? "Since they are an alpha dominate species, if we challenge and overcome the leader, then maybe the ranks will break as others will challenge each other to become the new Alpha? Almost like the idea of 'cutting off the head and the rest will scatter'." Lord Cephas was not sure if he liked this idea, but it was an idea.

As he continued to look for a shelter his mind started thinking about all the innocent lives that are at risk because of this invasion; countless lives of young men, women, and children. Some will die in defending their country while others will die as the causalities of war. And for what? Power? Land? What could possibly be the motive to mercilessly invade a peaceful land and show no value on the sanctity of life?

At this thought, Lord Cephas froze, for he heard a rustle that sounded like it came from a bush across the stream. As he scanned the area Lord Cephas landed upon a pair of yellow eyes beaming at him from within the dark secretes of a bush. The eyes that stared at him were small, nor was the dragon detector hot or giving off a brimstone scent. Lord Cephas felt confident that it was not a dragon. But this did not prevent the lord from drawing his sword and preparing for what creature may expose itself, for he knew that a delayed action may cost him his life. Calm and ready, Lord Cephas steered patiently into the eyes of this unsuspecting beast, as he waited for the creature to make the first move. The eyes disappeared and the bush began to shake. Suddenly, out popped a mouse. Lord Cephas did not flinch as he watched the rodent scurry toward the creek and then up stream.

"The amount of rustling could not have been created by such a small creature." thought Lord Cephas as he continued his gaze upon the bush. "The eyes were also much too big" he concluded, unmoved from the stance.

After a moment had passed, Lord Cephas was about to resheath his sword and continue his search when, without warning, the eyes light up within the bush again. Almost as quickly as the eyes reappeared, did a large muscular animal burst out from the shadows, declaring its presence. To Lord Cephas' delight, it was his horse!

"How did it ever find me?"

"Why did it not make straight for the castle after being released?"

These questions would have to remain unanswered, which did not bother Lord Cephas in the slightest, for he was thoroughly excited to be reacquainted with his steed. Without regard, Lord Cephas climbed down into the stream and embraced his horse in the middle of the waters.

"It's good to see you boy" expressed Lord Cephas as he wrapped his arms around its neck.

Pulling away and kissing its face, Lord Cephas grabed the reigns and gently stated, "Thank you for coming back to me. Now it is time to go."

53

Walking down the dark tunnels was no challenge for the dwarfs, for they had adjusted to dimly lit mines all their lives. The tunnel would be wide enough if it wasn't for the amount of people trying to squeeze down its corridors all at once. It wasn't long into the tunnels before they noticed the faded pictures on the walls; pictures of great hunts, the first bounty found within the mountains, and the first elected king. These were all ancient drawings that preserved the Dwarf's beginnings and the challenges that they went through to establish and preserve themselves as a nation. In fact, these were the ancient tunnels of Ubertyne that had been written about so much in Dwarf history. These tunnels had protected the dwarfs early on in their history from danger, helped them overcome enemies, and led them into the mountains in which they had established their kingdom.

It was all very fascinating at first, walking along and seeing the drawings of your heritage, and even having someone here and there recognize a drawing from a recorded event within the Dwarf archive and explain the significance of the event. It was like reliving your heritage, which deepened ones appreciation of who you are and where you have come from.

As wonderful as this was, it did not stop the inevitability of hunger pains resurfacing. Complaints grew among the people about the lack of food and water, about being exhausted, and that there seemed to be no end in sight of the tunnel. As they walked, scouts were sent ahead to make sure there was no danger and to see if the tunnel would to come to a split. Every report had been the same; thick walls of earth, rocks, and dirt is all that lay ahead.

After having heard these reports and the growing complaints of the people, Kithorah decided to speak up.

"Well Gurther, what do you say now? You are the one whom prayed and mother earth open up these doors. Do you think she will also give us a meal and a bed with a fire to keep us warm, or does she only delight in giving us a bit of hope that only leads to further despair?"

Gurther very much heard Kithorah, but chose to ignore him and keep on walking. Not because Gurther's faith was shaken or that he had doubt, but rather because he knew that just as their mother had provided, she will continually provide for them as well.

Seeing that he was not getting any response from Gurther besides a slight smile as he continued to press ahead, Kithorah decided to bring the concerns of the people to their assumed leader, Xoarah.

"The people are tired and hungry and long for something to drink," Kithorah began his plight. "What are we going to do now to satisfy the people? We cannot keep marching them with no provisions. They are not militant. If we cannot supply their basic needs, then they are likely to turn against us, and then what will likely become of our people? We need to do something to show them why they can follow us."

"And what do you suggest?" began Master Sergeant Xoarah, tired of being berated by Kithorah. "Is anything you can suggest that we are not already doing? If you have any ideas, please let me know."

Xoarah paused to hear what Kithorah may have in mind, but before he could say a word, Xoarah's frustration poured forth, "Do you suggest that we turn around and go back to the safe room to starve? Or maybe we can overwhelm the dragons with our sheer numbers. Never mind that most of our trained fighters have already been lost. Or how about we start digging with our bare hands through the earth, not knowing which direction we will be heading or where we would come out at?"

Seeing Xoarah's frustration, Kithorah made the only plausible suggestion, "It was Gurther who prayed to our mother and led us down this tunnel. Maybe if he were to pray again, our mother would hear our cry and supply provisions for our journey?"

Xoarah heard Kithorah's words, but knew that it was not wise to challenge their mother in such a way.

"She has always provided for us in every situation."

"Just as a parent would give their child necessities for survival, so will our mother grant us such provisions if we were to just ask for them" insisted Kithorah.

Kithorah's argument made sense. It was Gurther whom their mother responded to. And, if their mother was truly their mother, then she would gladly respond to the plight of her children.

"Ok." agreed Xoarah. "Not because I think it wise, but because the gravity of the situation and the lack of suitable options that are before us."

After hearing Xoarah's agreement, Kithorah wasted no time going back to Gurther and informing him that the Master Sergeant wanted to see him. Gurther did not question Kithorah, but went with him without delay.

"Yes, Master Sergeant, what is it that you wanted to see me about?"

"Gurther, you are a man of wisdom and faith. You have been the administrative assistant to the king's consul for many years. It was you that had prayed and opened the door that led us down the ancient tunnels of Ubertyne. Now, I come before you again. The people are tired, thirsty, and hungry. There does not look like there is any food or water within these tunnels or an end in sight. Therefore, I ask you, for the good of the preservation of our people, will you pray to our mother again for mercy and favor?"

Gurther did not think that it was wise to 'temp' their mother and that it was not good to be continually giving into the complaints of the people. But Gurther did not make any of these thoughts public, but rather, because the Master Sergeant had asked him to, agreed to fulfill Xoarah's request.

With Silas and Mendull's help, Gurther stopped the multitude and addressed them, "Children of earth. Our mother has heard our cry and rescued us from the mouths of death that invaded our city. For this, we never expressed thanks or gratitude. Let us now come together as one family and express thanks to our mother for what she has done."

Lifting his hands and looking up, Gurther prayed "Our mother, we give thanks to you. Although there has been a great distress this day, you have preserved your children. An enemy has attacked and devoured us, but you saved a remnant for yourself. By providing a way of escape from our adversary, you have shown us mercy and favor. And now, our mother, we thank you for all that you have done and all that you will continue to do. For you have not delivered us from our enemy just so we can die in these tunnels. No! You will provide all our needs, for you are a good mother that cares for her children. For this, we put our hope and trust in you."

"Let us all give thanks."

At first there was silence, but Gurther did not say anymore, for he knew that the people could not rely on his faith in their mother, but that they needed to show their faith in her as well. Nothing was said at first, but then, a faint voice rose from the crowd.

"Thank you mother for my mommy and daddy. Thank you for my friends and this tunnel. And please be with those who are sad and who are hurt."

Hearts could not help but to melt as everyone heard the prayer of this child.

Such simple faith.

It did not take long for the other children to follow suit with similar prayers, giving thanks for family and friends and asking for healing for those who needed it. With the children's example, it was not long before the adults joined in with their own prayers, thanking their mother for what she had done and what she will do to preserve her children.

The prayers grew loud and vibrant, so much that the tunnels shook all around them. This went on for a minute or two before all the prayers were concluded. When they were done, they opened their eyes to something wonderful. Food was hanging from above their heads, like a chandler in a dinning hall. Peanuts, turnips, beats, carrots, and potatoes hung from the ceiling in a spectacular array of beauty. Seeing the endless supply of food lining the roof of the tunnel, the dwarfs fell to their knees in awe and worshipped of their mother, for this was truly a miracle! Once again their mother provided for her children. If food was not enough to make one's heart believe in the provision of their mother, then the water that was now running down the side of the tunnel would have. Dwarfs cupped their hands to gather water before emerging their faces in the shallow pool while others lined the walls to drink to their hearts content. Some dwarfs had also climbed upon each other in order to collect food that was hanging from above. The cool draft of the tunnel had also dissipated with a warmth and glow that emanated from the gems and rubies that had surfaced from within the tunnel walls.

Gurther just stood by and watched as the people gathered their meals and quenched their thirst, knowing that it was not his faith, but their own that brought about this miracle.

Xoarah too, stood and watched, as he solidified his faith in his Mother and vowed to never again allow his faith and trust in her to be swayed by the people.

3
DAY 3 | ATTACK

54

The sun was shinning bright in Herms' chambers. There were not many windows in which the light could pierce through into his quarters, but the rays that did make it into his room seemed to find their way to lay softly upon his face. Herms was not ready for such an early start to the new day. For Murlynn and himself had only just arrived in the middle of the night, and now the sun was determined to have Herms rise up so that together they may start this new day. This is a fight you cannot win, for when the sun is warmly upon your face and is vibrantly persisting that you join her in this new adventure that awaits you, no amount of twisting and turning or covering you face will deny her the accompaniment of your presence. After a few minutes of resistance, Herms finally gave in to the suns persistence and decided to join her in this new day. Herms first course of action was to make his way to the dinning hall to put some much needed food into his growling stomach.

Herms followed his nose to the dinning hall, not knowing what to expect or who may be there or how the Lord King Titus may ask him to be of service this day. None of these thoughts stayed with Herms for long, for he could not concentrate on much else until his hunger was subsided.

The dinning hall was of good size and could sustain a multitude of people, but it was not near the size needed to hold the capacity of troops that had taken up post at the Castle Dorian. There were three long rows of tables with bench seating on either side. The kitchen was near the entrance and had a large opening were people could order what they liked. This is where Lord Cephas was waiting patiently as the cooks prepared his order. Why, to Herms surprise, all the Lords were here. And by the looks of it, they had already eaten as they now talked with Murlynn. Herms very much wanted to be apart of the conversation that they were having, but needed to take care of the first order of business before hand, his breakfast. Having made his way over to the kitchen, Herms stood next to Lord Cephas as he debated his order. To most people Lord Cephas was an intimating figure, but to Herms, he stood virtually petrified next to this towering individual. Lord Cephas stood taller than most. He is very thin, but very strong; with a square jaw and piercing eyes. Herms did not know what to say or even what to do. In so much that he did not even hear the chef ask him for his order. When Lord Cephas' food was up, Herms realized that he had missed his opportunity for a hot breakfast, and had to settle for some biscuits, pastries, and a few hard boiled eggs, for he did not want to miss anymore of the conversation that the lords were having.

Seeing that Lord Cephas and Herms were now joining them, Lord Titus stopped his conversation to greet them. "Lord Cephas, I am glad that you have made it back", he said as he stood up from his seat and put a reaffirming hand on the lord's shoulder.

Lord Cephas only nodded in return as he took a seat.

"Herms, I am glad to see you too this morning. I am sorry that I could not meet with you last night, I am sure you understand." Lord Titus paused their conversation for a moment out of respect for Lord Cephas as he whispered a blessing over his meal.

"Murlynn has told us all about what has happened" the lord continued, redirecting his comments toward Lord Cephas.

Again, only a slight nod of affirmation was all that was provided as the lord began to eat his meal.

"Given that your men are camped outside, I am sure you are aware of what is to come of us next."

"I am" replied Lord Cephas. "Upon my arrival within the night I had taken notice of my men and resided with them until the new day."

Lord Titus was a little surprised that Lord Cephas would make it to the castle so many hours ago and not make his acquaintance right away. Then again, it does make sense that if one would see their finest regiments camped in a foreign land, that you would stop for intell.

"My general reported of their summonce and the plans to launch a counter attack" added Lord Cephas.

Lord Titus was eager to hear Lord Cephas' opinion, for he is most wise and does not mince words. "And, what do you think?" he asked.

With a slight hesitation, Lord Cephas agreed, "I think it is our best defense."

Before Lord Titus was able to ask any more of Lord Cephas about their current strategy, or before Lord Cephas was able to inquire of Murlynn about any further about potions he might have been able to conjure up, a guard opened the door and announced the arrival of Lord Benaniah.

Wasting no time, Lord Benaniah made his way over to the table were everyone was gathered.

"Lord Benaniah", Lord Titus expressed with excitement, "It is so good to have you back!" spoke the lord softly as he embraced him with a brotherly hug.

"It is good to be back."

"Please join us so that we can consult before embarking on our mission."

Lord Titus was eager, now that all the lords had made it back safely. The lords were more than just neighboring kings of kingdoms, but rather saw each other as rulers of sections and divisions of Sahleam. They are five brothers of one family who function as one body that is made of many parts. Having all the lords return safely from their missions was a good sign on many accounts, but no reason more important than their ability to tightly knit together all the king-doms in this unified cause.

"Apollos," called Lord Titus as he waved for the guard to come near to him. "I have not seen Antheis yet this morning. I am not sure if he had dined before myself, but would you be able to call upon him so that he can be apart our discussion."

"Yes, my Lord," replied Apollos with a bow, and was off.

Lord Benaniah had already situated himself next to Herms on the other side of the table from Lord Titus. "My men are outside the castle familiarizing themselves with the other kin. We are ready to move when given the order." he reassured everyone.

The lords were feeling better and better about their plan, for it seemed that everything was aligning itself for a favorable outcome.

"I also wanted to let you know that I did meet up with Brutus." Lord Benaniah began to report. "After having convened with my Commander, Gillyad, I could not ignore the feeling of needing to know the current state of Endorah. If the dragons took hold of the city, it may take more than one battle to drive them back out of the land. I had requested for Brutus to lead my men here, but Chief Brutus persisted that he take on the mission instead, insisting that it would be better for me to lead my men here. After persuading me, I sent him along with a couple of my finest men to go and search out the city."

Lord Ekron's good mood started to fade as Lord Benaniah confirmed his own feeling of the dragon's more likely conquering of Endorah and establishing it as their stronghold. The thought of his people made his countenance fall and anger began to simmer within his veins.

"Murlynn is aware of how the carnivorous diffusion has been nulli-fied" Lord Titus began, trying to lead the conversation away from the thought of what may have happened to Endorah.

"Uh yes," interrupted Murlynn who was seated next to Lord Titus and could easily see the difference of expression on Lord Ekron who was across from him. "But, given all the accounts, the potion itself does not seem to be nullified as you have previously stated, but rather, it is not working because the potion is not able to penetrate the skin and enter the bloodstream."

Murlynn paused for a second, and instead of interrupting him, Lord Titus motioned for him to finish his explanation.

"As of now, although I have been working on it feverishly, I have not been able to come up with anything better than what I have already afforded to you."

Now all the countenances of the council fell as the jovialness from the lords' arrival and the hope in their plan was slowly being deflated as Murlynn shared his observations.

"But I do not think that the potion should be given up on entirely" Murlynn continued, trying to restore their hope. "I believe it to reason that the only rational explanation for the potions ineffectiveness is due to it not entering the blood stream." Murlynn paused briefly, gathering himself for what he was about to suggest, "So . . .all you have to do is find another way; a more direct way, if you will, to have the potion enter the bloodstream."

"Humph. That's a relief," remarked Lord Ekron. "And here I thought you were going to say something ridiculous." It wasn't that Lord Ekron didn't like the plan entirely, or that he wasn't up for a little crazy if it meant restoring peace in the land, but the thought of his people had already put him on edge.

Murlynn looked both shocked and puzzled by Lord Ekron's sarcasm.

"It's actually not as ridiculous as it may seem," said Lord Benaniah with refreshed hope. "If Murlynn's theory is correct, then we could not only continue to put the potion on arrows in hope that one may break through, but also on spears, swords, axes, anything really, that we will be using to arm ourselves with"

"That's right," agreed Murlynn.

"That's all fine and dandy," interrupted Lord Ekron, "but it doesn't improve our plan at all."

At first thought, it appeared that Lord Ekron was right. But this was only until Murlynn further revealed his proposal on how to ensure the carnivorous diffusions effectiveness.

"Well, there is one tactic that Lord Benaniah did not muse upon," began Murlynn. "The best and most direct way of ensuring the potions effectiveness is to direct the artillery into the creature's mouth."

"So I was right," exclaimed Lord Ekron in a sarcastic anger, cutting off Murlynn once again. "It's not ridiculous, it's ludicrous! It's not like these monsters fly around with their mouths open. You do realize," now directing his comments specifically to Murlynn, "that the only time a dragon opens its mouth is to either consume a meal or breathe fire?"

"It would be suicide" agreed Lord Augusta.

"My plan was to defuse their strengths and try to create an even battlefield, but Murlynn wants us to invite them to use their strengths upon us!" Lord Ekron exclaimed, allowing his anger to burst forth and overcome any restraint that he had previously shown.

Before the conversation could go any further, Apollos enters the room and briskly makes his way to Lord Titus, without any invitation, and whispers into his ear.

With seeing this unusual breach in protocol, the council subsides in its rising debate to hear of the news that was just delivered.

"What is it?" Lord Augusta asks.

With a confused and uncertain look, all Lord Titus could state as he processed the information was, "Antheis is missing"

55

Brutus and his company had wasted little time covering much ground since departing from Lord Benaniah. In a matter of one full night and a quarter of a day they traveled from the kingdom of Shaddonai, through the Mezpha forest, and were now in the Region of Vinyah.

This region has been left unoccupied since before the reign of Onesomus many years ago. Other than travelers and merchants passing through the land, Vinyah had been left to grow and develop as it pleased. Lush green vegetation sprang up from the earth as the

Podiseon River gave life to all that called upon it. Trees that had made their way from the forest of Mezpha dug their roots deep and spread their branches tall and wide. The grass had become vibrant and as soft as the clouds. Wildflowers had brought forth their perfume, making the air fragrant. The mighty river, Podiseon, herself let forth a soothing gurgle that lullabied the land, while Mount Endor watched over all from a distance.

Although one could enter into a lifelong state of rest within this beautiful paradise, Brutus and his company had only but noticed Mt. Endor towering in the distance. Their mission was to bring a report to Lord Benaniah of the state of the Dwarf city Endorah. For this mission, Brutus picked three of Lord Benaniah's finest men, whom he had gotten acquainted with very quickly in his short stay at the Kingdom of Shaddonai. First, there was Ichadad. Ichadad was a fine archer and had the eyes of an eagle. Next, Brutus chose Ashyer. Ashyer was quick and light on his feet, a fine tracker, and ingenious with his surroundings. And, of course, there was Nappitt. Nappitt was much like a younger Brutus. Eager to prove himself, not turning away from any mission, and always willing to do what was necessary for the overall good.

It was a tiresome journey, but one that they must make in order to successfully make an accurate report back to Lord Benaniah within a reasonable amount of time. Knowing that it would not be much further and that his company had made it a long way without pause, Brutus suggested to take a brief rest in a clearing not far from the Podiseon River.

No one disagreed with Brutus and got to work straightaway making provisions for camp. Ichadad went to the river to procure some fish, while Ashyer got the fire going.

"What am I to do?" questioned Nappitt as Brutus was gathering sticks to feed the fire.

"Are you not content to stand watch?" answered Brutus as he continued to gather wood.

"No sir, I am." quickly added Nappitt, not wanting to seem discontent or worse, insubordinate. "But it's just that everyone is doing something to contribute to the camp except for me. I may be young, but I am useful."

"Standing watch is useful."

"That it is sir, but even you are able to contribute by collecting sticks. Should not you stand watch and rest a bit and let me gather sticks?

"I may be older than yourself, but I am not that old."

Nappitt did not mean to insult Brutus. He knew that he was a man of valor and honor. Chief Brutus would never ask a person in his company to do something that he himself would not do. This was often shown in Brutus taking part in whatever task was before them, even if it meant gathering sticks. Nappitt though, wanted to feel that he was being productive and contributing to the camp in some way. Being a lookout was important, but all you did was just stand there.

"Well then, may I pick some berries?" asked Nappitt knowing that he was not likely to convince Brutus to allow himself to gather the wood. "I saw some hornthale bushes as we came upon the land. And you know what they say, 'Where there is one hornthale bush, there is another,' for they spread like ivy. I bet that there are some there, just beyond that small hill."

Brutus knew that Nappitt was eager to prove his usefulness. Seeing that they were in a rather flat portion of the land, and that there was a small likeliness that the enemy would be able to sneak up on them, Brutus granted his request.

"Hornthale berries are delicious and would go rather well with the fish" Brutus remarked.

"So I can go?" asked Nappitt surprisingly.

"You may go. But do not travel too far. If you are unsuccessful within one hundred yards, then give up and return back to the camp."

As quickly as Brutus gave the okay, Nappitt was off. Brutus knew that Nappitt was a fine solider who was more than capable of handling himself. If he did not think so, Brutus would have never elected him to come on the mission. But, in some way, Brutus felt a fatherly link to Nappitt. Maybe this was because Brutus did not have a son of his own, or that Nappitt's father died while he was still young. In either case, they developed a bond no sooner than Brutus' arrival at Shaddonai. This bond is also what made Brutus a little more cautious in what he would ask Nappitt to do while on their mission. Not because Nappitt was incapable, but because Brutus would have an undying regret if anything were to happen to him.

Shortly after Nappitt left, a southerly wind blew, carrying a dreadful smell with it. At first Brutus gave this smell no mind; *perhaps it was Ichadad cleaning the fish*, he thought.

But when he stopped and looked back at the camp, Brutus noticed two things that made him reconsider his position on this awful smell. First, the camp is downwind of him and the breeze that had carried the scent came from the north. Secondly, Ichadad was only now walking back to the camp from the river with the fish on his arrow and still needed to be cleaned.

With this new information, Brutus wasted no time in dropping his sticks and ran after Nappitt, who was walking upwind toward the source of the horrid stench.

Brutus knew this odor; it was of rot and decay. Death had claimed a victim. Although Brutus knew what the smell was, he did not know from whence it came. Since there had been no sign of a dragon, Brutus thought that the smell was emanating from a corpse that a predator was feasting upon. There are not many more foolish things one could do than to disturb a predator while it was devouring its prey.

Brutus ran as fast as he could, but had too much ground to cover in order to catch up to Nappitt before he reached the crown of the hill. To his surprise, when Nappitt reached the top, he stopped and remained motionless until Brutus had caught up to him.

Seasoned warriors know about the despair and anguish that come with war. Death and Loss are generals that consume the land during such times, with an undying hunger that can never be satisfied. For the soldier who encounters such circumstances for the first time, their reaction is no different than those who would encounter such tragedy in the home front.

Upon reaching the top of the hill, Brutus came to understand why Nappitt stood frozen in his tracks. It was worse than a predator gorging on its prey. It was worse than a stray dragon scouring the land. Here, at the bottom of this little hill, no more than one hundred yards from their camp, lay the Dwarf army, dead.

56

After a full meal and nights rest, the Dwarf remnant was on the move once again. Xoarah accompanied himself with his council, although Kithorah was not as talkative as normal. Since they had been in the tunnels, Xoarah had been sending scouts out ahead of them every so often just in case some sort of juncture or obstacle lay up ahead. This way, the council would have opportune time to make a decision beforehand. Ever since entering the tunnel the report had been the same: nothing but thick walls and darkness lie in wait. But ever since the provision of mother earth, Xoarah could not help but to be excited that they were going to find something else. This time, he was right.

A scout returned and said that there was light and that the end of the tunnel was in sight. Xoarah could not help but to express his gratitude to mother earth and share the news that would instill hope into his people.

Although it had not been more than a full day, the time spent in the tunnels was more than any Dwarf would care to spend in a single lifetime.

Excited to hear the report, Master Chief Xoarah could not restrain his excitement.

"Good news fellow dwarfs. mother earth continues to provide and lead us safely out of the mountains, for the scouts have just reported that the end of the tunnel is near."

A cheer emanated so robustly that it would have brought down the ceiling in the Great Hall, if it was still standing.

Everyone's pace quickened as they turned the bend and now could see light at the end of the tunnel. It was just a small light, hundreds of yards away. Yet, this sign of hope and life invigorated their spirits and rejuvenated their strength. Walking, jogging, and some even running, out of the mountain depths that had tested their faith and trust and toward the freedom that the light promised.

Anyone coming into the light from darkness would need time for their eyesight to adjust. This was even true for dwarfs, although dwarfs are used to working deep in the mines; to transition from the dark of the depths to the light of the day too quickly can be painful. It was worth the pain! For the pain meant light, and the light meant freedom. Even from a distance the light began to pierce their eyes. This did not slow them down or deter them. As they got closer to the mouth of the tunnel, the light only intensified and consumed the dwarfs as they left behind their fallen city and entered into their reconstructed future.

The light was so bright that they could not open their eyes. Even shading their eyes with their hands did not bring much relief. It took a moment, but their eyes eventually acclimated to the bright sun that was pouring forth in the land. When they were finally able to look upon the country without their hands over their face, it was quickly realized that the tunnels of Ubertyne had brought them out of the East Mountain Hurbon near the Podiseon River.

"Sir, what is it that you would have us do now?" inquired Mendull.

"It is not safe to stay in the open" added Silas. "The dragons would surely be scouting the land. We need to keep the people mobilized, find cover, and make our way toward aid."

"The kingdom of Vatoya is probably the closest, just due north of us," suggested Medull. "And the kingdom of Shaddonai would be a full day's journey just to the north and east of here."

"To travel through the plains of Elah would be suicide," interrupted Kithorah. "The dragons have taken Endorah and would easily be able to scout us out. We need cover if we want to preserve what is left of our people."

"It's settled then" replied Mendull eagerly. "Let's go toward the Nimrods. They are situated within the forest of Mezpha. We would have our cover and would be able to use the river as our guide to their kingdom."

"Actually, if I may," began Silas, "our best option would be to go the Castle Dorian. Raithyn and I came to Endorah with a message from the Lord King himself that also carried the seal of Lord Ekron. This document requested that armed men be sent to the castle in order to put together a retaliation force."

Kithorah's anger started to show due to this revelation. "Are you saying that this dragon invasion was known and instead of sending reinforcements to the most obvious city that would be attacked, they sent our men away?"

Dwarf anger is well documented within the kingdoms. Silas has read accounts of what Dwarf anger can do. Although Silas had never personally witnessed it, he hoped that his first encounter with such fierce rage was to see unleashed upon his enemies and not himself.

"I don't think anybody knew what we were up against. Let alone, knew how they were going attack." Silas suggested, trying to lower Kithorah's temperature.

Not interested in Silas' rhetoric, Kithorah had heard all he needed to hear to make his blood boil. "To take our best men and make us more vulner—" Kithorah started, but he was interrupted by a calming and reasonable voice.

"I don't think it would have mattered," Gurther stated flatly. "I had served many years in King Ekron's army, and much of the time was spent as a dragon specialist, helping guard our city from such creatures. I have seen and witnessed many things in my time, but never have I seen a coordinated attack as the one that we just endured. We are up against something more than just a couple of stray dragons."

All this time Xoarah was listening intently to the debate of his council, weighing all their words considerably in order to make the best decision possible. Having heard all that he needed to hear, Xoarah finally spoke.

"We should not be too far south of the Podiseon River. The lords requested that the armies of the land convene at the Castle Dorian. We have lost Endorah. We have no protection, no food, and no shelter. The Castle Dorian would be the most fortified and equipped destination to receive our people. We will head north toward the Podiseon River and follow it into the forest of Mezpah. The forest will give us the protection we need until we reach a point of crossing."

Xoarah spoke with confidence and wisdom as he laid out the plan of what they should do and why. No one questioned or second guessed his decision. The council received their orders, assembled the people, and started their migration north.

<u>57</u>

The lords have gathered their men, filed rank, and began their march out of the kingdom of Ev'ron.

War was none of the king's first option. They had all seen the effects of war. Families were torn apart. Husbands did not come home. Friends and loved ones returned mangled and maimed. Farms and fields destroyed. Houses and villages burnt to the ground. No one can hide from the cruelty of war. The only hope, the only satisfaction is if you are to emerge from the fray safely. What satisfaction is there in that? Most will have to live with having taken the life of another and also seeing the life taken from those in your company. No, there is nothing good about war, yet it is a necessity. For to have peace, is to prepare for war.

With those thoughts in mind, there was something magnificent and glorious about seeing this army march out of the kingdom. All the lands were represented: The Humans, the Fauns, the Sheppen, the Nimrods, and a Dwarf, all marching together to come against a common enemy. The numbers were vast, and the artillery was great, as so it needed to be. Skilled archers and master swordsmen filed in rank. Brilliant generals and fearless warriors marched out. Great crossbows and thunderous catapults were heaved among the troops. The ram's horn was blown loud and fierce in declaration of the freedom and love that they fought to protect. Many people gathered to see the army as it marched out of the kingdom. Some cheered, some cried, and some stood in silence. Everyone knew that this might be the last time that they would get to see their loved one or friend. Everyone hoped that their numbers and force was enough to vanquish this enemy from their land.

Lord Ekron marched with anger and pride, as he was the only Dwarf represented in the army. His men should have reached the Castle Dorian by now. If they had not, there are only two likely scenarios. First, the council decided not to respond to the letter that Silas and Raithyn delivered. Second, the men were diverted from reaching the castle. Both options reeked of death. For this reason, Lord Ekron marched with a fuming heart, revengeful mind, and determined soul.

Lord Ekron was accompanied by lords Titus, Benaniah, Cephas, and Augusta. The lords marched confidently in front of the men as a way to reassure them in the plan that they have trusted in. Murlynn, Herms and some other trusted advisors followed close behind the lords. Captains and lieutenants were placed among the divisions of men with direct orders for how to encounter and engage the enemy. Everyone knew what their assignment was. Spears, swords, and arrows were all dipped in the carnivorous diffusion. Weighted nets, carted cross bows, and catapults were all being transported to the battle ground in hopes that it would give them their best chance of success. There were few words uttered among the men as they marched throughout the kingdom. Only the sound of their boots pounding the earth kept their minds occupied from the fear of what was to come as they absorbed the farewell that the kin's folk were giving them.

It truly was an impressive collaboration of warriors.

The Nimrods were excellent marksmen, light and agile on their feet. Their job was to keep the dragons distracted and neutralize them with the carnivorous diffusion.

The Sheppen were strong and fearless. Thus, they were assigned to containing the beasts by securing them with weighted nets and muzzles.

The Fauns were very keen of sight and had mastered long range weaponry. Therefore, they were charged with the main aerial assault.

Lord Ekron marched as the lone Dwarf representative. Although his mastery of close-range combat was not favorable in this situation, it did not stop him from fantasizing about bathing in dragon's blood and where to mount their heads on his palace wall.

Lord Titus' men carted the heavy artillery and would assist the Fauns in their initial assault. After which, they would rely on their swordsmanship to assist in the ground attack.

Herms mustered up his strength, resolving within himself that this could be the end, and made peace with where his soul would come to rest if he were to fall.

Murlynn was confident that the carnivorous diffusion would work, but was still trying to come up with another formula that would be equally or more effective to their cause.

With all that there was to take in during this moment, both the glory and the somberness of it all, there was still one thought that did not sit well and lingered in Lord Titus' mind, "What happened to Antheis?"

58

Master Sergeant Xoarah and his men were marching north with vision and direction about what needed to be done. Now that they were out of the tunnels, the sun warmed their bodies and gave them hope, but their minds were still filled with sadness and their hearts filled with grief. Yes, their mother did provide and protect them in leading them this far, but it did not take away from the hurt and loss that they had experienced and the remorse that filled their hearts. Although hope lied ahead, the time of mourning over what happened had not yet passed.

As they drew near to the Podiscon River Silas perked up. Noticing something familiar and out of place he quickly ran ahead of the group. Fifty yards closer he could now definitely discern that something was not right. Returning to the remnant, Silas asked Xoarah to halt the exodus and requested if Mendull could accompany him to bring back a scouting report of what was up ahead. Silas reassured Master Sergeant Xoarah that it was not anything to worry about, but more of a precautionary measure. Agreeing, Xoarah sent Silas and Mendull on their way as he halted the remnant for a brief rest until their return.

"What is it?" asked Mendull as they made their way up the grade of the hill that was before them.

"Something fishy" replied Silas.

"Dragons?"

"No, fish."

"Like, dangerous fish?"

"No, like someone is cooking fish."

"Dragons are cooking fish?"

"Not likely. But someone is and I want to find out who," said Silas as they approached the top of the hill.

At the top of the knoll they could see a small fire just across the river, about one hundred yards away. Neither Silas or Mendull were able to make out who was occupying the camp, so they decided to move in for a better look to see if it might be a friend or foe. If it is a friend, then their mother has shown them favor once again. If foe, then they will need to be eliminated before the remnant can move forward.

It was not hard for Silas and Mendull to maneuver down the hill unnoticed, for bushes and trees spotted the hill and provided them with coverage.

Upon getting closer, they could tell that the camp consisted of two people who appeared to be Nimrods. But given all that had happened, Silas and Mendull were not about to trust anybody that they did not know. One seemed to be reclining while the other was on one knee by the fire, presumably cooking the fish that Silas smelt.

Suddenly two more people came running into the picture, another Nimrod and a human. Again, Silas was not able to tell who the Nimrod was for he was not acquainted with many of their kin, but the human seemed oddly familiar.

After a moment Silas realized that the human was in fact Chief Brutus.

"Fortune has smiled upon us." Silas began to tell Mendull. "I recognize the human. It is Brutus, one of Lord Titus' most trusted men. Come, let us reveal ourselves for he may be able to help us, or at least provide us with some information."

As Silas went to step out into the clearing Mendull grabbed his arm, "What if he is a mole"?

"Nonsense," said Silas shrugging off such an absurd accusation. Medull's charge was truly preposterous, but the essence of the claim held truth. Given the accounts of all that had happened, it would be reasonable to conclude that there was a mole within Sahleam.

"But," continued Silas after giving a second thought to Medull's allegation, "just in case he is as you suggest; you should remain hidden until I give you the okay to reveal yourself."

Medull did not like the idea of openly announcing their presence to an unknown group of kin. But if Silas was confident in believing that he knew who these folk were, then it would be best if it was he who would make himself known. This way the unknown group would not have the same suspicion that Medull had. And if it does not go favorably, then Medull would be able to go back and warn the dwarfs.

With that thought, Mendull agreed to Silas' plan.

Silas paused and gave thought as to how he would want to reveal himself. He did not want to barge down the hill in a brash or surprising way, for this may cause alarm and result in engaged combat. Silas needed to do something that would draw their attention his way out of curiosity, and not because they were startled. Remembering a particular whistle that was commonly used among the human army, Silas spread out his arms and began to whistle its particular tune.

The whistle percolated Brutus ears right away as he instantly gave his attention to trying to find its source. His company, on the other hand, were not familiar with the call and armed themselves, ready to take on whatever maybe approaching them.

It did not take Brutus long to locate Silas walking down a clearing just across the river with his arms spread wide, whistling that familiar call.

At first Brutus did not recognize Silas and would have taken him out. Not even his sign of surrender would have spared Silas from Brutus' marksmanship. Rather it was that distinguish tune that Silas was emulating that held off Brutus long enough for him to realize that this was a friend, not foe, who was approaching them.

Signaling for his men to lower their weapons, Brutus made way for the river.

"Brutus, it is good to see you," said Silas cheerfully.

"And you too, Silas." remarked Brutus cordially. "That was quite a risk you took."

"I knew that you would not fire upon a victim without knowing who it was first."

Brutus nodded in affirmation with a slight grin as he delighted in Silas' bravery.

Silas could not help but to wonder, so he asked the obvious question immediately. "What are you doing here? Last I recall you were sent out to the kingdom of Shaddonai in order to gather troops for the counterattack."

"And so I was until Lord Benaniah himself returned to the kingdom. Upon his arrival the lord shared with me his distress about the city Endorah. He himself wanted to journey here to see of her state, but I had convinced him otherwise and volunteered myself for the mission."

Silas' countenance fell.

Brutus stopped his soliloquy, waiting to hear Silas speak the words that Brutus knew he was going to say.

"Endorah has fallen. Dragons overtook the city, ambushing her with guerilla tactics. Mercy was not shown; rules of warfare were not heeded - killing men, women, and children."

Brutus' heart sank with hearing the news.

"Luckily, the Dwarf troops were sent out just before the attack. They will be able to get some retribution by unleashing some Dwarf furry on those beasts for what they did.

Brutus' heart sank all the more, knowing that he would have to tell Silas of what he just found.

"I am not the only survivor." Silas continued. "A remnant of dwarfs led by Master Sergeant Xoarah are just over the knoll, waiting for my report."

With that, Silas motioned for Mendull to reveal himself. After making his way to Silas, Silas told Medull to go report to Xoarah that it is ok to advance to the river.

Brutus' heart was very heavy with all the news that Silas reported. It seemed like the only good thing that happened in the past day was finding Brutus at the river, but even that came with bad news, for Brutus knew that he needed to relay what he had found. There was no good way to deliver this kind of news. In the years of experience Brutus discovered that when delivering bad news of this kind, it was best just to say it. There is no way to word this kind of news to make it any easier to receive. Therefore, Brutus told Silas straightforward the new he needed to hear. "Silas, the Dwarf army never made it to the Castle Dorian. They are dead."

Silas' countenance sank. He could not believe what he was hearing, the Dwarf army, dead. It seemed that there was no manner of luck for the dwarfs, but before Silas could fully take in the news that Brutus had delivered, Xoarah and the remnant came over the hill and down toward the river.

. . . .

Brutus and his men, along with Silas, had gathered privately with Xoarah, Mendull, Gurther, and Kithorah in order to inform them of the events that transpired.

"Are you sure?" asked Xoarah in disbelief.

"Yes," replied Brutus. "The remains were discovered by myself and Nappitt, one of my trusted men. At first, we did not know what had happened, but after looking upon the remains for some answers we discovered a scroll that was signed and sealed by Lord Ekron himself, requesting the Dwarf army to go to the Castle Dorian."

Utter shock took hold of the Dwarf councilmen. They knew that Brutus was telling the truth, but they did not want to believe it.

"I am sorry" apologized Brutus. "I know that you have been through more than any man should endure within the past night and day, but I thought you needed to know."

"I was hoping to be able to catch up with the army on our way to the castle." Xoarah said softly. "To see our army marching strong would have rejuvenated hope in the remnant. Instead, now I must tell them of the further death and loss that has consumed our people."

Seeing Xoarah's frustration and hope slipping from the councilmen, Gurther spoke up in order to prevent total despair and destitution.

"All is not loss. Do not forget nor belittle what you have done for these people," Gurther said, reaffirming Xoarah. "It was you who was elected by the council to be Master Sergeant. It was you who sounded the alarm when the dragons ambushed our people. It was you who led our people to the safe room. And it was you who led our people through the ancient tunnels of Ubertyne. But we cannot forget," Gurther now turning his words toward all the councilmen, "who we are, where we have come from, and what lies before us. There is no question that this loss will be gravely received, but we must not doubt ourselves, nor forget the provisions of our mother."

Xoarah found it hard to take comfort in these words, but did find himself encouraged to keep pressing forward. No matter what Xoarah thought of himself or his situation, their mother had proven herself too real and too faithful to turn his back on her. This did not mean that the news did not hurt. Xoarah's trust and faith in his mother did not change the fact that he knew many of the men in that company and was good friends with a number of them. His faith did not change the fact that they were alive and now they are dead. The recollections that he has of those he knew will now forever cling to his heart and rest in his mind. For no new adventures or memories await the dead among the living. No, his faith does not take away the sadness, the anger, the frustration, or the confusion that comes with such news, but there is still hope. Hope that one day, although they can never come back to him, that he may go to them.

"We will continue toward the Castle Dorian as planned," directed Xoarah. "Brutus, take Silas, Kithorah, and any other men you would like and go back to our fallen brethren to collect as much weaponry as possible. I will inform the people of what has taken place, and we will continue our march along the Podiseon River. Meet us at the southwest edge of the Forest of Mezpha and from there we will make way for the castle."

59

The once well-lit throne room of Lord Ekron, now was darkened by the destruction that had been exerted onto the city.

In the shadows, a dark figure sits casually; in a manner, disrespectfully on the throne of Lord Ekron. Silence filled the room as the figure remained motionless upon the throne, even sulking in his obtained victory.

The silence was only broken by the opening of the chamber doors.

"Ah, it is good to see you" said the voice from the throne, seething with malicious intent.

"Yes, my lord," said the man with a bow, not daring to move any closer than just a few feet in front of the chamber door.

"I assume you have rather important news to leave your post and visit me here." asked the man upon the throne rhetorically.

"Yes, I . . ."

"Well then, out with it" interrupted the figure irritably.

Without showing loss of confidence or intimidation, the solider continued with his report. "As you know the armies of the land have gathered at the castle Dorian, but instead of fortifying themselves they decided to launch an immediate counterattack."

"Do they really think that they can beat me? Thaddeous!" said the shadow of a man as he rose from the throne; his voice projecting through the chamber and his yellow eyes beaming. "How arrogant. For their arrogance, I will do them the favor of not making them march all the way down to me, but rather I will launch my own counterattack and engage them in suit."

"My lord, are you sure you want to do that?" questioned the informant, taking another step away from the door. "Why not let them exhaust themselves by marching through the Plains of Elah and down to Mt. Endor?"

Thaddeous had leisurely sat back in Lord Ekron's throne, "Do you think that it will make a difference whether we engage them in battle here or in the Plains of Elah?" he asked calmly.

"No, of course . . ."

"Then why even suggest such a time-consuming tactic." Thaddeous replied in annoyance. "We are not here on leave. We are here on a mission, a mission that I would like to complete sooner rather than later.

To this, the man said nothing.

"Besides, Antheis," Thaddeous said smugly. "If I recall, if it were not for me, you would be lying dead on the riverbanks."

Again, Antheis was able to say nothing.

"Well then, ready the fleet and alarm my commanders. We are moving out."

60

Xoarah knew that it would not be right to withhold this new information from the people. Although they would be better to be ignorant of what had happened, the people, especially the loved ones of the fallen, had a right to know what had happened, no matter how terrible the news would be.

As expected, there was great sorrow over the news of the fallen army. The once faith inspired hope had once again fallen to grief and despair. Depression and doubt fought their way through the people, vanquishing any glimmer of hope and optimism one may still have. It did not seem that it was their fate to survive this great battle. For every time it seemed the tide may be changing, it came crashing back in to remind them of their cruel reality.

But Xoarah knew that he could not let the mourning go on for long. The people needed to march; to march on past this devastation and to march on toward their new beginning. For to stay in a place of mourning and grief would only lead one to be consumed by doubt and depression, thus killing any manner of life that would be left in them. No, they needed to march. So Xoarah had Mendull and Gurther helped him encourage the remnant to march on.

Xoarah himself was not unmoved by everything that had happened. He knew that he needed to be strong for the others. Within himself, he was asking the questions that everyone else was asking aloud: Why was all of this happening to them? Why would their mother allow such a thing? Will they be able to recover? Will they be able to fully drive the dragons out of Endorah? With one thing after another happening, what else was going to happen to them?

These thoughts came and went in Xoarah's mind as they marched on toward the Forest of Mezpha. Xoarah did not spend much time entertaining the questions of "what has happened". One cannot change the past. We can only use the past to help make a better future. The questions of "why" Xoarah also dismissed. Unless he could talk to a dragon, he would never know "why". And to think that their mother "allowed" this to happen is unthinkable. If someone has the ability to choose the right decision, then they also have the ability to choose the wrong decision. If you take the ability to make the wrong decision away, then you are taking away the ability to choose in totality. If you take away one's ability to choose, then you are more like a marionette who only comes alive when the puppeteer wants to enact its will on you rather than a living being. Furthermore, making the right decision is only beautiful because we make it in spite of being able to make the wrong decision. With such reasoning, Xoarah did not think about the question any further.

The questions Xoarah thought about most to occupy his time was not 'will they' but 'how can they'. How can they vanquish the dragons from Endorah? How can they rebuild their cities? How can they help to drive out the dragons? How can they rebuild their nation? Looking forward to the future is what fueled the fire burning in his heart.

With his mind so preoccupied with such thoughts, it seemed that only moments had passed since talking with Brutus, as they were now approaching the Forest of Mezpah. It was this place, just before the Podiseon River enters the forest, that they crossed the river and waited for Brutus and his men to meet up with them.

Although the current had slowed, the water was still several feet deep. This made it challenging for dwarfs who typically stand under five-foot-tall, especially for those who were carrying supplies or children. But, with little falter, they were able to pull together and help each other out so that everyone was able to cross safely.

To stay out in the open was not a good idea, so Xoarah had everyone head just beyond the tree line of the forest. They took shelter and rest as they wait for Brutus and the rest of the men to return.

. . . .

Brutus and his men hurried as fast as they could to catch up to the dwarfs. With two humans, three Nimrod's, and a couple of dwarfs, the company was able to gather quite a bit of battle axes, short swords, and bows and arrows from their fallen brethren. Each ran as fast as they could, being sure not to drop any of the weaponry that they were transporting. The amount of arms they collected were certainly not enough to arm the entire remnant, but it would be adequate to put up a fight against any creature that may consider trying to finish them off.

It was a sad sight, seeing the Dwarf army dead as they removed their weapons from their cold hands. As dishonorable as this was to do to a fallen solider, let alone a Dwarf, they all knew why they had to do it and moved on.

For having much shorter legs than Brutus and the rest of his company, the dwarfs did well in keeping up, even with hauling their own heavy load.

The Region of Vinyah quietly passed them by as they ran east northeast, up the Podiseon River and back toward the Forest of Mezpah.

When Brutus and his company first arrived at the tree line of the Forest of Mezpah, it appeared that they had arrived there before Master Sergeant Xoarah and the remnant. As Brutus and his men slowed their stride, approaching their destination; Mendull, Gurther, and Xoarah revealed themselves from just within the forest. There was no time for cordial pleasantries; they went straight into a brief council before moving onward to the Castle Dorian.

Seeing the axes, bows, and swords stirred emotions in Xoarah, Gurther, and Mendull once again. They believed Brutus when he had told them that the army was dead, and they even believed it in their hearts. But seeing these weapons only solidified what they already knew, for a Dwarf warrior would never give up his weapon unless it was pried from his cold, dead hands.

Keeping their emotions at bay, Xoarah started the dialogue on how to approach what must happen next.

"Brothers, thank you for completing such a dangerous mission. Now, we need to make a decision: which way should we proceed to the Castle Dorian? Should we travel through the Mezpah Forest or cut up the Valley of Kurdish and along the Plains of Elah?"

This was a perplexing question, for both paths come with their own risks and danger.

After some thought Nappitt finally spoke up, "I think that we should stay in the Mezpah Forest. It makes the most sense. There is constant water, food, and shelter. Also Ichadad, Ashyer, and I grew up in these woods. We are very familiar with the wildlife and paths that would lead us closest to the castle."

This was a compelling argument, but Silas knew that something even more important than their safety needed to be considered. Thus he was quick to speak up before Nappitt's suggestion took grip on their minds.

"This may be true, young master, but you are forgetting one very important factor: time."

"Oh, yes, this is true" you could hear the council mumble among themselves.

"Time is not a luxury that we have, nor can we afford to waste" added in Gurther.

"Well, what if we did go through the Valley of Kurdish and up the Plains of Elah?" added in Mendull, leading the other Nimrods to make apparent the wisdom in staying in the forest.

"For starters," quickly added Ichadad, realizing what Medull was doing, "there is not a ready supply of food, shelter, or water."

"Our mother has shown her faithfulness to us in our time of need both in the safe room and in the ancient tunnels of Ubertyne," cut in Kithorah before Ichadad had the ability to say much more. "I have no doubt that she will continue her faithfulness in the Valley and in the Plains if that is the way we choose to go."

"I am sorry, I did not mean . . ."

"Also," continued Kithorah, not wanting to hear Ichadad's political sentiment. "I do not think that we need to worry about an attack. The dragons would need to go through the Kingdom of Vatoya before they would be able to attack us. Besides, I am sure that they know that the armies of the land are gathering at the Castle Dorian. It would not be wise on their part to risk getting that close to the castle after it had been fortified."

"Unless they want to attack it" Medull said flatly.

"Enough." Xoarah interjected. "Both points have been made and received. Although safety is a high priority, in this case, it is not the ultimate factor. Time is not our friend. If the dragons are planning on attacking the castle, then we need to make sure to beat them to the finish. I do not think the risks are great enough to require us to go into the Mezpah Forest."

With that, everyone agreed.

"Gather the people. We move onward to the Valley of Kurdish"

. . . .

Staying close the tree line of the Mezpah Forest, it was not long before the remnant came to the Valley of Kurdish. The view was one of the most beautiful sights that any of them had seen in what felt like a lifetime. To their south, the Podiseon River raced down the Mountain of Endor and maneuvered its way through the Region of Vinyah as it made straightway for the Mezpah Forest. To their west, the Plains of Elah proclaimed their subtle beauty; connecting with the most basic of desires within all of us, to own and work the land. Behind the remnant, to the east, was the Mezpah Forest standing tall, dark, and mystical. It was from this view that many have called the Valley of Kurdish the Valley of Life.

At the top of the valley you could smell the fresh grass and almost taste the clean air. The sun reaches down from the heavens to refresh your soul as you stretch out through unhindered skies. The valley itself was not a steep, but rather an accommodating grade that made the decent and ascension manageable. With time of the essence, cutting through the Valley of Kurdish and continuing north through the eastern edge of the Plains of Elah was their most direct path.

One may think that it would not be wise to position yourself on the low ground knowing that you may have an enemy spring upon you, and you would be right. But knowing that the dragons would have an aerial assault, it did not matter much whether they stayed on the hills of the valley or not.

Down the hill and into the valley they went, moving as a heard of wild beasts migrating through the land. The smell of fresh air and grass became more and more faint as they drove from the heights of the hills to the depths of the valley. An odd smell, one not too familiar with the average Dwarf, but had become all too familiar within the land of Sahleam, greeted them as the remnant arrived at the base of the valley. Brimstone, ash, and rot filled the air and overtook any natural pleasantries that emanated from the valley. It did not take much of an investigation to discover why the pleasant smell of nature was replaced with decay. Corpses lay scattered throughout the valley. Some burnt beyond recognition, some mangled and maimed, and others torn by scavengers that had come to feast on the massacre that was left behind.

It was obviously that this was the result of another dragon attack, but this time on one of Lord Titus' Dragon Retaliation Platoons.

Seeing this all too familiar sight, once again brought sorrow to Xoarah's heart. This time though, the sorrow did not last for long. No, this time the sorrow went through a metamorphosis, transforming into anger and revenge. Xoarah had no more tears to shed, nor groans of anguish within him to give for these dead.

"What is all of this for?" thought the Master Sergeant as his anger boiled.

"All this killing. All this murder. For what? For land? To exhort dominance? For revenge on those who had exiled the species from the land?" Xoarah's anger now was boiling over.

"Even still," he continued, "how many lives need to be lost? How many families need to be torn apart? How much blood needs to be spilled before a resolution is rectified?" Xoarah could not hold in the anger, frustration, sadness, and grief any longer. All that he had seen and experienced within the past two days had finally reached its breaking point. No longer could he hold back what he could not show to the remnant as he led them out of Endorah here to this valley. What once was considered a Valley of Life has now become a Valley of Death. With a loud yell that echoed through the land, Xoarah finally released all that which he could hold back no longer.

Although Xoarah's yell caused a tinge of fright and made everyone look to the sky, Xoarah felt some relief after having released some of his pent-up frustration. No sooner did Xoarah take a deep breath, he saw Chief Brutus racing down the hill toward him.

"Brutus, what is it? What's the matter?" inquired Xoarah after Brutus had finally made his way to him.

It took a moment for Brutus to catch his breath, for although his position as Lord Titus' guard was held in high esteem, it was not the most rigorous post that one could be assigned to.

"Dragons are coming!"

61

It truly was a beautiful day. The skies were calm, and the sun was shining high. A gentle breeze swayed the tall grass of the Plains of Elah as Lord Titus and the army of Sahleam marched through the land. Clouds dotted the sky, looking as if they were painted on by God Himself. The rhythmic sound of boots pounding the earth created a sense of tranquility as they marched through the land. This beauty, this land, this home all served as a constant reminder of why they marched on, willing to pay the price of freedom with their blood.

"Lord Titus," approached Lord Benaniah from within the ranks. "I have just gotten urgent news from Chief Brutus. A fleet of dragons are heading our way."

Without hesitation, Lord Titus told his commanding generals to dig in and prepare for combat. Commotion quickly filled the air as orders were given and the divisions made themselves ready for battle.

With all the commotion Lord Titus stopped to address Lord Benaniah privately. Although Lord Titus trusted Lord Benaniah emphatically, which is why he gave the immediate order to make ready, there were no real evidence that dragons would soon be upon them.

"Are you sure dragons are nearing us?"

"Yes," replied Lord Benaniah assuredly. "When I had met up with your Chief in the Kingdom of Shaddonai I had given him some of the communication spell that Murlynn had given me to use in order to relay what he found to be of Endorah without delay."

Lord Titus said nothing, but just nodded in agreement.

"I am glad for this new magic that Murlynn conjured up, or else we would have been the ones hit by surprise"

It did not take much time for the army to position themselves and to be at the ready.

"This is not where I was hoping to engage them," mentioned Lord

Titus aloud, more talking to himself than to those around him as he surveyed the land, "but it will have to do."

Turning his attention toward Lord Benaniah, Lord Titus continued his thoughts, "At least we are in position and ready for what may come. We no longer have the element of surprise, but nor do they. Hopefully our numerical and tactical strategy will be enough."

"It will be," chimed in Lord Augusta. "Because our army is fueled by something greater than strength and skill; we have hope, faith, and love."

Looking out among the men you could see many different expressions on their faces. Some looked nervous as their eyes dotted the sky looking for any sign of their fate. Others mouthed words of prayers that were only heard by the ones to whom the prayers were addressed. Still, others sat quiet and stone faced, waiting for the opportunity to be noted in history as a dragon slayer. No matter how they felt or what they thought, every man was ready to do what needed to be done. For they knew that they were the best that the land had to offer, and they were the best chance Sahleam had at overcoming this foe.

Lord Titus himself could not help but to find himself in astonishment as he witnessed the men's eagerness to prove their courage and honor as they tried to stop this juggernaut.

"How many ants does it take to overcome an aardvark?" asked Lord Benaniah, interrupting Lord Titus' thoughts.

"It depends on the ant" the Lord responded.

"Well, we will get to find out soon enough" replied Lord Benaniah, as he pointed to the black dots in the sky.

62

The dwarfs clamored to get into position in anticipation of the dragon attack. Some of them were fearful for what may happen as others were eager to get a chance to enact some revenge, and others were just caught up in the sudden excitement of what was happening. Orders had been given for the men to form ranks and for the women and children to be sent into the forest of Mezpha to take cover.

Xoarah knew that he needed to put someone in command over the division that was to take cover in the forest of Mezpha, someone that he could trust and that the dwarfs would listen to.

"Here is Isadoorah, as requested, Master Sergeant," announced Mendull. Then he left abruptly to continue to make ready the troops.

"Isadoorah, I am glad you are here." began Master Sergeant Xoarah. "We do not have much time, so I need you to listen carefully. You are the daughter of General Durstin of the Dwarf Army. Your father was held in high regard and highly respected among our people. Because of this, I know the people will not only look to you, but listen to you," said the Master Sergeant. "Therefore, I need you to take command over the division of people retrieving into the woods."

Isadoorah's slight smile turned into a slight frown on her hardened face. Isadoorah was not like many of the other Dwarf women. Being brought up in a military family had given her a strong will and determination to achieve anything she set her mind to. She was just as smart and beautiful as she was strong and tactical. "With all due respect, Master Sergeant, when Medull fetched me to be brought before you, I relished in the idea that you were in need of more warriors to help stave off the dragons." Isadoorah began her refute. "Not just myself, but many of the dwarfettes are prepared to die in battle."

Xoarah listened intently as Isadoorah made her plea.

"They murdered my father, and destroyed my home," she continued. "For that, I protest under any other circumstance that does not afford me the opportunity to enact my revenge on these monsters."

Xoarah took a deep breath. "Your father, General Durstin, was a great man. You know that he was like a father to me. I was taking great hope and comfort in the idea of rendezvousing with him. When Chief Brutus relayed the news of his death and the loss of the entire Dwarf army, the final piece of my heart was broken."

Xoarah placed his hands on Isadoorah's arms and looked her square in the eyes. "I know the pain you feel. That we all feel. Most of the remnant share in your experience and sentiment. Under any other circumstance I would oblige your request. But it will do us no good if the dwarfs are eradicated from the earth here today.

Xoarah released Isadoorah's arms as he took a moment to allow his heavy words to sink in.

"As the Master Sergeant, it is my responsibility to vanquish any foe who threatens our kin, but it is also my responsibility to ensure that there are kin to protect. We are all that remains of who we are. If we perish in battle, then who will preserve our lineage? Who will preserve our heritage? We are a remnant, and from that remnant a few must remain at all cost."

Isadoorah's emotions were stirring within her like a gale tossing the ocean. The loss of her father, her hatred for the dragons, her sympathy for her people, and her respect for Xoarah were all mixing within her like a vile concoction trying to escape its cauldron.

Xoarah could see Isadoorah's thoughts in her eyes. "You are a leader." he reinforced to her. "This much is obvious to me and to our people. And as a leader I need you to help in the greater cause of our people. You will have your chance to repay these beasts for their actions, but not here, not today."

With that, Isadoorah gave a nod in agreement and put her fist over her heart in acceptance of her new post and marched off to ensure that the dwarfs were in place and ready for when the attack came.

It took a moment, but after some order was restored, the men were able to situate themselves in what they thought was their best defense in a timely manner.

With the dwarfs now in position and the dragons approaching, Xoarah felt it necessary to encourage the men for what was about to take place. For these men were not warriors, but tradesmen and businessmen who were willing to lay down their lives for their wives, their children, and their fellow countrymen; to preserve their nation and stop the further on slot of their people.

"Men. Brothers. The time has come to put an end to this vile evil that has come upon our land. Endorah lies in ruins. Our people were mercilessly butchered. Even now, after we have been driven out of our beloved city and torn from the people that we love, we are being hunted in pursuit of extermination. I will not tell you of the size, and strength, and of other advantages that the dragons have. For those things only win the battle, but they will not win the war. It takes heart, honor, and courage to win a war. Of which the Dwarf has more per stature than any other known being in this universe. Do not let the death of our people be in vain. Do not afford these beasts the opportunity to attack our women and children. Do not fear death! For in death we will have honor. In death we will prevail. In death we will live on in the hearts and minds of those whom we have protected. So let us show them, here today, why it is well known throughout the land 'to never ignite a Dwarf's fury'"!

With that the dwarfs gave a loud cheer that resonated throughout the valley. If the dragons did not know where the dwarfs were, they certainly would not have any trouble locating them after such a proclamation.

It would not be long now before the dragons were upon them.

The dwarfs were ready. They were ready to fight. They were ready to die, but they were not ready for what happened next. After the cheering had died down, they all waited with bated breath watching the dragon fleet get closer and closer. Finally they were upon Xoarah and his men. Just as quickly as the dragons came within battle range, they also passed the dwarfs without as much as turning their heads or batting an eye. This left the dwarfs confused and relieved. They were relieved because a battalion of untrained men did not need to overcome insurmountable odds, which would mean that the preservation of the nation would still be in order. Otherwise they were confused because if the dragons were not after the dwarfs, then who were they after?

63

Although the Army of Sahleam did not wait long before the dragons were upon them, the anticipation made it feel much longer than it was; like when one takes a journey to a destination in which they are excited about arriving at. Although, when the dragons finally arrived, everyone would have much preferred a more prolonged anticipation. There were no negotiations, nor offered terms of surrender, or any other formalities before engagement. As soon as the dragons arrived, the battle had begun.

The dragons started diving toward the army at top speed. Lord Titus had already given the order not to open fire until the dragons were within artillery range and not until their wings were opened. Their ammunition had already proved useless just the other day when the Dragon Retaliation Platoon had gotten ambushed. Lord Titus did not want to make that same mistake twice.

It was hard for the men to continue to hold fire when such fierce beasts were diving straight at them with blood lust filling their souls. But the men held their ground. They did not give into fear or nervousness, prematurely igniting the counterattack. Rather, they held fast until the best opportunity was afforded to them.

Holding off fire while the dragons were rapidly diving toward them proved valuable for Lord Titus. As the dragons drew close, Lord Titus was able to realize something that he was otherwise ignorant of while preparing for this battle; the dragons had riders on them. Never before had there been an account when a person of any sort was able to mount a dragon and live to tell about it. He did not know who they were or where they had come from, but that did not matter. What mattered was that this new information needed to be relayed to the other lord's and generals. Instead of facing the dragons, which was daunting enough, now they had to worry about these mercenaries as well.

All thoughts and sounds faded away as the men waited for their signal to unleash their fury on these beasts. Their thoughts were consumed with keeping the dragons in their cross hairs. Their only audible existence was the pounding of their hearts and the deep soothing breaths they took in order to try and stay calm.

"Fire!" came the command, breaking through the rather tranquil state of the men. The twinge of the arrows leaving their strings filled the air like a pin drop until the thud of it hitting its mark and the screech of the dragons brought the reality of the situation roaring back into focus. The bombardment was so fierce that it looked like there was a thick black cloud rising from the land in the aid of Sahleam.

Some of the dragons had been brought down from the Faun's aerial assault, while others had made it through the barrage to release their transport. Knowing that it was unlikely that the dragons would willingly ground themselves again, the Nimrod's and the Sheppen gave a loud cheer and went straight to work on the second part of the battle plan: keeping the beasts grounded with muzzles and nets.

The battle had begun. The struggle for the land and their lives was in full contest. The Sheppen and the Nimrod's led the ground assault as they tried to neutralize as many dragons as possible. The Faun's continued to lead the aerial assault as they tried to bring down the airborne dragons with a barrage of arrows and boulders. The humans and Lord Ekron were engaged in close range combat with this new enemy that the dragons had brought into the battle. Yes, the onslaught quickly became a massive fray.

....

Amidst all the action, a warrior arose in a black hooded robe. He moved through the army of Sahleam with relative ease, fearlessly slashing through any that would challenge him. Neither human, nor Nimrod, nor Sheppen was able to match this adept solider for any length of time. Lord Titus knew that this skilled foe needed to be brought down if they wanted any chance of winning this battle.

When Lord Titus finally made his way over to this black knight, he could not help but feel a sense of acquaintanceship as they locked eyes, sizing each other up for the encounter that was to come.

"Who are you? Why have you invaded Sahleam and waged war on its people?" asked Lord Titus, hoping to get some sort of information.

There was no response from this dark figure as he just continued to stare down Lord Titus with his sword drawn at his side.

Lord Titus could not shake the familiarity of this foe, as he tried to pierce the black shadow that his hood created over his face. There was no more time for that though, and it did not matter, for this enemy needed to be brought down. With no more words, Lord Titus began the fight with a swing of his sword.

....

Herms was a bundle of nerves until the first twinge of his bow.

It's just another day at the shooting range, Herms told himself. Words like these were what Herms would tell himself when he was lined up for a race at a major event. Nervousness was something Herms never got used to over the course of his racing career. Ever since his first race, he got nervous. Even now, years later and a multitude of races won, depending on whom he was racing and at what event he was racing in, Herms would still get nervous. The crowds, the cheers, and the venue still could be very overwhelming, even for an experienced runner such as himself. Herms had learned, though, that when the race started, all of the external factors became irrelevant and it became just another race. There were no more stadiums. There were no more spectators. There were no more competitors. It would be just himself on a track racing against himself. This same technique was how Herms tried to calm himself as dragons roamed the earth and swooped through the sky, thinking, *It's just another day at the shooting range.*

He was by no means a marksman archer by any sorts, but he was far better in archery than he was in swordplay. Therefore he was stationed with the fauns and was doing his best to bring down the remaining dragons and to find an opening to strike those that had been grounded.

Although the fauns were doing a good job of grounding and even keeping the dragons at bay, Herms was having no such luck with the aerial assault. He just could not find his mark. Realizing that several dragons had landed, Herms decided to survey the battlefield to see if there was a dragon that he could help detain. To his surprise, Herms noticed a dark green dragon that was isolated on the perimeter. Not being too far away, the dragon had its back to the company Herms was in and was rather immobile. This did make Herms rather curious as to why it was not engaged in battle. Herms could tell that the beast had not been muzzled, but was not sure if it had been affected by the carnivorous diffusion. He thought that it might have been injured and could no longer contribute to the battle, so it pulled itself away to die. This thought made Herms feel braver than he really was, and so he decided to break from his company, sneak up on the beast, and stick it with the carnivorous diffusion so that they could properly detain the animal.

It is rather easy to sneak up on someone or something in the middle of a battle, especially when they had your back to you. With all the clinging and clanging, and screaming and groaning, you can barely hear your own thoughts let alone the soft steps of one trying to go unnoticed. Still, Herms was being extra cautious and careful to mind his distance. There was no need to be closer to this beast than what he needed to be. It would prove quite impossible to shoot an arrow into the beast's mouth when you are sneaking up on it from behind. Although sneaking up on the beast meant getting closer to the dragon than Herms would have ever dared, he also knew that he would rather stab it in the back than to try and shoot an arrow into its mouth. I am not sure if one part of a dragon is safer than another in the field of battle, but Herms felt more comfortable and confident with the idea of jabbing the dragon in the tail over any other part of the beast.

The dragon had not moved, and Herms was only about an arm's length or two away from the bravest act he had ever done when the monster suddenly turned around and locked eyes on him.

Herms froze. He was now face to face with a dragon! Stiff as a board, all of his thoughts and muscle coordination seemed to have lost their basic function. Fear gripped his heart as his body trembled in trepidation.

Oddly, the dragon did not pounce. Instead, it just stared at Herms with its yellow beady eyes that pierced his soul and struck horror into his heart. Those old tired eyes felt strangely familiar as they barrowed into the recesses of his mind.

Without warning, emotions overtook Herms. Thoughts that were not his own entered his mind: thoughts of a young man and a small hut, of flying over fields and a rush of freedom, of armed farmers and fright, of sadness and loneliness, of wondering and wearisome, of manipulation and a hooded figure. The feelings were so strong and vivid that Herms felt as though he was there for each one of these sensations with the dragon, experiencing each of these memories.

As quickly as the emotions came, they were gone. When all the images and sensations had run their course, Herms felt emotionally drained. Exhausted and weary, for a moment Herms forgot that he was on a battlefield face to face staring into the eyes of the enemy.

Or was it the enemy.

As Herms looked back at the dragon, he thought he could see moisture in its eyes.

"Is the dragon crying?" thought Herms. "Can it be sorry and remorseful for what it has done?"

Before anything more could cross Herms' mind, the old dragon had lifted its long, green, spike ridden tail high into the air. It seemed to rise in slow motion as Herms watched its massive tail ascend to such a height that it eclipsed the sun. No sooner was this barbed club of death raised to its full extent, did it fall again with all the force and might that the dragon could muster. Herms stood gripped in terror as the dragon's tail of death passed over his head and collided with another dragon.

Unbeknown to Herms, another dragon had snuck up on him during this time and was amidst pouncing upon him when the spiked tail of the old green dragon crashed into its jaw and killed it.

Herms was stunned with disbelief, "Did the dragon just save me?" he thought.

As he locked eyes with the old familiar dragon one more time, he felt happy relieved, and satisfied. Almost like a burden had been lifted off of its shoulders.

How could such a mindless, blood thirsty beast experience such complicated emotions? thought Herms.

This redemptive experience did not last long. All too suddenly pain and anguish raged through Herms' body. Having come back to his own senses and realizing once again where he was and what was going on, Herms looked and saw that a solider had come upon the dragon and given it a fatal blow to its underbelly right between its shoulders, piercing its heart.

The dragon let out a ferocious roar as Herms gave an immutable "NO!" while the solider extracted his blood ridden sword from the dragons chest and moved on to his next victim, leaving the dragon there to die.

The massive beast fell to the ground with a solid thud. Its life was coming quickly to an end. Unexpectedly, Herms felt sad and even grief for the loss of this beast. Everything that Herms had experienced over the past three days, especially here on the battlefield, led him to question what he was taught to be the fundamental principles of dragon behavior. "Dragons are not mindless, blood thirsty animals that roam about aimlessly, ravaging the land. For whatever reason, for whatever purpose, this one spared my life, not once but twice. Why it felt the need to do so, I do not know. But what I do know is that I would not be here if it were not for this friend?"

With the life quickly escaping from the dragon, Herms looked the dragon in the eyes one last time. His old friend was tired, in much pain, and letting go. It had lived its life and no longer had anything to hold on for. Herms did not feel or experience this, but could tell it just by the look in its eyes.

Knowing that its final moments were upon them, Herms gave a gentle "shh" as he placed his hand on the cheek of the dragon, trying to give it some comfort and ease of mind as its life ran out. This did seem to bring some relief to the dragon as it closed its eyes and gave a slight grin that could easily have been interpreted as a smile. With that, Herms put his head on Korel's forehead as she gave up her last bit of life that was left to give.

....

Although many of the dragons were grounded and some even captured or killed, the battle was not proceeding in the army's favor. There were still dragons in the air that were proving difficult to bring down, and the dragons that had been grounded were proving very difficult to detain. The carnivorous diffusion was working as Murlynn had theorized, but getting it into the dragons' mouth was no easy task, for the dragons were not frequently utilizing their fire due to the cost of hitting their own men. In order to get a direct hit with the carnivorous diffusion, some gave their lives in noble sacrifice, charging the beasts in order to get the closest shot possible. Many lives had already been lost and the remaining men were getting tired and seemed to be starting to lose their courage.

Not Lord Ekron though. He fought with all the might of the dwarfs that had gone before him, and all the dwarfs that would come after. He was fearless and courageous on the battlefield. Some would even say quite stupid at times. He helped as many as he could that were struggling in battle and showed no fear as he ran upon the dragons so that they too may taste the blade of his axe. The thought of his people, what they had lost, and how they had been killed fueled Lord Ekron with such adrenaline that his that his strength, stamina, and courage on the battlefield would go down as legend for generations to come.

It was with this display of effort by Lord Ekron that the army continued to hope and press on in their cause.

Even still, some of the men did not hold onto hope, but let it go in the wake of the battle. Hope in itself is not a plan of action, but hope is a great asset and can prove to be very powerful and help overcome obstacles as fuel for a course of action. Hope is also not something that someone or something can take away from you. It is not tangible. It is not a thing. It is a strong desire and passion for something that is not yet. Therefore, the only way to 'lose hope' is if you were to let it go.

This is what was happening on the battle front. They knew that the dragons were an impressive enemy, and even that they were going up against more than one dragon, but they thought that their numbers and amount of artillery would even out the odds. They were wrong. The dragons, along with their riders were skilled and fierce. Some of their best fighting men had fallen and the strength of their assault was diminishing rapidly. This was draining hope from the army's heart. It would only be a matter of time before the battle was lost.

Some of the ranking officers, not the lords mind you, began to wonder if it would be better to accept defeat and live to fight another day? That is, of course, assuming that the dragons would not pursue them. Even still, if they retreat, who is to say that Sahleam has enough soldiers left for another attack? Or do they water the ground with their blood until the last man has fallen? Neither option was favorable.

Something needed to be done.

Just when it seemed the last shred of hope was slipping away, even out of the most believing hand, a yell echoed through the battlefield like a resounding roar of triumph. This was not a surge from the army nor was it an overcoming roar from the enemy. No, this was a new yell, one that had not yet been heard. With a curious eye Lord Ekron looked to the south east toward the Valley of Kurdish from which the yell came, and to his eternal surprise he saw a band of dwarfs flanking the dragons, running up for battle.

. . . .

The arrival of the Dwarf remnant brought a new hope to all of the Army of Sahleam. The army itself could not help but to reciprocate with a jolting yell of excitement and reception. No one thought that the dwarfs had survived the dragon attack on Endorah. Surely, if they did survive the attack, the dragons would have laid siege on the city until their imminent death. Yet, there were the dwarfs running into the fray as if they were resurrected from the dead with the sole purpose of being a deliverer of death.

As for Lord Ekron, there were no words that could express the emotions that ran through his bones when he saw the Dwarf remnant. His family that he thought was dead was still alive. Not only alive, but bravely running into the battle, led by Master Sergeant Xoarah, to aid in a fight against an enemy that does not give favorable odds of survival.

Although the Dwarf's arrival revitalized the Army of Sahleam's spirits and rejuvenated their hearts, the biggest advantage that came with the Dwarf's arrival was that the dragons and their men were now flanked. Every person and creature on the battlefield was stunned by the sudden turn of events, but it was the Army of Sahleam who gained the upper hand and attacked while their enemy was still distracted.

. . . .

The arrival of the dwarfs caught the attention of all who were in combat, including both Lord Titus and his antagonist. Lord Titus as well took advantage of the opportunity and reengaged in attack while his rival was still diverted. With a couple moves, Lord Titus disarmed the hooded figure and had him grounded, wounded, and at sword point.

Lord Titus would have slain this menace at once, but was taken aback by whom his eyes now laid upon; for the hood had fallen off of his head and fully revealed the face of he who laid there in defeat.

"Antheis" Lord Titus said in disbelief.

"Lord Titus, is that you?" replied Antheis as if he did not know where he was or what had transpired.

Lord Titus said nothing. He was a bit shocked by what was going on. Even still, he did not lower his sword from Antheis' neck.

"Where am I? What's going on?" Antheis protested in befuddlement.

Lord Titus still did not answer as his mind tried to make sense of the current situation.

Seeing Lord Titus' bewilderment, Antheis slowly started to get up as he continued to plead his case to his executioner, "The last thing I remember was falling asleep at the Castle Dorian, and now I am here."

"We are at war. You and I have been at battle." Lord Titus said at last.

"I must have been under a curse of some sort or trans," implored Antheis, "for I do not know about what you speak." Antheis was now fully standing with his hands in the air, not wanting to give Lord Titus any reason to believe otherwise. "Surely you are not going to run me through."

Lord Titus did not know what to think. He did not fully believe Antheis' plight, but neither could he bring himself to kill Antheis either. Antheis was like a brother to Lord Titus, one of his personal bodyguards, and one of his closest friends.

Finally Lord Titus spoke, "I am glad you're okay. Come. Redeem yourself and join us in this fight against terrene."

With that being said, Lord Titus lowered his weapon and turned to continue in battle. This came as a complete shock to Antheis and he could not believe that Lord Titus did not end him right then and there. This was an opportunity that Antheis was not going to let pass him by.

As soon as Lord Titus turned his back, Antheis pulled a dagger from his side and lunged for Lord Titus.

Before he could plug the dagger into the back of his lord and friend, Lord Benaniah, who had been fighting nearby and had taken interest in what was unfolding, interjected and deflected the attack and ran Antheis threw.

Lord Titus turned to see Antheis' lifeless body fall to the ground. A tear came to his eye and his emotions began to swell as he remembered many of the good times that they had together. But Lord Titus did not let that show. Antheis was a traitor and had betrayed them all. Instead, Lord Titus mustered out an inaudible "thank you" with a slight bow of his head to Lord Benaniah. Then they both turned and were back off into battle.

....

Thaddeous sat back and watched the battle, not feeling that he needed to bother with combat in order to obtain victory. That was, until the dwarfs arrived.

When remnant arrived, the tide had changed, and it was now evident that Thaddeous needed to do something in order to regain the upper hand. He did not panic, nor did the thought of possibly losing the battle ever enter his mind, but the hope that the dwarfs brought with them needed to be crushed. Therefore, Thaddeous began walking through the fray, not paying any mind to what was going on around him, and waving off those who would try to oppose him. Until, at last he found who he was looking for, Murlynn. Thaddeous concluded within himself that if he could take down their wizard, then all hope would be crushed, and this skirmish would quickly be over.

Murlynn was not engrossed in the battle, for he was not much of an offensive weapon. Yet, he was armed with a sword that he knew how to use quite well in defending himself. "So, it is you then," said Murlynn after he turned around and saw Thaddeous walking toward him.

"Yes, it is I, Thaddeous." he said, as they now were standing about ten yards away from each other. "And your time has come."

"Oh," said Murlynn surprisingly, "come for what?" this was said with such genuineness that anyone might have believed that Murlynn was not sure what was about to happen.

"Don't be a fool!" replied Thaddeous irritably. "You knew that it would come down to this. The age of tyranny is over. The time of war is here. A new era is now upon us."

"Yes, the times are changing." Murlynn agreed, seemingly oblivious to what Thaddeous had just said.

"We have been cast out and held down for far too long." Thaddeous ranted. The anger, frustration, and even compassion were unmistakable in his voice. "All we ever wanted was to be left alone so that we could live a prosperous life, but no! The dragons are killed at first sight in Sahleam. We were cast out to a cruel land that does not yield a crop according to our labor. You lay heavy taxes on the people so that you can live in luxury while you rule with an iron fist from a faraway land. No more!" at this Thaddeous' rage boiled over and the duel began.

Thaddeous threw his hands forward, sending a surge of energy that caught Murlynn off guard and sent him airborne and to the ground.

Thaddeous capitalized on the opportunity by grabbing the dagger from his waist and immediately rushing upon Murlynn. Just before he fell upon him and plunged the dagger into his heart, Murlynn crossed his arms and created a shield of light that deflected Thaddeous and sent him flying backwards and disarming him.

Thaddeous and Murlynn got up at the same time, but it was Thaddeous who continued with the offensive. Lifting his hands as if trying to pull something from the ground, rocks of different shapes and sizes rose around him. One by one Thaddeous swiftly launched the projectile missiles at Murlynn.

Murlynn countered the attack by lifting his hands and bringing them together for a clap that sent out a crescent shape light that looked something like a boomerang, which turned all the rocks into dust.

Seeing that his second attempt failed; Thaddeous' frustration grew rapidly, blinding him with anger. He quickly grabbed a sword from a nearby fallen solider, pressed the blade between his hands and multiplied it. Then, all at once threw them at Murlynn. Murlynn quickly formed the shape of a ball with his hands and then stretched it out as far as his arms would allow him and pushed it forth toward the swords and braced himself for impact. The swords hit the magical sphere with a great force, but when having entered the ball they turned into long blades of grass, making them lose momentum and fall to the earth.

When Thaddeous witnessed that Murlynn had countered all three of his attacks, he became furious.

"How is it that this old man is able to sustain the energy needed to deflect my attacks?"

But while Murlynn was countering his last attack, Thaddeous realized that his guard was down due to the amount of focus and energy his spell required. With that, Thaddeous waved his arms in front of him and created a vortex out of the dust and grass from his previous attacks, and encapsulated Murlynn within it.

Realizing that he had finally gotten Murlynn, Thaddeous capitalized on the opportunity and picked up his dagger and made a mad dash for him.

When Thaddeous came upon the grass and dust peppered whirlwind, he took his opportunity to end Murlynn and change the course of this battle by killing him then and there. He gripped his dagger with both hands, raised it high above his head, and thrust it down into the tornado with all of his might. As he plunged the dagger deep into the earthly vortex, a dagger also emerged at the same time, stabbing him in the chest.

Immediately the vortex stopped, letting the grass and dust fall to the ground from which it came. Murlynn stood perplexed as Thaddeous let out a thunderous scream and dropped to his knees with his own dagger sticking out of his chest.

It was as if the whole battle had stopped and witnessed this event.

Murlynn looked down at Thaddeous, truly a little sad, for he did not mean for Thaddeous' death when he had put up the mirror spell. Murlynn did not know what Thaddeous may continue to throw at him and wanted to make sure that he was protected.

Murlynn knew that the wound was a fatal and did not see the need to "finish him off". Thaddeous' deception was so great that it led him to his own demise as Murlynn left him to die alone, with only his thought to comfort him.

. . . .

When Thaddeous was struck, the whole battle froze as his yell echoed through the Plains of Elah. Seeing that Murlynn had overtaken Thaddeous, the army of Sahleam doubled their efforts in one last surge of attack in order to overtake the enemy then and there.

With the fall of their leader, the dragons and their riders that remained did not see the purpose in continuing the attack, so they counted their losses and fled in retreat.

This was a great victory for Sahleam. Knowing they needed to be at full strength in order to chase down and conquer the enemy, the army did not pursue, but filled the land with cheers of triumph.

They had great joy in their victory, and were even amazed themselves that they overcame such insurmountable odds. They congratulated each other, bumped forearms, and even gave each other hugs as way to express their overwhelming happiness.

All were very happy, but none happier than Lord Ekron as he ran toward his kinsfolk and gave Master Sergeant Xoarah a mighty hug (which was not a proper thing to do for a king).

Yes, there was much to celebrate, but as the moment passed a somber feeling came upon them as the cheers faded and the groans of the wounded rose from the earth. Only now did the kings and the surviving army fully realize the hefty price that had to be paid in order to obtain such a victory. The dead and injured where scatter across the Plains of Elah. It was now the job of those who were able to try and save the injured and bring the dead back to the living so that they can be claimed by their loved ones.

64

After the wounded had been cared for and the dead had been collected, Lord Ekron asked Lord Titus for leave so that he could go with the Dwarf warriors back to the woods to be reunited with his people before marching out for to the Castle Dorian. This, of course, was enthusiastically granted by Titus and the other lords.

There was much to report as they walked from the Plains of Elah to the Forest of Mezpha. Master Sergeant Xoarah told Lord Ekron extensively about all the events that had taken place over the past three days. First there was the arrival of Silas and Raithyn and the sudden ambush on their beloved Endorah. This led to Raithyn's sacrifice outside of the safe room and their predicament of being trapped within its very walls. Xoarah went on to tell Lord Ekron of how their mother revealed the hidden doors that lead to the ancient tunnels of Ubertyne and how their mother provisioned within the tunnels. After which, the Dwarf remnant met up with Chief Brutus at the Podiseon River, who had revealed to them the finding the dead Dwarf army. From there, Xoarah told his lord how the dragon fleet had passed them in the Valley of Kurdish, which led to them following the fleet and joining the army of Sahleam in the battle against the dragons. Lord Ekron was amazed at all that had happened as he listened patiently and intently to Master Sergeant Xoarah, who left nothing unsaid.

Lord Ekron could not believe what he heard. His emotions went from mountain peaks to valleys, and all within the confines of his utter joy for the remnant of his people. Pride swelled up within Lord Ekron for Master Sergeant Xoarah as he told him all that had happened. Xoarah turned out to be more of a leader than anyone had expected. Lord Ekron was furthermore in awe of their mother and all of her provisions that ensured the survival of her people. Even still, all of these positive emotions were dampened as he heard of all the lives that were lost in the horrific invasion of Endorah. It was very evident to Lord Ekron that taking Endorah and exterminating the dwarfs was a top tactical priority.

When Xoarah and his men finally got back to Isadoorah, they were so happy that they could not help but to cheer. Although Isadoorah and the rest of the division of the dwarfs waited for Xoarah as he had commanded them to; they essentially counted them for dead when they had left and only waited out of respect. Seeing Xoarah and his division return was the first good thing that the remnant had experienced in three days. And when they finally realized that it was not just Xoarah and his men, but that Lord Ekron was with them as well, they gave such a thunderous roar that filled the whole forest.

A tear came to Lord Ekron's eye and trickled down his face. He was back with his people. A moment that he thought he would never realize again.

The dwarfs had survived the battle with the dragons with minor causalities and the division within the forest did not have to face any attacks. Since there were no urgent matters at hand, Lord Ekron put together a council so that they could quickly decide in what they must do next.

It was not Dwarf custom to have a dictatorship, but rather a balanced monarch rule. Since Xoarah had led the people out of Endorah and exhibited excellent leadership skills, it was obvious that he should be on the council. Master Sergeant Xoarah saw it fit to include Mendull, Gurther, and Kithorah on the council as well since they had been a resounding board for him over the past three days. Some did wonder about Kithorah and the skepticism he has shown, but his recent actions had proven to Xoarah where his heart now stands. Lord Ekron agreed with the wisdom in this decision. The only problem was that to have four councilmen left them one short of what was required by Dwarf law. Therefore, Lord Ekron invited Isadoorah onto his official council as well. This was unprecedented. Never before had a dwarfette been on the king's council. Master Sergeant Xoarah held her in high enough regard to put her over a whole division. Also, with her pedigree and zealousness for her people, Isadoorah would make a fine addition to Lord Ekron's council.

With his council set, Lord Ekron and his council gathered next to a small cluster of trees just far enough away from the remnant so not to be heard, but close enough that they could still see all that was happening.

"Councilmen and councilwomen," Lord Ekron started. "I am overwhelmed with emotion. I thought I was marching against the dragons as the lone representative of the Dwarf kin. I figured that by the end of the day I would join you in the company of our mother. But with her favor and blessing, I now find myself here with you."

"Here, here!" the councilpeople cheered.

"We have beaten back the dragons," Lord Ekron continued. "But now we must decide what's next? Now, I know that you know that we must go to the Castle Dorian and rest for a while. But the castle is not our home. No matter the outcome, dwarfs must have their own land. We do not know if the dragons have fled back to Endorah or fled out of the land of Sahleam altogether. If they did hunker down in Endorah, then we must think of a way to reclaim our beloved city. For we are not nomads, nor herdsmen, nor gatherers, nor hunters, nor farmers. No! Dwarfs are miners and need to bring forth elements out of the earth for trade and craftsmanship. When one knows their purpose, it is all they can do to fulfill that purpose. For to do anything else, no matter how glorious would leave them empty and unsatisfied."

They all nodded in agreement, knowing the truth that Lord Ekron brought forth.

"Do we leave now and push the people until we get to the castle, or do we wait and allow everyone to refresh before marching on?"

"We move on" said Xoarah without hesitation and with no uncertainty

"Even though we had been in the woods for a short amount of time," Isadoorah concluded, "it has been difficult to find enough food and shelter for the amount of people that are with us."

Lord Ekron only nodded as he listened to the council discuss the situation.

Kithorah was not shy about giving his input either, "The people just had a great victory. Their spirits are up and the people are energized. I am not sure if we did stay that we would actually accomplish the reason for our staying."

"Kithorah is right," Medull quickly agreed, expanding Kithorah's thought. "If we stay, the people will celebrate. There will be fires, singing, and dancing of the likes that we have not seen. If we stay, the people will not rest. Plus the commotion will only be a beacon for predators and possibly dragons."

"But if we leave now, we become a traveling feast" Lord Ekron said more as if he was thinking out loud rather than trying to interject. "Plus there is no cover in the Plains of Elah besides the dark of night."

With those words, Lord Ekron paused for a moment. With that

pause, Xoarah quickly rebutted his concerning thoughts. "With all due respect, my king, the route we would need to travel was previously discussed and decided earlier when we were with Chief Brutus and his men."

Medull, Kithorah, Gurther, and Isadoorah whispered in agreement.

Lord Ekron was not offended or taken aback by this, but instead impressed with their organization and decision making as they moved through the land.

"Our mother has provided." Gurther's soft and wise voice broke through the council. "She led us out of Endorah and into the saferoom, out of the saferoom and into the tunnels of Ubertyne, through the tunnels of Ubertyne to the Podiseon River, and along the Podiseon River to the Plains of Elah" continued Gurther as the council hushed in order to hear his soft voice. "She had led us this far; she will make sure that we get to the castle."

No one doubted, nor had already forgotten what Gurther spoke of, but his words resonated deep within them.

"It is settled then. Gather the people. We head for the Castle Dorian right away," said Lord Ekron, concluding the council.

....

As soon as it was evident that the dragons were not going to come back, Lord Titus sent a messenger off right away to notify all the king's folk at the Castle Dorian of their victory. It would still be some time before the army of Sahleam would be able to begin their march back to the castle due to the amount injured and dead that needed to be tended to. Only after every person: dead, injured, or alive, was accounted for, did the army march back out to their loved ones.

The end of the day and the start of the night was almost at hand when the army finally arrived at the Castle Dorian. The people had been packed outside of the city gates to greet them ever since the messenger had arrived and told them of the great news. Every kind was represented as they waited in anticipation to see the Army of Sahleam appear off in the distance. It felt like hours upon hours had passed as loved ones waited outside the gates peering off into the distance. Although the wait felt longer than it actually was, the people did not mind, for they knew that the army would be breaking the horizon soon.

Then, what looked like a swarm of flies invading from the south came into view. All at once the entire land of Ev'ron erupted into jubilation! Deafening cheers shook the ground as rams' horns blasted through the sky and drums thundered with each powerful strike. The wait was over. The army was back. Many of those who were waiting outside the gates ran toward the army in hopes that their loved ones would be among those who were marching back to them. Soldiers could not hold back their excitement either as they broke ranks and ran out to meet them while they were still a way off. For some, it was great relief and joy that filled their spirits as they embraced the ones they loved once again. For others, it was a crushing moment when they realized that their loved ones had paid the ultimate sacrifice in obtaining this great victory. They were not coming back to the Castle Dorian. Instead they had entered their eternal home. They were no longer going to see their loved ones again upon this earth, but one day they will embrace them again when they too enter their eternal home. Although grief filled their hearts and tears of sadness moistened their face, they knew that those who were not returning died with great honor and as a hero that will be immortalized in monuments, histories, songs, and legends for generations to come. Their physical presence would no longer be with them, but their memory and what they did would live on forever.

....

After having settled in at the Castle Dorian, Herms found himself sitting in front of a fire watching it dance as he contemplated the past three days, especially this mysterious connection that he had with the dragon. He had not told anyone about it, but yet wondered if he should talk with Murlynn to see what his thoughts were about it.

Herms could not help but think that the dragons were not acting on their own accord. For the dragon he encountered had many chances to kill him but did not. And what about all those feelings that he had experienced? Herms did not know that dragons were capable of such emotions. There were too many thoughts and questions that needed to be answered that left Herms unsettled, so he finally resolved in himself to seek out Murlynn and hopefully get some answers.

Herms did not have to search the castle long before finding Murlynn in the War Room looking at the paintings on the walls.

"Every one of these paintings show a significant part of Sahleam's history." Murlynn stated without taking his eyes off of the paintings. "They will now have to make room for a new painting."

Herms took a moment to look at the paintings. They were beautifully done, capturing both the glory of victory and the pain of defeat.

"Murlynn, I wanted to ask you a question." Herms began as Murlynn just stood fixated on the painting of Onesomus' and the Battle of Ezerek. "I do not think that the dragons were acting on their own behalf."

Murlynn turn and looked at Herms with a quizzical look.

"I mean," Herms continued in further explanation, "there has been several times when the dragons, I mean one specific dragon in this case, had a chance to kill me and it did not."

Murlynn pierced his eyes trying to understand what Herms was getting at.

"I mean, there was one dragon that I kept coming in contact with, and I felt like I had a connection with it." Herms was starting to get frustrated, because he himself did not understand what he was saying, so how was Murlynn supposed to understand his babble. "I don't know how to explain it, but I felt like I had a connection with a dragon, and it was able to share its thoughts and emotions with me."

To Herms surprise Murlynn cracked a slight smile, "I too once had such a connection. It was a great and terrifying experience."

Herms stood shocked, partly because Murlynn was able to make sense out of what Herms had said and partly because he was not the only person who has had such an experience.

"It was long ago, when I was a boy," Murlynn continued. "I had found a dragon egg and kept it. I helped the egg hatch and then nurtured the hatchling. Ever sense I found the egg I felt a profound connection to it. I had dreams and visions of the creature that was inside. After it hatched the connection got stronger as my love for the creature grew. Inevitably, the dragon got too big and started exploring the land and its abilities. No matter what I did, no matter what I tried the dragon always went back to its natural instincts. One night she had an incident with a group of farmers. Her identity was now made known. No matter what I may say or do, the perception of the dragon was now ingrained into the minds of the people. So, Korel had to go. At first I thought I could still sense her. I would still have dreams of flying and hunting, but as time went on, the connection faded. Dragons are not mindless savage creatures. Rather, they are misunderstood."

Herms was stunned by Murlynn's proclamation. It was obvious that his connection with Korel was deep and strong, for Herms could still see his care for her in his eyes.

With the revelation that someone else had also experienced this same kind of connection that Herms had experienced; Herms thought about what had happened over the past three days and asked the next logical question, "Do you think that the wizard you fought had a connection with the dragons?"

"Possibly," said Murlynn contemplatively. It was obvious that he himself was already mulling over this idea and its ramifications. "It would make sense as to how the dragons were acting while they were invading Sahleam. It would also explain why the dragons left after his death."

They both paused and mused over the idea of someone, somehow being able to manipulate not just one, but a fleet of dragons. This was not only beyond Herms' cognitive grasp, but his imagination as well.

Too many questions of "how" and "why" streamed through his mind that he was not able to answer. All of these unanswered thoughts stacked within his mind and began to give Herms a headache, like trying to solve a very hard math problem without all the variables and factors. So, to free himself from these thoughts, Herms shared with Murlynn his experience with the dragon.

"For the past three days I have had a connection with an old green dragon. Many times I did find myself unwillingly standing before it. Not once did it try to kill me. Instead, I think, it was helping me so that the army of Sahleam could pull together and fend off the attack. None of this did I realize until after I had encountered the dragon on the battlefield and it saved me from another that was coming upon me by killing it!"

Murlynn smiled. He was not sure if Korel was alive, for it had been a long time since he was able to connect with her. Even if he did see her, Murlynn was not sure how dragons aged and could have looked right at her and not known it. Yet, to hear of Herms' experience brought closure to Murlynn's heart. For he believed that, if given the opportunity, his beloved Korel would have behaved in such a redemptive manner.

Not much more was said after that. In fact, Herms left the War Room shortly afterwards relieved, knowing that he was not the only one to experience such a connection. He was sad that the dragon died, but knew that it died with honor and retribution. Sometimes in life the right thing to do is not the easy thing to do. Yet he wondered. Herms was glad that this race was over, that he finished it alive.

. . . .

Lord Titus prepared himself as best he could for the mixed emotions upon his arrival. Their freedom came at a high cost. Although everyone was elated about winning the battle, he could not overlook the hefty price of victory. Lord Titus celebrated with those who welcomed back their loved ones and mourned with those who had seen their loved ones for the last time. Lord Titus truly loved the people and was not isolated from all the emotions that they were experiencing. He encouraged the families to bury their dead and mourn in whatever way they thought best. After each family had their time of mourning, Lord Titus would hold a memorial service for those who had served in that great battle. This service was dedicated to all: dead, wounded, and those who came home. It was not only dedicated to the humans, but to all the races within Sahleam, for it was through their alliance that they able to overcome this enemy.

4

SEVERAL DAYS THEREAFTER

As the families took their time in grieving, Lord Titus also used this time reflect and process all the emotions that this battle stirred within him. To be a good king you must love the people you serve. On the other hand, to be a good general you must be willing to kill the thing that you love most. There was no doubt that attacking the dragons head on was the best possible plan, and there was also no doubt that death and war go hand in hand. To know the coming of death does not take away the shock or sadness of it when a loved one finally passes. All of this he could feel. All of this he could express to his council and lords, but to no one else. Not because showing these emotions are weak, but because the people needed a strong leader to lean upon as they themselves went through the same struggle.

Then, there was Antheis. Lord Titus was still in disbelief about his betrayal. There had to be a reason why someone so close to him would commit such high treason. Lord Titus treated Antheis like a brother and held him in high regard. Antheis' betrayal cut Lord Titus deep. And with Antheis' death, Lord Titus would never know "why". But, then again there is no reason "why" he had done what he did that would make sense to Lord Titus, nor would there be any reason "why" he had done it that would not hurt Lord Titus even more than what he was already feeling. In that thought, it would probably be best if the question of "why" was left unresolved and Lord Titus could further conclude that Antheis was just not acting in his right mind.

Amongst the feelings of happiness, sorrow, and confusion there was pride for people like Xoarah, Brutus, Silas, and Raithyn who showed great courage and bravery as they willingly put their life on the line to procure the defeat of this enemy. Especially Raithyn, who deserves double honor for the sacrifice he made to ensure the dwarfs lineage. He will forever be remembered and honored in song, legend, and with a great statue that will read "Raithyn: the only person in all of Sahleam to ever slay a dragon single handedly."

All of this filled Lord Titus' mind as he reflected over the past several days in preparation for the memorial service. But now as he sat in reflection of all these accounts, Lord Titus readied himself to address not only his own kin, but all the people of Sahleam.

He made his way from his chambers of contemplation to the podium, where Lord Ekron, Lord Benaniah, Lord Cephas, and Lord Augusta where seated to the right and Brutus, Silas, Xoarah, Murlynn, and Herms were seated to his left. The murmuring and chatter of the vast crowd of people died down to a still silence were a whisper would have been clearly heard amongst all who were there. Looking out among the people, Lord Titus settled his thoughts, took a deep breath, and began.

"Fauns, Sheppen, Nimrods, Dwarfs, and Humans, we are gathered here today, not as five distinct kingdoms, but as one people group that is banded together by Sahleam herself. You are all my people. You are all my kin. You are all my brothers."

"A recent attack on this land has helped us pull together in an unprecedented way. Not since the time of Onesumis has the land been unified for a common cause. Each kin represented here today is strong, resourceful, and cunning. But not any one kin would have been able to drive out this enemy by themselves. It was by our alliance, being united by a singular objective that we were able to stand up and fight back against such tyranny. Through the sacrifice of some, and the bravery of all, we were able to overcome insurmountable odds. But as comes with war, so comes death and destruction. I will not tell you that the pain you feel or the loss that you have experienced will get better over time, but I will tell you, if it were not for the courage of those who marched out to battle, we would not be gathered here today. Many have died, and many more were wounded, but none will be forgotten. Do not remember the anguish of death, but remember the joy of their victory. Let us keep those who had fallen alive in our thoughts, our prayers, and in our hearts. Let us now also help those who have come back suffering the causalities of war. Just as we united for this battle, so now must we stay united in helping each other in the days to come."

"Brothers and sisters, I thank you for all that you have done. It is not one lord or one kingdom that make up the land of Sahleam. Rather, the thread of commonality that flows through our veins is the idea of a free people that love their land, love their people, and love their god."

"Because they attacked, we came together. Because we fought, we live. Because of our death, we will always remember."

THE END

ACKNOWLEDGMENTS

I never thought I would one day write a book. It has been one of the hardest things that I have ever done. If it were not for God, none of this would be possible. It is through His love, grace, kindness, and forgiveness that I am the man I am today. I want to thank Him for His continual belief in me, which inspired the thoughts and ideas that fill this book.

I want to especially thank my wife, Lisa. She is the only person who has read this book more times, other than myself. She has been an encouragement and sounding board for me through this whole process. I definitely could not have done this without her.

Next, I would like to give a special thanks to my children, Joshua and Caleb. Your creativity and imagination have kept my mind young as I grow old.

I would also like to thank Rod VanBlake for persisting me to publish this book and being a resource to help make it a reality.

I want to thank my editor, formatter, and artist for their time, dedication, and expertise in helping make this book more than what I ever thought it could be.

Finally, I want to say thank you to my family, friends, and everyone

I have met throughout the years. All relationships are influential, and it is those influences that shape us into who we are.

CPSIA information can be obtained
at www.ICGtesting.com
Printed in the USA
LVHW081910290121
677494LV00005BA/82